FIRST DEGREE

A Cass Leary Legal Thriller

ROBIN JAMES

Robin James Books

Copyright © 2020 by Robin James Books

All Rights Reserved

No part of this book may be reproduced or transmitted in any form or by any means, electronic or mechanical including photocopying, recording, or by any information storage and retrieval system, without the written permission of the author or publisher, except where permitted by law or for the use of brief quotations in a book review.

This is a work of fiction. Names, characters, businesses, places, events, and incidents are either the products of the author's imagination or used in a fictitious manner. Any resemblance to actual persons, living or dead, or actual events is purely coincidental.

For all the latest on my new releases and exclusive content, sign up for my newsletter at:

http://www.robinjamesbooks.com/newsletter/

Chapter 1

NOTHING BAD HAPPENS HERE. People think it. They might even say it. Only, we know it isn't true. Sure, Delphi, Michigan is far quieter than nearby cities like Jackson or certainly Detroit. But evil finds us here too. On an unseasonably cold Labor Day weekend, it found Lauren Rice and brought her into our nightmares.

Nearly three weeks later, it was still cold. Cold enough that as I stood outside Delphi's one and only Presbyterian church among a group of mourners that seemed to double the population, even my wool jacket didn't keep me warm.

"You should have worn gloves," Eric said. He gave me a sad smile. "Come here."

He slipped an arm around me, pulling me against his solid warmth. He was like my own personal furnace.

"I'll be fine," I said.

Ahead of me, my brother Joe stood with his wife, Katy. Katy dabbed at her eyes with a tissue she had the foresight to bring. Joe leaned down and kissed the top of her head. Standing a few yards away from them on the first step leading up to the church was their daughter, my niece, Emma. No amount of tissues would have helped her.

Ashen-faced, Emma huddled with two of her classmates. Red-headed girls, sisters. I remembered seeing them huddled together like this in joy just three months ago at their high school graduation.

Emma's boyfriend Cole towered over the three of them. He pulled Emma against him, just as Eric had done to me. She leaned on him for support, just as I had.

"I don't know if I can do this," Katy sniffled.

"We have to," Joe said, stoic. "For Gil."

The funeral home doors opened, and the crowd made way as the first group of mourners came out. It meant the next group could go in. Two deputy sheriffs manned the doors to make sure the building stayed within capacity for the fire code. It was going to be a very long day.

Katy's breath hitched. Joe closed his hand around hers. We moved.

As we made our way through the doors, I could see Gil Rice's thick head of gray hair standing near his daughter's closed casket. One by one, the crowd moved forward and stepped up to pay their respects.

Shell-shocked parents, numb from horror and guilt. *This could have been my child. Thank God this wasn't my child.*

Gil stood alone, shaking their hands, hugging them, receiving their grief as he struggled to process his own. A huge, blown-up color photo of Lauren rested on an easel beside the casket. She was beautiful, of course. Shining blue eyes and thick, straight blonde hair. She wore a Delphi High cheerleading uniform holding silver and green pom-poms at her hips as she smiled for the school photographer.

Eric put his hand on the casket, his lips moving in silent

prayer. I joined him, struggling to remember the words of the
Hail Mary and hoping it would help.

"Gil doesn't believe in God anymore," Eric had told me.
"Not after he lost Julie to breast cancer."

This was all there would be. No funeral mass. Just a small
graveside service at a tiny, non-denominational cemetery
where Julie Rice had been buried just six years ago.

We made our way out of the building and joined Joe and
Katy. Cole and Emma followed close behind. Emma's face
had gone purple from crying. Cole looked awful himself. He
comforted her. But he didn't know what to do.

"How close were they?" I asked Joe after we'd made our way
back to the parking lot across the street. We had some time to
wait before we moved into position for the cemetery procession.

"Close enough." Joe shrugged. "I mean, obviously."

"Eric," Katy said. "Can you tell us anything? Have they
caught the guy?"

I knew what else she meant. It's what everyone meant. All
the parents of daughters today wondered the same thing. *Is he
still out there? Is my child safe tonight?*

"Katy," Eric said. "You know I can't comment on an
ongoing investigation. Even if I could, it's not my case."

"But you'd know," Katy said. "I know you'd know. This is
Delphi."

"I can only share what's already been made public," Eric
said, lowering his voice. He put a light hand on Katy's
shoulder and the group of us stepped away for privacy's sake.
It didn't really matter. Everyone here spoke in hushed
whispers about the exact same thing.

Lauren Rice went missing Labor Day weekend. She'd
been at a party attended by probably half of the kids at this
funeral. She never came home.

"Was she ... raped?" Katy said, mouthing the last word.

"She was found with ... um ... she was partially nude when they found her," Eric said.

"In a ditch," Katy sniffed.

"The drainage ditch off Lumley, yes," Eric said.

"Did he ... God. Did he cut her?" Katy asked.

"Katy," Joe said, pulling his wife away from us. He whispered in her ear. She squeezed her eyes shut.

"I'm sorry," I said to Eric. He shook his head and lifted his hand in a dismissive gesture.

"It's okay," he said. "She's just trying to make sense of it. We all are."

"They're good kids," I said, knowing evil doesn't care. But, like Katy, I was trying to process it.

"Emma was at that party?" Eric asked.

"I don't know," I said. Just then, Emma and Cole started walking toward us. Cole, God bless him, had managed to get my niece under control a bit. Though the color had drained from her face, she had stopped crying for now.

"A bunch of us are going to head over to Mr. Rice's tomorrow," Cole said. "Everyone's bringing him food and all, but we thought maybe he'd need his lawn mowed. You know, or some work done around the house."

"That's a good idea," Eric said.

"I'll head over with you," Joe said. "He might need my truck."

It was at least ... something they could do.

"Aunt Cass?" Emma said. Without even seeming to think about it, she moved into my arms. I smiled. Emma was eighteen years old, but she still had the same scent about her I remembered from when she was a baby. I remember my mother once told me she could have walked into any of our rooms blindfolded and known whose it was.

"What, sweetie?" I asked.

"A group of us ... after this is over today. We want to get together. Not a party. We just ... we need a place to be. There are about twenty of us. Maybe twenty-four. There isn't ..."

"Of course," I said, knowing what she wanted. "You're welcome to come to my house for a while. It's the only place big enough for all of you."

"I'll take care of ordering some pizzas," Eric said. "Let you guys go on ahead and set up whatever you need."

"We can set up some tables and chairs in the pole barn," I said.

"I'll go there straight from here," Cole said. "I can grab Trace and Marcus to move everything around. We'll stay and clean up after."

I deposited Emma back under Cole's arm. "Thanks," I said. "That'll be a big help. You know where I keep the spare key?"

Cole nodded. He'd been doing some work for me this summer under Joe's supervision. Joe planned on teaching him how to pull the dock and winterize the boats in a few weeks. I didn't know Cole's whole story, but the kid found ways to stay away from his own house more and more. I was grateful for the extra pair of hands.

The funeral home doors opened. Gil Rice walked out. He wasn't a big man to begin with, but now his suit hung off of him. He'd aged twenty years in the last two weeks. I hadn't yet seen him cry.

"She was his whole world," Joe said. "It was just the two of them after Julie passed. Lauren got accepted to Valparaiso on a track scholarship but wouldn't go."

"God," Eric muttered. "He'll blame himself for that. If she hadn't ..."

Eric froze beside me. Lauren's casket came into view.

Eight pallbearers struggled to keep it straight as they made their way down the stairs.

"They're all ... they're all girls?" Katy whispered.

My brother made a choked sound. "Gil told me ... God. He's worried whoever did this to Lauren was someone she knew."

Cold tendrils of dread curled around my heart.

Someone she knew.

There were dozens of young men in attendance. All were friends of Lauren Rice's, and Gil Rice was terrified that one of them was responsible for putting her in that casket. He wasn't about to take the chance and let them carry it.

"Let's go," Eric said, nudging me. Blinking back tears for Gil Rice, I followed Eric to his car and climbed inside. We waited in silence, watching as eight young women slid Lauren Rice's casket into the hearse.

WORD GOT out about Emma's plan. Her twenty-four friends turned into roughly fifty and included many of their parents.

But the sun came out. By six o'clock in the evening, it was warmer than it had been four hours before. I leaned against the porch railing and looked out at the water.

"It's so beautiful here," Katy said as she walked up beside me. "I hope you never take it for granted."

"I don't," I said, sipping a glass of white wine. It was only my first. I had a feeling there might be at least one more before the night was through. I'd built the home just last year following plans my great-grandfather had left. The house faced west now, giving me dazzling views of each and every sunset for the rest of my life.

Some of Emma's friends stood out on the dock. Too cold

to swim, a handful of them threw poles in the water with Joe and Cole's careful direction. Eric stayed out in the barn, making sure our pizza and pop supply never dwindled.

Emma sat on the swing near the water, leaning her head against one of her friend's shoulders.

"I wish Gil had come," Katy said. "It would do him good to see how these kids have come together on their own to honor his daughter."

"He'll see," I said. "It won't end just today."

"I just can't stop thinking about it though," Katy said. "To throw her away in a ditch. Like she was garbage or something. You know it was those two who found her?"

I followed Katy's finger. She pointed to two of the boys standing on the dock.

"Jake and Mitch Bradley," Katy said. "Brothers. Mitch is only fourteen. Jake just got his driver's license. They were part of the search party Delphi P.D. organized."

"They were alone?" I asked.

"No," Katy said. "One of the officers was with them. But ... Cass, they saw her. Her body. Face up in that ditch."

"How awful," I said. Just then, the smaller of the boys, Mitch, I assumed, reeled in a sizable smallmouth bass.

"Sebastian," I said.

"Huh?" Katy asked.

"Sebastian the Bass," I said. "That's what Jessa calls that one. He hangs out under the dock. She's caught him a couple of times and decided he needed a name."

Katy laughed. Mitch took the hook out of Sebastian's mouth and threw my eight-year-old niece's favorite fish back in the water for her to catch another day.

"I was just hoping for a little peace around here, you know?" Katy asked. "We've been through enough."

I got quiet and sipped my wine. It was the closest my

sister-in-law had come to mentioning some of the marital tension I knew she and my brother had experienced of late. But Katy loved Emma in spite of their difficulties. Though Emma often bristled against it as teenagers do, Katy had stepped in and mothered her as best she could when Emma's biological mother abandoned her. No matter what, I would always love and fight for Katy because of it.

Cole walked down the dock toward Emma. She smiled up at him and left the swing.

"That's getting pretty serious?" I asked.

Katy took a sip of her own wine and nodded.

"She wants to move in with him next year."

Her words dropped like a bomb. "She's eighteen!" I whispered. "Joe's got to be out of his mind."

"She's eighteen," Katy answered. "She wants to finish her freshman year in the dorm, then get an apartment. Joe doesn't know yet."

"Oh Lord," I said. "Remind me to find a way to be out of town when that happens."

I would have asked her for more details but Eric came out of the barn just then. A car pulled up my driveway. Even from this distance, I could see Eric's expression turn grave.

Katy was still talking as I stepped around her and edged closer to Eric. The car slowed to a stop, and I saw the source of his concern.

It wasn't another guest. It was an unmarked patrol car just like the one Eric drove while on duty. Detective Megan Lewis stepped out. Katy had stopped talking, becoming frozen to her spot.

Lewis went to Eric. A muscle jumped in his jaw and I recognized the sober expression on his face. This was bad news. Very. Bad. News.

Eric nodded, receiving whatever message Lewis had to convey. He looked toward the dock.

The events of the day replayed in my mind. Gil Rice was worried one of the mourners today was his daughter's murderer. Mitch and Jake turned, going sheet white as they saw Eric and Megan Lewis heading down the yard.

"Stay here," I said to Katy. I raced down the steps. Emma rose from the swing.

"God," I whispered to myself. "They're just kids."

Eric broke off and came to me. He took my elbow and gently pulled me aside as Megan kept walking toward the dock.

"Eric ..." I started.

"They want him for questioning," he said. "And I swear to God I didn't know about this beforehand. I never would have been okay with her coming to your house in front of all these kids but ..."

"What?" Emma shouted, her voice cracking.

Then everything made sense and broke apart at once.

Detective Lewis wasn't here for the Bradley brothers. Cole had made it up the yard. He turned to my niece and told her everything was going to be okay. Then he followed the detective and walked toward her car.

"Aunt Cass?" Emma shrieked.

"Cass?" Eric said.

"Right," I answered them both. "Just let me get my coat."

Chapter 2

"Ms. LEARY, I swear I don't have anything to hide," Cole said.

He appeared outwardly calm as we sat in the lobby of the Delphi P.D. Public Safety Building. Being a Sunday evening, the place was fairly empty. Eric had followed me. He and Detective Lewis disappeared into their inner offices.

"Do you want me to get a hold of your parents for you?" I asked, pulling out my cell phone.

"No," Cole said. "They're not even home, anyway. My mom spent the weekend with her friend in Manitou Beach. My dad's been on the road a little while. We haven't seen a lot of him lately. You know he's a truck driver."

"Do you have any idea what this is about?" I asked, hating that I had to.

"I was at that party on Labor Day weekend," he said. "They've been talking to everyone from it. Somebody probably told them I was there. I think I even told them I was there."

"You've talked to the police before?" I asked.

My cell phone buzzed. My brother Joe had texted me four

times already. Emma wasn't handling these new developments well at all.

"I'll tell you something when I know something," I texted back. "I'm with Cole. Everybody, just calm down."

Eric strode down the hall, looking grim. It sent my pulse racing. This didn't feel like a run-of-the-mill fact gathering.

"Wait here," I said to Cole.

I moved down the hall to meet Eric. He took me gently by the elbow and steered me into the nearest interview room.

"Lewis just wants to ask him a few questions," he said.

"About Lauren Rice?" I asked, still holding out hope this was unrelated.

"Yes," Eric answered, dashing those hopes in an instant.

"Eric ..."

"Stop," he said, putting up his hands. "He's not in custody. Cole's free to go. You know full well it's in his best interests to cooperate. We're letting you be here as a courtesy."

"A courtesy," I said.

"Don't start," Eric said. "I mean it. I'm not your enemy. I'm not Cole's enemy. We're trying to figure out what happened to that girl, Cass. You want that as much as anyone."

"It's okay," Cole said. He'd left the bench and followed the sound of our voices. "Ms. Leary, I told you. I don't have anything to hide. If there's something I can do to help, I want to."

Detective Lewis emerged from deeper down the hall. She held a pad of paper and a pen in her hand. If I thought Eric's expression was grim, hers was downright funereal. After the events of the day, that was saying something.

"We can talk in here," she said. "Ms. Leary, you're

welcome to sit in. Mr. Mathison, can I get you a bottled water or anything before we start?"

"No," he said. "I'm fine. I'm happy to do whatever I can."

"I'll wait for you in my office," Eric said. Cole brushed past me, his stride confident, unafraid, at ease. I followed behind him.

Megan took the seat closest to the wall so she faced the door. Cole sat opposite her. I took the chair beside him.

Megan was smaller than I was, barely topping five feet. She had pale blonde hair she wore in a tight bun at the back of her head. The only woman in the Delph P.D. Detective Bureau, I knew she'd pushed against the small-town patriarchy to get there, even in the 21st century.

"Mr. Mathison," she started.

"Just call me Cole," he said. "Mr. Mathison sounds weird. Nobody even calls my dad that."

"Fine," she said. "Cole. I want to be clear that this is just an informal interview. You're free to leave if you so choose. I just want to ask you a few questions about Lauren Rice. Is that okay with you? Do you understand?"

"I get it," he said. "And like I said. Anything I can do to help. Lauren was my friend."

"Okay," Megan said. "I'm going to record this interview." She took out a small hand-held recorder and placed it in the middle of the table.

"It's Sunday, September 15th. Uh ... 6:48 p.m. This is Detective Megan Lewis. I'm here with Cole Mathison. His lawyer, Cass Leary, is also present."

"She's not my lawyer," Cole said. "I mean, she's a ..."

"It's okay," Megan said. "You can work all that out later. I just want to make it clear that Ms. Leary is present. Are you acting on Mr. Math ... Cole's behalf?"

"Yes," I answered.

"Thanks," Cole said. He sat with his hands folded, his back straight, his eyes focused on Megan. He looked more like he was here for a job interview. I took it as a good sign.

"Okay," Megan said. "Cole, can you tell me how you knew Lauren Rice?"

"We were friends," he said. "Close friends. Lauren and I went to high school together. I graduated two years ago this past June. She was a year behind me."

"Did you travel in the same peer group, would you say?" Megan asked.

"Yeah," Cole answered. "You know Delphi's small. We're all in the same peer group. But if you mean clique. Sort of. Yes. I was on the football team. Lauren was a varsity cheerleader."

"I see," Megan said. "Were you just friends?"

Cole chewed his bottom lip. He never changed his straight posture, though.

"We, um, we did date for a little while. Mostly during her senior year."

Cole remained at ease, but my palms started to sweat.

"She was your girlfriend," she said.

Cole looked at me. "Emma knows about all of this," he reassured me.

"It's okay." I smiled. My legal spidey senses were tingling big time. I wanted to pull the kid out of here. At the same time, I was damn curious about what else he had to say.

"Yes," he answered. "I guess Lauren was my girlfriend for a little while. That's fair to say."

"How long did you date?" Megan asked, scribbling on her pad.

"Gosh," Cole said. "We were friends for a long time. Like I said, we were in the same clique, if that's what you want to call it. I'd known her since junior high, at least. I'm trying to remember when ... we started hanging out kind of exclusively before I graduated. So that was over two years ago. And then through that summer before I started college. Then, I took her to homecoming. After I was out, it would have been her senior year homecoming. We dated off and on throughout that fall and winter."

"Do you remember who broke it off?" Megan asked.

Cole shook his head. "You know, I can't say that either of us did specifically. There wasn't one thing that ended it. I was just ... I was probably not very, uh ... attentive. I was in the swing of it with college classes. I just didn't have a lot of time. Lauren was in the swing of the high school thing. And she was gonna go to a different school that next fall. I don't know that there was ever a formal break-up. We just stopped going out. I think she even started dating somebody else. I took her to homecoming. But she went with some other guy to prom."

"Do you know who that was?" Megan asked.

"I don't," he said. "Gosh. I don't think he was from Delphi High. I didn't know him. I just saw on social when she posted pictures of them at the dance. Ben something."

"How did you feel about that?" Megan asked.

"About the pictures?" Cole asked. "I think I remember thinking Lauren looked pretty. Happy. Like she was making the most out of the final days of high school. I think I texted her that. Or maybe I commented on the picture. You can check."

"I see," Megan said. "Cole, when was the last time you saw Lauren?"

"Oh, at the bonfire at the Pits."

"The Pits," Megan said. "You're referring to Shamrock Woods? I know there's a section out there where kids go." We all knew it. There was a large clearing where a couple of huge trees had fallen and rotted out. They formed big depressions in the ground. Pits. The name stuck.

"We're not supposed to," he said. It was the first time I noticed his posture change. The Pits was a notorious party hangout for teens. It had been that way since well before my time.

"Tell me about that party," Megan said. "Who hosted it?"

"Hosted? Nobody hosted. I just started getting texts that there'd be a bunch of people out there the Saturday of Labor Day weekend. It was BYO. It's always BYO. Look, I'm sorry. I'm not twenty-one for a few months yet. I want to be honest. But am I in trouble if there was beer?"

"No," Megan said. "That's not what I'm here to talk to you about. I'm just trying to get a sense of who all was there. Who Lauren interacted with. That's all."

"She wasn't there with me," Cole said. "I didn't bring her. I didn't actually stay very long."

"What time did you arrive?" Megan asked.

"Gosh. Maybe ten?"

"Where were you before that?" she asked.

"Um, I was at home. Playing *Call of Duty*. To tell you the truth, I hadn't even planned on going to the Pits. But I was getting frustrated with my game play so I'd say it was around ten I just logged off and thought I'd go to the Pits after all."

"Did you go on your own? Did you pick up other friends?"

"I went by myself," he said. "It was supposed to be a bunch of alumni. You know, kids from my class and the older ones. When I got there, it was mostly people from Lauren's class."

"Did you speak to Lauren that night?" Megan asked.

Cole looked at the ceiling in thought. "We hung out a little. She was ... I don't know. This is going to sound bad. But

I was just over it after about a half an hour. I stayed until maybe eleven. Twelve? It was just all Lauren's class, is what I'm saying. I didn't have a lot of friends in that group."

"Cole," Megan said. "If someone else at that party remembers you having an argument with Lauren, do you know what they'd be referring to?"

Before I could interject, Cole answered. "Yes." He pursed his lips but stayed tall in his seat. He didn't fidget. He wasn't sweating.

"Can you tell me what happened?" Megan asked.

"Lauren was a little drunk," he said. "She ... uh ... she got a little clingy. A little overly friendly. And not just with me. But yes, she kind of tried to hang off me at one point. That wasn't cool with me. I don't know. I got a weird vibe. Like maybe she was trying to make someone jealous. I kind of peeled her off me and told her I was leaving. She yelled something at me. I don't even remember what. I just ... it's part of why I left. It was all ... uh ... I know this makes me sound bad. I'm only twenty. But it felt really high school. I've moved on. So, I took off."

"Where did you go after that?" Megan asked.

"I went home," he said.

"Was anyone else at your house?" she asked.

"My mom was home. But she was asleep. She usually turns in by eight. My dad's truck was in the garage. We had a brief conversation. I don't remember specifically. I kind of ... I have sort of my own place in the basement. It's not easy being twenty and still living with your folks."

"Of course," Megan said. She made more notes, pursed her lips, then found a smile as she looked back up.

"Is there anything else you need from Cole?" I asked. I wish I knew more about the timeline of Lauren's disappearance. I only had what I'd read in the papers. Lauren went to the party in the Pits. When Gil Rice woke up the next morning, she wasn't in her room like he expected. She didn't answer any texts or calls from him. Her car had been found parked along the side of the road, not far from the Pits, but Lauren herself had vanished.

"What did you do after you came home?" Megan asked.

"I don't remember if I went straight to bed or went back online. I might have gone online for a little while. I was kind of keyed up after leaving the party."

"Why is that?" she asked. I wanted to kick Cole under the table.

"I don't know," he said. "It was just ... like I said. The party was kind of sad to me. A bunch of kids trying to hold on to high school. I wasn't keyed up because I was angry. I was just ... it occurred to me I'm not that kid anymore. It was just weird, and I was feeling ... reflective. To be honest, that's the most notable thing to me about that party."

"Do you recall who else Lauren was hanging out with while you were there?" Megan asked. Cole dropped his head. It was the first sign of discomfort I'd seen in him. It raised alarm bells.

"Cole?" Megan asked.

"This is ... I'm not. She's dead. What does it matter what I thought of her that night?"

"What did you think of her?" Megan asked.

"Lauren had too much to drink. I'd never really known her to drink at all when we were closer. I should have offered to drive her home. I'm kicking myself because of that. If I had ... maybe none of this would have happened. Maybe she'd still be alive. But I have a girlfriend. This is a small town. I didn't want rumors to start flying."

"Cole," Megan said. "What do you think happened to Lauren?"

"Okay," I said. "Is this really productive anymore?"

"It's okay," Cole said. "I told you, I want to help. Maybe if I'd done more that night, it would have ... I don't know. I don't know what happened. But Lauren seemed different. Just the whole thing of her throwing herself on me. She doesn't act like that. She's not like a lot of the other girls. She's not a partier. Just her being there. Lauren Rice isn't the kind of girl you'd expect to hang out at the Pits, you know? Something was off. At the time, I just chalked it up to maybe she was feeling a little unsettled about college or whatever. We hadn't really talked much recently."

"I see," Megan said. "I'll ask again though, was there anyone else you recall her specifically hanging out with ... or off that night?"

"No," he said. "She was everywhere. Working the crowd, if you know what I mean. I saw her in just about every little group. Laughing. Talking. Just having what outwardly looked like a good time."

"Okay," Megan said.

"That's all I know," he said. "I swear."

"Okay," she said again. "Cole, there's just one more thing I need to ask you. We're asking this of everyone who attended that party."

My stomach twisted, knowing full well where this was going.

"Would you be willing to provide a DNA sample before you leave? It's just a cheek swab. It'll take less than a minute."

I opened my mouth to answer for him. Cole spoke up at the same time. "Of course!" he said. "Seriously. I meant what I said. Whatever you need. I just want to help."

Megan smiled and gathered her notes. She excused herself, promising to come right back with the swab kit.

"You can say no," I told him.

"I'm not scared," he said. "I'm not hiding anything. They can take whatever they want from me."

"Okay," I said.

"I'm not ... what I said ... I need you to know I'm not saying she asked for it. God. I feel like a jerk."

"I didn't get that impression," I said. "I think you're concerned for your friend. You think you could have done something different and it would have changed things. Maybe it would have. But probably not."

"I don't do that a lot," Cole said. "Hang out at the Pits. And I never would have let Emma go. I need you to know that. She doesn't drink, Ms. Leary. I swear. I shouldn't have gone. I knew it was a bad idea. I'm sorry. I just don't want you to think ... ugh. Emma's dad is going to kill me if he finds out I was there."

I smiled. "He won't hear it from me. For one thing, I'm sort of here in an official capacity ..."

Megan came back in. She opened the swab kit. Cole opened his mouth. She scraped the inside of his cheek and bagged the sample.

"We're good then," she said. "If I have any other questions, I'll let you know."

"Please do," Cole said.

We rose together, and I led him back down the hall. I passed by Eric's office. I poked my head in. "I'll see you tomorrow," I said. "I'm going to make sure Cole gets home. His car is still parked at my place."

Eric opened his mouth to protest, but saw the look in my eyes. Instead, he gave me a half-hearted salute.

Cole was mostly silent on the fifteen-minute drive back to my place. Everyone had cleared out. Even Joe had left with Emma. My motion lights came on as I pulled my car alongside Cole's.

"You did the right thing," I said. "Don't beat yourself up too much."

"I'll try," he said. "But I meant what I said. About Emma."

"Oh, I know," I said, sliding out of my seatbelt. We got out of my car and Cole started toward his.

"And one other thing," I said, just as he was about to climb into his driver's seat. "If I find out you ever *do* take Emma to one of those parties, it's not my brother you'll have to worry about."

I shot him a wink as I turned to walk back into the house.

Chapter 3

Monday morning I faced the first of two panels of inquisitors I would encounter that week. I'm fairly sure the stern eyes of Jeanie Mills and Miranda Sulier were the more formidable. They waited for me in Jeanie's downstairs office with a big pot of coffee between them. I went for it.

Jeanie snatched it away. "Nothing doing," she said. "Not until you spill the beans about your weekend."

"And your meeting with the governor's office," Miranda said. She was far more worried about the latter.

A few weeks ago, I'd been approached by Governor Christine Finch's office about a vacancy on the Woodbridge County District Court bench. They'd put me on a short list to fill it. I hadn't come close to making a decision on it.

"I meet with the governor's office on Thursday," I reminded her. Though as my office manager, Miranda knew my schedule better than I did.

"You were supposed to meet with them two weeks ago," Jeanie said. "You want to tell me why you keep putting it off?"

"I like it here," I said, smiling. "I find your charm irresistible, Jeanie."

She rolled her eyes. "It would be just like you to pull my ass out of retirement, then leave me just when I was starting to have fun again."

"Fun?" Miranda said. "We've been having fun? Nobody told me."

Jeanie's expression grew serious. She put the coffee pot back down and let me fill my cup. "Okay, enough small talk. Why don't you fill us in on what happened at the police station last night?"

"How is it you already know about that?" I asked. Though it was a futile line of questioning. Miranda had ears all over town. All over the state. Jeanie, on the other hand, had a sixth sense about when I was ready to stir things up. Which was often.

"Spill," Jeanie said. "You should have called us right away ."

"Yeesh," I said, blowing over my cup. "It's Monday morning. I figured I'd give you guys an actual weekend off. Where's Tori, by the way?"

"Down at the probate court looking up some filings for the Downing case," Jeanie answered. "I go to trial on that one in two weeks."

"You need any help with that one?" I asked. Fred Downing was one of Jeanie's oldest clients. Heck, I'd done work for him back when I was in law school and she took me under her wing. He finally died, and his greedy nieces and nephews filed a will contest.

"Not so far," Jeanie said. "And you should keep your schedule clear until you get through the selection process with the governor's office."

"I thought you didn't want me to leave you?" I asked, smiling. Jeanie was hard to read on this one. I couldn't tell for sure whether she wanted me on the bench or in the office above her. I didn't know myself. That's why I'd rescheduled the governor's office three times already.

"Are they going to arrest Cole Mathison?" Miranda asked, steering the conversation back to our most immediate gossip.

The bell over our lobby door rang as someone walked in. I looked at my smart watch. It wasn't even eight o'clock yet.

"Did you unlock that?" I asked Miranda. She shook her head no. Troubled, I started to rise.

My brother Joe strode in, his key in hand. He did maintenance work for me often enough, I'd given him his own set. He froze and had the decency to look sheepish when he saw Miranda and Jeanie.

"Sorry," he said. "I didn't mean to barge in."

"Like hell you didn't," Jeanie said, echoing my own thoughts.

"Cass," he said. "You didn't answer my texts last night."

"I got home late," I said. "It was a long day."

My brother narrowed his eyes. He wasn't having it.

"Better talk to him," Jeanie said. "We both know he'll be insufferable until you do. Cool your jets, Joseph. I know that look. You've been throwing the exact same one since you were about ten years old."

"Younger," Miranda chimed in. "He used to drive Lynn out of her mind with that one. I seem to recall you standing buck naked at about two years old looking just like that when she wanted to hose you off. You went frog hunting in the swamp over by the public boat launch. Stripped down to your birthday suit and caked yourself with mud for camouflage. She was two seconds from calling the police when she couldn't find you."

"Face it," I said to Joe. "You're outnumbered, big brother."

He let out an exasperated breath and made a sweeping gesture toward the stairs. "Ten minutes. That's all I'm asking for."

"She had a paddle she repurposed from one of those string-and-ball sets. The kind you'd get at the five and dime," Miranda went on. She had a mischievous twinkle in her eye. "Oooh, boy, did you run. Like a little greased piggy."

Steam came out of my brother's ears though the tips of them turned red with embarrassment.

"Stop it," I laughed, whispering to Jeanie and Miranda as I rose. Joe had already stormed up the stairs. "You'll just make him worse."

I topped off my coffee and headed up to join him, leaving the rest of my coven cackling behind me as I closed Jeanie's office door.

I found Joe pacing in front of my desk. I closed *my* office door and slid into my comfy leather chair.

"How's Emma holding up?" I said, trying to get serious. "Everyone was gone by the time I got back."

"How's she holding up?" Joe asked. "Not great, Cass."

"How close was she to Lauren Rice?" I asked. Joe shrugged.

"They were friends. Not best friends or anything. But they knew each other. They had classes together. And this is Delphi."

"Right," I said.

"Katy's out of her mind," he said, still pacing. "So am I. So is the whole town. Now they're all talking about Cole."

"You know Delphi," I said. "There's never been a rumor people didn't like to spread."

"What happened yesterday?" Joe asked. Finally, he took a seat opposite me. I took a good look at him. Lord, he was starting to look more and more like our dad. Only a year and a day older than me, we were what they called Irish twins. But Joe had a new sprinkling of silver just at his temples. Lines had begun to harden around his eyes, making him look distinguished and, dare I say it, downright handsome. Gross.

"They asked him some pretty routine questions," I said.

"He was at that party at the Pits," Joe filled in. "Cass, he came over to the house late last night. He wanted to talk to me, not Emma. I think he came straight from your place."

"Oh?" I asked.

"He said he was at that party. That he saw Lauren and that she'd been drinking. He blames himself for not offering to drive her home."

I found it comforting that at least Cole's story to the police had been consistent with what he told Joe.

"He's torn up over it," Joe said. "I've never seen him like that. He and Emma have only been dating since late last spring. I've pegged him as a good kid. Eager to learn. His old man ... there's some turmoil there. He and Cole's mom have been separated on and off. I get the impression he's a lot like ... well ... our old man."

"In what way?" I asked, bristling. On his good days, my father had been absent. The bad ones had been very bad indeed, and I knew Joe still bore some of those scars.

"Emma says she's seen bruises on Roxanne, Cole's mom. Cole won't talk about it."

"Oh," I said, my heart sinking.

"He's a hard worker," Joe said. "And he picks stuff up easily. I've been teaching him on small engines. He's been a big help. Quick study. And he seems, I don't know, starved for it."

"What do you mean, starved for it?" I asked.

"Well, like I said about his old man. He's never taken time with Cole to teach him anything. Hell, Emma complains that half the time, Cole wants to come over to hang out with me more than her. She and Katy laugh about it."

"That's a good thing, Joe," I said.

Joe got quiet. He ran a hard hand over his face. He hadn't yet shaved this morning. Those bits of silver shaded his cheeks and chin now, too.

"What did he tell the cops?" Joe asked.

"He told them about the same thing he told you," I said. "They're just trying to figure out who all was at that party. Establish a timeline as to when she left. See if anyone might have seen her leave with someone."

Joe got quiet. "Emma told me. She said Cole and Lauren used to date. When he came over last night, I asked him about it."

"And?" I asked.

"I told you, he's torn up. He said it wasn't a rough break-up or anything. They were still friends. She was dating some other guy after Cole."

Good, I thought. One more point for Cole for keeping his story straight. I could view it all clinically in my defense lawyer's brain. Except for one glaring thing. This was my niece's boyfriend we were talking about. If there was even a chance ...

"He's a good kid," Joe said. He seemed to say it more for himself than for me.

"It wasn't an interrogation, Joe," I said. "It was just an interview. They've interviewed lots of people. They'll probably want to talk to Emma too. You let me know if that happens. I'd be happy to sit in on that."

"I just ... God. To leave that poor kid in a ditch like that. They're not saying how she died. Did Eric ..."

"No," I said. "It's not Eric's case. Beyond that, he's not going to disclose details of an ongoing investigation to me. No matter how close we are."

"Yeah," Joe said. "No. I know. I just want ... she was Emma's age, roughly. Nineteen. Cass, I don't know if Gil Rice is going to survive this. I'm really worried about him. We all are. He's got guns ..."

"You don't think he'd go after someone on his own?" I said.

Joe shook his head. "I'm not worried about him using them on somebody else. I'm worried about him eating one of them."

I winced. "Joe ..."

"We're taking turns," he said. "I'm still in the Football Dads Facebook group. You know, from when Emma was a cheerleader for like five seconds. Anyway, there's a group of us keeping an eye on his place. So far, he's letting us. There's a bunch of ladies on the bereavement committee at First Presbyterian. They're taking meals over there. Checking in on him."

"Good," I said. "No. That's really good, Joe."

Then, my brother did something I hadn't seen him do since we were kids. He broke.

It came out of him so suddenly, it went through me like a shock wave. Joe's shoulders bunched and he let out a racking sob. He buried his face in his hands. I came around my desk and put my arms around him.

"Hey," I whispered. "Joey. It's going to be okay."

"It isn't," he said. "Not for that poor girl. I don't know what I'd do. Lauren was all he had. She was the thing that made it all bearable for Julie Rice when she got sick. She counted on that kid to be there for Gil. She was only thirteen at the time, but she stepped up. We all saw it. You weren't here for that funeral. You were still in Chicago. But I swear I saw that kid grow up in one afternoon when they buried her mom."

My blood turned to ice for a moment. This wasn't just about Gil and Lauren Rice. My brother and I had lost our mother at roughly the same age Lauren had. We, too, had been forced to grow up in the span of a day.

"You're a good friend," I whispered. "But more than that, you're a good dad. Emma's okay. She's more than okay. But she needs you now. You can't make sense of this for her, but you can be there. That's all she needs."

"He's going to kill himself," Joe said, lifting his eyes to meet mine. "And in his place, Cass, I don't know if I'd be able to get out from under it either. So if you know something. If you have to do something ... you've done it before."

I straightened. "What do you mean?"

"I love that kid," he said.

"I know you do. Emma's ..."

"No," he said. "I love Cole too. But if you hear something ... if Eric ..."

"What are you asking me?" I asked. "Joe, if you and the rest of these football dads are planning some kind of vigilante crap ..."

Joe's eyes hardened. "Don't take the moral high ground with me. I know what world you live in."

I jerked my head back. It was a not-so-veiled reference to my days working white collar defense for the Thorne Law Group back in Chicago. I knew what Joe thought. I knew what everyone thought. I worked for powerful men who sometimes used nefarious means if it fit their agenda.

"Joe," I said. "I think you need to go home. Be with Katy and Emma. Keep an eye on Gil. Will you promise me you won't do anything I have to try and clean up after?"

I meant the last bit as a light-hearted joke. My brother's eyes seemed to turn to stone though, unsettling me.

"I promise," he finally said. Then his face softened, and he kissed my cheek. I felt far from reassured.

Chapter 4

"Ms. Leary?" a bright voice echoed through the cavernous rotunda of Michigan's Capitol Building. I pulled my eyes away from a giant, frowning portrait of William Woodbridge, Michigan's second governor and my county's namesake.

"Ms. Leary." The woman attached to the bright voice drew closer and extended a hand to shake mine.

She had bright eyes to go with the voice, slicked-back black hair and wore a crisp blue suit and sensible shoes. I pegged her close to my age. Mid-thirties, but probably on the front half, while I edged toward the back.

"I'm Jane Witherspoon," she said. "We spoke on the phone. I'm Governor Finch's deputy chief of staff. Thanks so much for driving all the way up here."

"My pleasure," I said, shaking her hand. I'd worn my tried-and-true black Alexander McQueen power suit. I'd never lost a trial in it ... so far. Ms. Witherspoon's eyes stopped on the beat-up, brown leather bag I carried. I would weather every dirty look on that score. They'd have to pry that bag off my cold, dead shoulder to get me to give it up.

"We're meeting down the hall," she said. "Just a small informal group today."

"Hmm," I said. "Informal." My eyes went up and up, taking in the ornate tiered floors above me.

Jane led me halfway down the hall and stopped at a large double door. She opened it and ushered me into a conference room where mahogany apparently went to die. Two other staff members were seated at the massive oval table. One man, deeply tanned with salt-and-pepper gray hair; one woman with dark eyes, even darker hair, and a wide, friendly smile.

"Ms. Leary?" Jane said. "This is David Carmichael, the governor's communications director. This is my boss, Salina Jarvis, Governor Finch's chief of staff."

"Good to meet you," I said, shaking each of their hands. After waving off refreshments, I took a seat on one side of the table. Jane moved around it to squeeze in next to the others, making the thing feel a lot like a tribunal.

"You know why we're all here," Jane said. "We're here to answer as many of your questions."

"I appreciate that," I said.

"We've heard great things about you," Salina Jarvis said. I knew she'd been around Michigan politics forever. She'd mounted her own failed bid for a state congressional seat about a decade ago. Since then, Salina Jarvis was considered one of the shrewdest political operatives around.

David Carmichael I knew little about. Miranda had figured out he'd started as a beat reporter with the *Free Press*. But that was eons ago in the days when most people still preferred a physical paper. Governor Christine Finch had been elected two years ago during what was known as a youth wave. So far, she'd managed to survive major political scandals and positioned herself as a true moderate and rising star within the party. If one concerned themselves with things like that. I didn't.

Which was why I, more than anyone, had no earthly clue why I was even here.

"We're considering a few names," Salina Jarvis continued. "But we're very excited to talk to you today, Ms. Leary."

"You can call me Cass," I said.

"Good," she said. "I think I can speak for everyone that we can all be on a first-name basis. Now, why don't you tell us how you feel about our offer."

"Offer?" I smiled. "You said you were looking at several potential candidates for appointment to the district court seat."

"Right," David chimed in. "Let's not get ahead of ourselves. First off ... um ... Cass. You haven't directly answered whether you'd be interested in the position."

"Well," I said. "I have to be honest, this really came out of the blue. I truly hadn't thought about becoming a judge. So I'm curious; why me?"

The three of them exchanged looks. They remained friendly, hard to read, but I got the impression I'd just asked the million-dollar question.

"Woodbridge County can be a tough nut to crack," Salina said. "The governor really feels that the community would be best served by a judge with deep roots in it. You were born and raised in Delphi. You have a stellar reputation among your colleagues."

"Not so much the town, though." I smiled. "I'm sure you've done your research. You know my last name doesn't usually provide me with much of an advantage."

"We're not looking for another elitist judge," Jane said. "You have the kind of background that we think would well suit the job. You've got the legal pedigree. You've got name recognition. And you care about the community."

"Are you interested?" David said. "Forgive me for being blunt, but I don't see the point of going through this exercise if you're just ... curious."

"I'm interested," I said, blurting it in a way that surprised even me.

"That's great!" Jane gushed. "So why don't we talk about what you can expect from the nomination process."

She reached for a thin file folder sitting on one end of the table. She slid it across to me. I opened the flap. It contained a multiple page questionnaire.

"It starts there," Jane said.

"What is your timeframe?" I said, closing the file and sliding it into my messenger bag.

"We'd like to install an interim judge to the bench within the next few months," Salina said. "You understand that Governor Finch will have the ultimate say. And she's going to want to meet with you, but she'll rely heavily on our recommendation. After that, if she chooses to appoint you, a special election will be held in November of next year to fill the remainder of Judge Tucker's seat. He was up for reelection in three years."

"I remember," I said. And this was the part that gave me pause. I'd never considered myself a politician. "Forgive me, but so far all of this we could have discussed over the phone or by email. If you don't mind, what's your real purpose in wanting to meet with me face to face today?"

Again, the three of them exchanged a look. David Carmichael cleared his throat and spoke for the group.

"Well, the first of it you've already addressed. We wanted to know directly from you whether you're interested in the job. Beyond that, you understand there's a formal vetting process. So we'd like to know, once again, directly from you, whether there's anything you'd like to share with us before we go down this road."

"Any skeletons in my closet?" I smiled.

"So to speak," Salina said.

I sat back in my seat and folded my hands in my lap. They still hadn't really answered my question about who put my name forward. I didn't know how these things normally worked, but I had no doubt they'd solicited inquiries from other members of the Woodbridge County Bar. I felt a lump in my throat thinking about who I would have considered the front runner. Our late prosecutor, Jack LaForge, had always dreamed of taking the bench. He tragically died of a heart attack just last month. We were all still feeling the impact of his loss.

"I think my history is well known," I said. "I told you, I don't usually win points in Delphi for being Joseph Leary's daughter. My dad was an Olympic-caliber drunk. He wasn't so nice to my mother and brother. He's got a record. He was recently accused of murder, falsely, I might add. And most of the world assumes I got my start as a mob lawyer. And I assume you do too. Is that what you're really here to ask me about?"

Salina Jarvis dove right in. "We're aware that you were lead counsel for the Thorne Law Group, yes. And we're aware of your past relationship with Killian Thorne, head of the Thorne family businesses. But ... as far as we're aware, he's operated above board."

"Rumors notwithstanding," I said.

"Exactly," David answered.

"But you're no longer associated with the Thornes," Jane helpfully added.

"No," I said. "I am not."

"Good," Salina said.

"Is there anything about your past, your family, your current life that you wouldn't want to become public knowledge?" David asked. "Because it will. I can assure you of that."

"I'm an open book." I smiled.

"Your political affiliations," Salina started. I cut her off.

"I have none," I said. "See, that's the part in all of this I don't fully understand. I'll fill out your questionnaire, of course, but I suspect you've already done your research on me. Fully. I'm a true independent. I don't even put political signs in front of my home or my business. I intend to keep it that way. Mind you, that doesn't mean I don't have strong convictions. I can assure you, I do."

"Would you care to enlighten us on some of them?" Salina said. "The governor's come out very strongly on hot-button issues like abortion rights, gun control, etc."

I smiled. "And last time I checked, county district court judges don't really rule on constitutional issues."

"They don't," David said. "But you'd be kidding yourself if you think your opponent, whoever that may be, won't use whatever they can to win."

"Understood," I said. "And like I said, I'll be happy to fully answer your questionnaire. After that?"

"After that," Salina said, "we'll expect you to submit to a formal interview with us and other members of the governor's staff. And as I said, the governor herself."

"I look forward to it," I said, rising. The trio rose to join me. We shook hands again. I had no idea whether they still thought I was a good bet or not. But I meant what I said. My life was my life. If it didn't mesh with the governor's agenda, it was better we all knew that as soon as possible.

"Let me have one of the pages show you out," Jane said.

"Or if you'd like a behind-the-scenes tour while you're here
..."

"Thank you," I said. "I'm actually due in court back in
Woodbridge County later today. May I ask, how long do I
have before you need this back from me?" I lifted my bag and
patted it.

"Would sixty days be ample?" Jane asked.

"More than," I smiled. Then, I left Jane Witherspoon,
Salina Jarvis, and David Carmichael behind as I made my
way to the door.

I got halfway down the Capitol steps before my phone
rang. Miranda already. I swear that woman was psychic. She
always knew exactly when to call.

"Just got done," I said as I answered. "Nothing major to
report. But yeah ... I told them I'm interested in Tucker's
seat."

Miranda paused before answering. That alone should
have clued me in to the nature of her call.

"That's great, honey," she said. "I'm happy for you. It's
just ..."

"What?" I said, my heart filling with dread at the tone of
her voice.

"You're going to want to head on back just as soon as you
can. Word just came down. They've arrested Emma's
boyfriend, Cole."

Chapter 5

I ARRIVED at the Delphi Public Safety Building just as a patrol car pulled up carrying Cole Mathison, handcuffed in the back.

Megan Lewis's unmarked gray sedan slid into the spot next to mine. She emerged grim-faced, bracing no doubt for whatever I had to say.

"Ms. Leary!" Cole said, breathless as two patrolman helped him out of the vehicle. "I don't know what's going on. They think ..."

"Stop," I said, putting a finger to my lips. "Just cooperate with these officers. They've read you your rights. Use them. Don't answer any questions other than your name and date of birth. Got it?"

His Adam's apple bobbed up and down and he gave me a nod. The kid was terrified.

"Why didn't I get a phone call?" I said to Megan after they led Cole in the building.

She pulled a piece of paper out of the inside pocket of her blazer and handed it to me. It was her arrest warrant. I scanned it quickly, but it was almost a moot point.

"You could have served this on me or given me a heads-up it was coming," I said. "I would have arranged for that kid to surrender himself. My secretary said you picked him up at the lumberyard in the middle of his workday."

"I wasn't aware you were officially his attorney of record," she said.

"Megan, come on," I said. "You know that kid is a friend of the family. This wasn't necessary."

"Nobody is keeping you from doing your job," she said. "I'd appreciate it if you didn't get in the way of mine." With that, she brushed past me and charged up the stairs.

"What the ever-loving ..." I muttered. I grabbed my bag out of the car and started to head up.

Tires squealed behind me. I turned to see my brother Joe's truck slide in crooked to a spot further down the sidewalk.

"Perfect." I sighed. "Might as well invite the whole circus."

Joe rushed toward me, white-faced. Over his shoulder, I saw Emma in the passenger seat, still strapped in and bawling.

"Joe," I said. "You shouldn't be here. She definitely shouldn't be here."

"I know," he said. "But she was about to tear off without me. Short of tying her to a kitchen chair, this was the best I could come up with. I promised her I'd make sure you got here."

"Promise kept," I said. "Now disappear. There's nothing you can do right now. Let me go in there and see what's what. I saw Cole for two seconds. He seems to understand, keeping his mouth shut. Same goes for you and Emma. Have they already asked you for interviews?"

"Yeah," he said. "Emma. Detective Lewis left a voicemail on her phone. Emma hasn't called her back yet."

"Okay," I said.

"What are they saying he did?" Joe asked. "What's the evidence?"

"I don't know yet," I said. "I haven't even had a proper chance to review the arrest warrant. I'm not even sure what the charges are. Let me do that. Let me get Cole through the booking process."

Joe waited while I took a second look at the arrest warrant. My heart did a little flip. Good Lord. They were going for murder. I slipped it into the outer pocket of my bag.

"Please just take Emma home. Tell her I'll do whatever I can. Where are his parents in all of this?"

"Cass," Joe said. "I know Vic Jankowski. I got Cole that job out at the lumberyard. He won't have him back after this. He's already texting me. They led him away in handcuffs in front of the whole day crew."

"Great," I said. I knew Vic well enough too. No matter what else happened, Cole would be lucky to still have a job by the end of the day.

"Let me go do my job," I said. "That is ... I'm not saying I'm agreeing to defend Cole. If I do that, you know we're done having conversations about this. He's probably better off with a public defender or ..."

"Just find out what you can," Joe said. "Like you always tell me, one step at a time. I'm going to head over to Cole's folks' house after I get rid of Emma. They probably don't even know about this yet."

"Right," I said. "Good idea." I repositioned my bag and headed up the stone steps.

By the time I weaved my way through the desk sergeant and the bull pen, Cole had already been through the initial booking process. They had him installed in an interview room. I found Detective Lewis waiting in the hallway in front of it.

"You're not interviewing that kid outside my presence," I said.

"Oh, he's already asking for you," she said. She held another piece of paper out for me. By the color of it, goldenrod, I could already guess what it was. The district court still typed up court scheduling documents the old-fashioned way before they were logged into the online system. I took a glance at it. Cole's first court appearance was scheduled for eleven a.m. tomorrow morning.

"It was the soonest I could get," she said. "Sorry, but your boy will have to spend the night in jail."

"I haven't even seen the charging document yet," I said.

"You can call Jack's ... um ... the prosecutor's office as soon as you're finished here," she said. Jack LaForge's death was still so fresh in everyone's mind. It would take a long time before any of us stopped calling it Jack's office.

"You can take your time," Megan said, giving me her first concession. "I don't need this room for a while."

"Thanks," I said. I slipped the docket schedule in my bag next to the arrest warrant. Cole Mathison looked like he might get sick as I walked into the interview room and closed the door behind me.

I slowly sat down in the seat opposite Cole. He looked generally scared. Terrified, really. Tears played at the corner of his eyes and he struggled to keep his hands still as he folded them in his lap.

"I didn't kill Lauren," he said.

"I'm still trying to figure out how they made probable cause to arrest you," I said. I ran my finger down the list on the arrest warrant. They had cell phone records. Standard. They had his statement from the interview earlier in the week. In all likelihood, they'd caught him in a lie. Though I'd have to look at the case file, I had every suspicion Cole's DNA sample might have clinched it.

"Cole," I said, folding the arrest warrant. "I need brutal honesty. What was going on between you and Lauren Rice?"

His face fell. So did my stomach.

"They subpoenaed your cell phone records as well as Lauren's."

"How could they get that?" he asked. "I had my phone until they came and arrested me at Vic's this morning."

"They only need your cell phone number to start with," I said. "That will show them everywhere your phone has been within the timeframe leading up to and after Lauren's disappearance. I'm going to go out on a very short limb here and guess you've been communicating with her recently. And a lot."

He pressed his thumb and forefinger to the bridge of his nose. "Yeah," he said. He looked up. "I didn't kill her. I don't care what they think my cell phone shows. I didn't kill her."

"All right," I said. "Let's take this step by step. They'll get you through the rest of the booking process this evening. After that, you're scheduled for an arraignment tomorrow morning. It'll happen in district court. The judge will determine whether it's appropriate to set bail."

"Whether it's appropriate? Ms. Leary, do I have to spend the night in here?"

"Yes," I said. "You'll go to a holding cell until they take you over to the courthouse. If you want me to represent you at least this far ..."

"I do!" he said. "Please. Oh ... I have to pay you ..."

"One step at a time, remember? I haven't completely decided whether I want to take your case. It could get complicated. If my niece is called ... when my niece is called as a witness if this goes to trial ..."

"I don't trust anybody else but you. I don't know anybody else but you," he said, his voice breaking. It was hard not to feel for him. He was just a kid. At the same time, so was Lauren Rice. Could my entire family have been so horribly wrong about Cole?

"We'll get through the arraignment," I said. "I'll take a look at the charging document. I can make a case for bail. Cole, do you have anything else in your past I need to know about? Tell me about every single parking ticket."

"Nothing," he said. "I swear."

"If you're lying, it'll take my staff about five minutes to find out," I said.

"I'm not lying," he said. "No parking tickets. No speeding tickets. Ms. Leary, I helped run Safety City with the sheriff's office for the last two years. They gave me a junior deputy badge."

"Okay," I said. "That'll work strongly in your favor. I know you've also done volunteer work with your church. You have strong ties to the community. But the prosecution is going to argue the severity ... the brutality of the crime and what happened to Lauren. You need to be prepared to hear it. And you need to keep your cool. No outbursts. You let me do all the talking. Where are your folks?"

"I think the police were going to go over to my house. They had a search warrant."

"Great," I said, expecting as much. I just hoped my brother didn't make a nuisance of himself if he stopped by. It would be one in a row.

"Another thing," I said. "And this is probably the most important. You cannot discuss this matter with anyone. Not your parents. Not friends. Nobody. Do you hear me?"

He nodded. "Of course. Yeah. Yeah. I know that."

I sat back in my seat. He had to feel like the walls were closing in.

"All right," I said. "So for now, tell me why the police think you killed that girl."

He squeezed his eyes shut. "I didn't lie," he started. "But they just asked me about the night of the bonfire at the Pits. That's all they asked me about so I didn't think they cared about the rest of it. I mean, don't they have Lauren's phone or something? Wouldn't that detective already know all of this? There were ... Ms. Leary, Lauren started texting me a few weeks ago. A lot. She ... she was ... she wanted to get back together. Her texts got kind of aggressive."

"Aggressive how?" I asked.

"She started sending pictures. God. They're going to find them all. I deleted them off my phone. But if they have Lauren's ..."

"What kind of pictures?" I asked, though I already knew.

"Of her naked," he said. "I was clear with her. I wasn't into that. I'm with Emma now. She was ... persistent. I started hearing some things that had me worried about her. But I didn't want to get involved. Lauren and I ... at least on my end ... we weren't that serious. We were convenient."

"Cole," I said. "When was the last time you had intercourse with Lauren Rice?"

I didn't think it possible, but Cole Mathison's face went even whiter.

"I don't remember the date," he said.

"But it was recently," I said.

"Last winter, I think. It wasn't intercourse. Not how you think. And ... I didn't lie about it. Emma knows everything, I swear to God."

"If the cops found your DNA on Lauren's body," I said. "Do you know how it got there?"

He finally broke. Tears streamed down his cheeks. "They can't. It can't be mine."

Those walls closed in. Cole's shoulders crumpled as he must have felt the weight of a two-ton anvil dropped straight on his head.

Chapter 6

I HAVE a knack for taking on cases the citizens of Delphi hold against me. I represented the woman accused of murdering the town's most celebrated coach. I defended a stone-cold contract killer. I defended the most hated man in town, my father. So, when I walked into the district courthouse on Thursday morning ready to get Cole Mathison at least through his arraignment, I expected the usual vitriol and heated stares.

Instead, I got hugs. Actual. Hugs.

"He's in good hands. I know it." This from Patrice Willoughby, Delphi High School's Spanish teacher. Reverend Ned Maynard from the First Presbyterian Church came in right behind her.

"Um ... thanks," I said. I didn't want a scene. I didn't want anything. It all happened as Gil Rice made his way down the hall, looking even skinnier than he had a week ago. He hadn't combed his hair, hadn't shaved. He wore an ill-fitting suit with sleeves so long they covered the bases of his thumbs. He froze, eyes glistening as he watched Patrice and Reverend Ned. They at least had the decency to look chagrined as they made their awkward way into the courthouse. A few minutes from now, they would stand ready to serve as character witnesses for Cole if it came to it.

The elevator doors opened behind me. I braced myself, expecting to see my brother again. I'd threatened him within an inch of his life to stay away. Emma too.

I let out a breath of relief as Eric strode out. He shot me a wink that sent my blood humming. Then he saw Gil. Eric turned all business and took Lauren's father gently by the elbow.

Eric had a light touch and reassuring manner that put most people at ease. It made him a devastating interviewer. It also made him a great friend. He was that for Gil Rice now.

"Come on," Eric said. "We'll find a place for you. Do you mind if I sit with you?"

Gil let Eric lead him into the courtroom, his shoulders sagging with gratitude. The man needed someone to help him through what to do. God. I didn't want to cause him more pain. I wanted justice for Lauren as much as anyone else.

The elevator doors opened once more and Cole came out. He wore a suit Joe brought over for him. It fit him well enough. He looked freshly scrubbed and terrified.

"Remember what I said," I told him as Deputy Poehler brought him over to me. "Nothing out of you. We've got a good case for bail."

Taking my advice to heart, Cole didn't even verbally respond. He nodded, and we walked in together.

I felt Cole stiffen as he caught sight of Gil. He started to turn. I could feel the anguish coming off of him. My God. He wanted to comfort Lauren's father. It was as if he momentarily forgot why he was here. Why we were all here.

"This way," I said abruptly, clearing my throat. If Gil

understood what almost happened, he didn't show it. He kept staring straight ahead. Only Eric gave me a pained look.

We made our way to the defense table. Across from me, the newly installed acting prosecuting attorney for Woodbridge County gathered his papers.

"Hi, Rafe," I said. Rafe Johnson. Young. Bright. Ambitious. A new hire from Washtenaw County, his installment had been a bold choice. Everyone expected it to be someone local or one of the existing assistant prosecutors. But when the dust settled after Jack LaForge's death, no one had wanted to throw their hat into the ring to take over his office.

"Cass," Rafe said, giving me what I can only describe as a professional smile. He was forty. Good-looking, with a thick head of closely cropped black hair and angular features, Rafe had political ambitions that wouldn't keep him in Delphi for long. Unless ...

Rumor was, he also had an interest in the district court seat I'd just interviewed for. Oh yes. This trial could get interesting indeed if it went that far.

Rafe handed me a thick file. "Preliminary case file," he said. "We were going to courier it over, but this was faster."

"Thank you," I said. I stuffed it into my bag, feeling it burn a hole already.

"All rise!"

Judge Mark Colton's bailiff announced his presence. Everything from then on felt paint by numbers.

Cole stood tall and straight as the judge read the sobering list of charges against him. First-degree murder. Abuse of a corpse, stemming from Lauren's presumed removal from the site of her murder to the ditch where she was found.

"Do you understand the charges against you, young man?" Judge Colton asked.

"I didn't ... Oh. I'm ... I didn't kill Lauren."

I tugged on Cole's sleeve. Then, remarkably, Rafe Johnson didn't object to setting bail. Jack LaForge never would have gone for that. Ever.

"Fine," the judge said. "We'll set bail at two hundred and fifty thousand. Standard conditions apply. Mr. Mathison, you are under a no contact bond. That means you're to have no communications with the victim's family. Do you understand?"

"Yes," Cole said quickly.

"Your lawyer will go over the rest of the bail conditions with you. Do you have a bondsman in mind?"

"We do," I said. I came prepared. Cole's distant cousin owned one of the best-known bonding companies in the county. I just hoped his family could come up with the twenty-five thousand needed to get him out. Once that happened, Cole would be able to stay at home.

"Fine," Judge Colton said. "My clerk will get true copies to everyone. Make your decisions on prelim. We're scheduling into late November, I think."

"Thank you, Your Honor," I said.

"Bailiff," Judge Colton said. "What's up next?"

And we were adjourned.

"Okay," I said to Cole. "I don't have a lot of time. I've got another hearing in about twenty minutes upstairs. They're going to take you back to holding. Your next step is figuring out how to come up with ten percent of your bond."

"Um ... there's been a fund set up, I think. I didn't do it. Reverend Maynard did. There's been a donation from someone from the church."

"Good," I said. "I'll speak with him. Once that's clear, you'll be processed out. You'll stay at home with your parents.

They should have been here today, Cole. Your mother, at least."

"She ... she's not in great shape. She would have just sat here sobbing the whole time. I didn't want to put her through it," he explained.

"Well, if it comes to it, she'll need to be by your side in court. You need a show of support at hearings. She can't come to meetings with your lawyer, but ..."

"Won't that be you?" he asked. "If it's about the money, the reverend said ..."

"I need to see what we're up against," I said. "Then I'll make a recommendation. I promised to get you this far for Emma's sake. But this isn't so clear-cut for me ..."

"I understand," Cole said. "And I really appreciate what you've done so far."

I looked over my shoulder. Eric had wisely gotten Gil Rice out of Dodge. I wasn't so much afraid of Gil saying something to Cole as I was the reverse. The less drama the better at this point.

Deputy Poehler came into view. "Judge needs the courtroom," he said. "You can talk to your lawyer back at the jail if you need to ..."

"We're done for now," I said. "Thanks, Pat."

I gave Cole a reassuring pat on the sleeve, then made my exit.

As luck would have it, my Circuit Court hearing got postponed, freeing the next hour or two to review Rafe Johnson's file on Cole.

By the time I made it back to the office, I found it empty. Jeanie had a few house call estate planning appointments. Miranda took an early lunch, and I had Tori doing research from home.

I made my way to the conference room so I could lay out

the file. I found myself holding my breath a bit as I pulled out the report.

Cole's transcripted interview, I knew by heart. I was there. Rafe included seven witness statements, primarily from people who had attended the bonfire at the Pits. I skimmed them for now. The consensus seemed to be that everyone had seen Cole with Lauren at one point or another. Every one of them commented on how they appeared to be arguing, but nobody knew the substance. One witness claimed she saw them talking away from the party by the side of the road. I noted her name. She might be the last person to have allegedly seen them together. Cole hadn't mentioned leaving the party with Lauren. If true, that would hurt.

Cole's phone records provided no real surprises either. The tracking corresponded with Cole's statement about where he'd been. The phone was stationary at his parents' house from just after three until seven the next morning when he left for work.

It wasn't an alibi, but at least it wasn't an obvious lie.

Lauren's phone records, on the other hand, made the floor drop out from under me.

She'd been at home most of the time during the day of her murder. There was a trip to Target that lasted about an hour. She had texted Gil to tell him that's where she was headed. The cell data tracked.

She went out again after five with friends. Then, just before ten p.m., she went to the Pits. She appeared to have left within ten minutes of when Cole did. The data dropped out right after that, like she'd turned it off. The phone itself had been found in her empty car about a mile from the woods in the driver's-side door cup holder.

None of those things alone would rise to the level of probable cause to arrest Cole. I flipped to the end of the report. The tenth addendum after the witness statements and cell phone data contained transcripts of Lauren Rice's texts to Cole Mathison in the two weeks leading up to her murder.

Sweat beaded the back of my neck as I read. Most of the texts went unanswered.

From two weeks before her murder.

Lauren: Hey, we need to talk. I don't like how we left things.

From thirteen days before her murder.

Lauren: I came by your house. I know you were home. Either pick up your phone or meet me somewhere. I miss you.

It went on like that for several days. Lauren kept reaching out, wanting to talk. Cole remained unresponsive.

From four days before the murder.

Lauren: You're not going to get away with ghosting me, asshole. This little problem of yours isn't going to go away. I've been more than patient. I'm not trying to ruin your life. I'm trying to get you to do the right thing.

Do the right thing. Lord.

The conference room door opened. Miranda poked her head in. The smell of freshly baked bagels wafted in. Miranda waved a brown paper bag.

"Figured you'd want to eat in," she said. "I heard about the hearing."

I sat back in my chair and managed a smile. Miranda's dropped.

"Uh-oh," she said. "I sure know that look."

"Miranda," I said. "Can you find out what's holding up the full autopsy report on Lauren Rice? I need to know if she was pregnant."

Miranda let out a sigh. "Lordy," she said. "Looks like I better order dinner too. It's going to be a long day."

Chapter 7

It took almost the rest of the day for Cole Mathison to get processed out of the county jail. Dave Carver, the bail bondsman, called me at ten p.m. to tell me he'd finally got it all taken care of. Cole was spending the night at his place. He called it a family favor. He didn't think I'd want to meet with Cole with his parents around. By then, I was spent. Cooked. I ignored half a dozen calls from my brother and Emma before falling asleep at the conference room table.

A stiff cup of coffee and Tori's smiling face holding it woke me up. I had notebook paper stuck to my cheek as I lifted my head. "That bad?" Tori asked. She slid the mug my way.

"Might help if I just injected it straight into my veins," I said. I pretty much scalded the roof of my mouth as I took the first sip, but figured it was a small price to pay to enter the land of the living again.

"Can you have Miranda shuffle my appointments this morning? I'm going to need to make a house call at David Carver's," I said. "Cole's staying there today. It's more private so we can talk."

"Already handled," she said. "Only other thing you've got today is a pretrial on the Kinsale license suspension case. Jeanie's gonna take care of it. She's got a couple of motions on the domestic docket right around the same time. Unless you're expecting surprises on Kinsale."

"I always expect surprises," I said. "Wait, isn't that an oxymoron?"

"I get it." Tori smiled. "You want me to head over to Carver's with you?"

"Not this time," I said. "Cole trusts me. I'll have a better shot telling if he's lying one on one."

"Do you think he's been lying?"

"I don't know," I said. "That's the truth. I know he's been holding back. Any word on the full autopsy report?"

"Not yet," Tori said. "Miranda's got a call in to Dr. Trainor's office. Several, actually. The best news I can give you is it hasn't been released yet. Not even to Rafe Johnson."

"Well, let me know if that changes," I said. "Let me run a brush through my hair and over my teeth. I don't know how long I'll be at Carver's."

"Take your time," Tori said. "We can hold the fort down here."

"Thanks," I said. I sniffed under my arm. I'd smelled worse. I always kept a change of clothes and essentials here for the occasion. Lately, I'd been using them more often.

I gathered the notes I made last night, downed more coffee, then headed out the door. A quick text exchange from Dave Carver, and I knew Cole was ready for me. I just wasn't sure if I was ready for him.

David Carver lived at the very edge of Delphi. He had a deep, twenty-acre wooded lot. To the east, he owned another forty acres of corn fields he rented out to a local farmer. His house was one of the oldest in the county. A few years back, it had been registered as a historical site. His great-great-grand-something had actually been one of the town's founders but had lost some vote to name it Carverton instead of Delphi.

I pulled up and parked in Dave's driveway circle. He waited for me on the front porch with a friendly wave. I knew he'd likely seen me coming minutes ago. He had trail cams installed everywhere.

Dave was a prepper. He kept an apocalypse room underground. My brother Matty was one of the few people Dave had ever allowed down to see it. He'd been sworn to secrecy about all of its contents, but Matty held it in awe.

"Hey, Dave," I said.

Dave was one of the good ones. He put off a prickly vibe and most people in town were scared of him. He liked it that way. But our families went way back. I used to babysit his younger brother Garth. He'd been killed by a roadside bomb outside of Kandahar during the first years of the Afghan War.

"You can use the office," he said. "You want Max to bring you some lunch?"

Dave's wife Maxine ran a catering business. My stomach growled at the mention of her.

"Not just yet," I said. "Cole's mom or dad show up yet?"

Dave shook his head. "Neither. We haven't seen Rudy for a while. They've been on and off again for years. Roxanne is pretty fragile. That's why I thought it was a better idea to just have Cole here for the night."

"How close are you to her?" I asked.

"She's my mom's cousin's daughter, I think is how it goes. She's sweet. I don't know if I'd say she's very worldly, if you know what I mean. It's Rudy we have a problem with. I'll be honest. Rudy Mathison is ... not a good person. Most of the family won't have him over. So Roxanne's been pretty isolated."

"I'd heard something similar from my brother," I said. "I really appreciate you stepping up for Cole. Roxanne's on my list of people to talk to."

"Just give a holler when you want lunch," Dave said. "Maxine's fixing up some of her gourmet chicken salad. Wedding shower tomorrow."

"I'll keep that in mind," I said.

I walked through the living room and found Cole already sitting on one of two leather couches in Dave's home office. He'd converted the original master bedroom for the purpose. He kept an antique cherry wood desk in one corner. I sat on the opposite couch and plopped my messenger bag beside me. I took out a notepad, pen, and selected printouts from Lauren Rice's text transcripts. I tossed them to Cole. I was in no mood for lengthy preambles.

Cole caught them and began to read. He bit the inside of his cheek. His fingers shook as he flipped the pages. Then he set them down on the table between us.

"I need to know everything," I said. "Every single thing. I'm not Emma's aunt right now. I haven't fully decided whether I want to continue being your lawyer. For now, I still am. Anything you tell me I'm bound by law to keep confidential. Do you understand? The worst thing you can do right now is lie or withhold facts. The absolute worst. Yesterday, you were charged with first-degree murder. That means you could go away for the rest of your life. No parole. Maximum security prison. Forever, Cole."

He trembled as the weight of my words settled around him.

"I was trying to do the right thing," he said.

"About what?"

"I know how this will all sound. It all looks so bad after everything that happened. I know that. But it's not what you probably think. It's not what the police think. It's a nightmare."

"Cole," I said. "The truth. Or I'm leaving. I'm done."

"Lauren and I were talking," he said. "Just talking. She gave up a lot for her dad. She worried about him being alone. She turned down a partial scholarship at Valparaiso so she could stay home and take care of him. I told her it was a mistake. Everyone told her it was a mistake. I can't believe her dad let her do it. But then ... I don't know. Earlier this year, I think it all started catching up with her. She started to regret it. She started to regret a lot of the decisions she'd made. Including ... at least she told me ... me."

"She regretted you?"

"Yeah," he said. "She said she missed me. This was ... I think, early spring of this year. A few weeks before I started going out with Emma. Lauren wanted to get back together. I felt ... I felt sorry for her. She seemed depressed. I was worried about her, really worried. She ... Ms. Leary ..."

"She what?" I asked.

"She tried to kill herself. She told me she did, anyway. She said she swallowed some pills. I went over there. I made her throw up. I never saw a pill bottle. And it's not like I inspected anything after ... but she was in bad shape. I brought her to my house that night. Her dad was gone, visiting his sister."

"When was all this?" I asked. The cell phone records only went back six months, to mid-March.

"Late January, early February," he said. "There was snow on the ground still. After that, I felt like Lauren just needed a friend. I don't know why she felt like she could confide in me. I tried to be there for her. I tried to get her to talk to her dad. Or a counselor. She wouldn't. She said if I tried to force her, she'd just finish what she started."

"That's a lot to put on you," I said.

"Yeah," he said. "After a while, I just got exhausted. If I tried to pull back, she'd freak out, threaten to hurt herself again."

"Did you start things up again with her?" I asked. "Romantically?"

"A little," he said.

"A little? There's no halfway with that, Cole," I said.

"We hooked up, yes," he said. "Again, that was before I started dating Emma. I swear. And I ended things with Lauren. For good. That was late January, early February, at the latest, I think."

"You started dating Emma just before Memorial Day," I said. I knew that because she'd brought him around to the lake house that holiday weekend.

"Yeah," he said. "And at first, it was all okay. She and Lauren were on friendly terms. I thought she was in a better place mentally. Then, it changed again a couple of months ago. She started sending me these texts." He picked up the stapled papers and waved them at me.

"I met her once at the Worley Street diner. I think that was late July, early August. I told her this had to stop. I wanted to be her friend, but that was it. I was happy with Emma. I thought she understood it. Well, Lauren got really angry with me. She said, 'We'll see about that.' Then she kind of stormed off. Then I got that last round of texts."

"Was she pregnant?" I asked.

"I don't know," Cole said. "If she was, and she was claiming it was mine, I haven't been with her in that way since the winter, Ms. Leary. What is that, five months ago? Six? I swear, there was nothing since."

"I don't know what the autopsy shows yet," I said. "I'm working on getting that."

"Everything else I told you was the truth. I swear it on my

life. I didn't tell you all the rest of this because I didn't want to say bad things about Lauren. She was a sweet girl. She had a good heart. She was just ... feeling overwhelmed. Kind of desperate. I blame myself. I didn't kill her, but I still blame myself. That night, at the bonfire, she was showing off for me. She draped herself around every guy she could, trying to get a reaction out of me. That's why I left. For her. I should have seen her home. I'll regret that for the rest of my life. But I didn't kill her. I swear I didn't kill her."

I let out a sigh. "Cole, I'm going to be honest with you. So far, the case against you is weak. anemic, from what I can tell. These texts from her are damaging. You lied to the police in that interview. You were the last one seen with her. And you weren't honest about when the last time you and Lauren were intimate with each other was. If she was threatening you with a pregnancy, they see it as a motive to get rid of her. But ... even taken together, I see lots of room for reasonable doubt. There's no crime scene. The police can't prove where Lauren was killed, only where she was found. Your car is clean. Your house is clean. Lauren's car is clean."

Cole's whole posture changed. His spine crumpled with relief. But it was far too soon for that.

"So you'll help me? You'll stick with this case?"

"I don't know," I said. "That's the truth. I have more questions than answers. And I'm still not sure you're telling me everything I need to know. Let me do more digging. Let me take a look at that autopsy report."

"Of course!" He sat up straighter. "I swear. I'll do anything you need. I won't try to hide stuff to protect Lauren. That was dumb, I get it. I just never in a million years thought anyone would try to pin this on me. I thought ... I thought I was being a gentleman."

"Don't," I said, leaning forward. I looked Cole Mathison

straight in the eyes. "Now, I'm going to ask you one more time. Is there any reason why your DNA would show up on Lauren Rice's body?"

Cole took a beat. He kept his unblinking gaze fixed on mine.

"No," he said. "I swear."

I'd like to say I'm one of those people who could read a liar a mile away. But I can't. Still, everything in my gut told me Cole Mathison was telling the truth.

Chapter 8

FOR THE NEXT TWO WEEKS, I worked on gathering a list of witnesses to interview and statements to nail down. The M.E.'s office was waiting on final toxicology results to release the official autopsy. Cole was back at home and I tried to keep my brother and niece from full-tilt meltdowns. In other words, things were as normal as they could be.

On Monday, the second week in October, I finally pinned Roxanne and Rudy Mathison down to an interview. We met at their house. Cole left to do their weekly grocery shopping. It was better if he wasn't around for this. Roxanne opened the door just a crack after I knocked, even though she'd been expecting me.

"Hi, Roxanne," I said, "Thanks so much for meeting with me." She hesitated a moment, scanned the street behind me, then finally opened the door wide enough to let me in.

I smelled fresh-baked cookies as I walked in. The Mathison home was a mid-century ranch with crooked black shutters and peeling paint on the front porch. I found that odd. Cole had spent most of the summer doing little side home improvement projects with Joe at his house. There was a detached garage behind the house, a yard with a chain-link fence, and a wooded lot beyond that.

"Let's sit in the kitchen," she said. I immediately saw why. Roxanne Mathison's front room was cluttered with newspapers, sheet music, and various knick-knacks in need of dusting and proper placement. She had the makings of a hoarder.

The kitchen, though, stood in stark contrast. Not so much as a crumb littered the yellow Formica countertops. I took a seat in a green vinyl kitchen chair and declined when Roxanne offered me coffee.

"I know this must be a rough time for you," I said. "I'll try to answer whatever questions you have, but understand that I represent Cole. There are certain things we won't be able to discuss."

"Of course," Roxanne said. She was a pretty, tiny woman with jet black hair she wore pulled back in a giant, tortoise-shell barrette. She had small hands she kept folded in her lap while we talked.

"He's such a good kid. He's been more worried about me during all of this than he is about himself," she said. "I'm sorry I didn't make it to court that day. We just thought ... Cole was worried I wouldn't be able to stop crying."

"I understand." I said. "Is Mr. Mathison on his way in?"

I saw a family photo sitting on a credenza in the living room. It was one of those awful studio ones with the fake outdoor backgrounds. It was hard to see from here, but I guessed Cole wasn't more than five or six in it. Roxanne looked almost exactly the same. I was pretty sure it was the same barrette in her hair. Cole's father, Rudy, was his spitting image.

"Rudy's working," she said quickly. "This has been hard on everyone."

"Sure," I said. "When we spoke on the phone, I was under the impression that he'd also be here. I asked you to make sure he was."

"He's working," she said abruptly. "He's on the road."

Okay, then.

"Mrs. Mathison," I started.

"You can call me Roxanne," she said.

"Good. Roxanne. I wanted to go over the statement you gave to the police a few weeks ago."

"I said everything I remember," she said. "Cole was home that night."

"Right," I said. "Do you remember him leaving at any point on the night of August 31st?"

"He came and went as he pleased. He's twenty, after all. Almost twenty-one. Cole never gives me any trouble at all. He has a room down the hall still, but he's been living in the basement. I can take you down there if you'd like. He fixed it up as an apartment. There's a separate egress out the back."

"I saw it when I pulled up," I said. There were steel BILCO doors on the side of the house. I had to figure they made a lot of noise when open and shut.

"So you're saying Cole usually came and went through that egress?"

"At night, for sure," she said. "I go to bed early. I'm usually asleep by nine. That always frustrates Rudy. That I can just lay my head down and be asleep within a few minutes. I've been that way since I was a kid. Rudy tosses and turns."

"And Rudy was working the night of the thirty-first?" I asked.

"Yes," she said. "I think so. You know we've been separated for a while on and off. Not formally. But since the summer, Rudy's been staying with friends most of the time. We're trying to work it out."

"Where?" I asked. "What friend is he staying with?"

"I ... he lives down in Columbus, I think."

"Okay," I said. "Let's get back to Labor Day weekend. So you don't remember hearing Cole leave the house on the thirty-first?"

"I said goodnight to him like I always do, probably eight o'clock. He was playing one of his games. He told me he might go meet some friends later. I remember telling him to try not to wake me."

"Got it," I said. "When did Cole come back?"

Lines of worry creased her face. "I don't know. I was asleep. I wish I could say I heard him come back. When I'm out, I'm out."

"It's okay," I said. I leaned over and tried to put a comforting hand over Roxanne's. She jerked away, startling me. Then she plastered on a smile and tried to cover.

"Sorry," she said. "I'm just a bit jumpy with everything that's going on."

"I'm sorry," I said. "I just wanted to say it's okay. You remember what you remember."

"Sometimes I do wake up though," she said. "And I go check on him. I've done that since Cole was a baby. I check on him. Maybe I did that night. If I think harder, maybe ..."

"Roxanne," I said. "Only if you really remember. You're probably going to be called as a witness if this case goes to trial. It's important that you tell the truth. No matter what. Even if it's not what you think will help Cole."

She nodded and squirmed in her seat. Something seemed off about her. Of course, it could have just been the circumstances. Her only child was facing a life sentence for murder. But she didn't seem worried, she just seemed, well, squirmy.

"Roxanne, how well did you know Lauren Rice?" I asked.

"It's just so awful," she said. "So young."

"It is. Did you know she and Cole were dating?" I asked.

"He had a few different girlfriends," she said. "Nice ones. At least, they seemed nice. But Cole didn't usually bring them here. Only sometimes."

I already knew that indirectly. She and Cole usually hung out at Joe's. Come to think of it, that seemed a little odd, given the circumstances. If Cole really had an apartment set-up downstairs, I would have thought most red-blooded straight twenty-year-old guys would have preferred the privacy that afforded. I knew my brother wouldn't have let the two of them alone for a second.

"Do you know why that is?" I asked. "Why was Cole more comfortable spending time away from home? You said Rudy's not home a lot. And you said you go to bed relatively early."

"You'd have to ask Cole about that," she said. "It's just what he's always done. I always figured it was just because the girls' fathers would rather keep an eye on them. I know I would."

I smiled. "I think my brother would agree with you there."

"She's a sweet girl, your niece," Roxanne said. "And so pretty. She comes over sometimes too."

"Thank you," I said. "What about your husband? Cole said he was home too."

"He came home sometime late that night. He was there when I woke up for a bit. But he left again. I'm sorry I can't give you exact times. When he comes home late, I don't see him. I go to bed so much earlier than the boys do."

"Mrs. Mathison ... Roxanne. I need to talk to Rudy. I need to know what he saw that night. What he heard. Cole gave a statement that Rudy and he spoke when Cole got in. I need to talk to him. That needs to be nailed down. You understand how difficult this is?" I didn't want to flat out say her kid needed an alibi. I only wanted the truth.

"Oh, I know all that," she said. "But Rudy won't have anything to tell you either. He and Cole are ships passing in the night, even when they're under the same roof. And ... they haven't been for a while. I'm sorry if this all sounds strange. It's just ... this is all very personal. I wasn't raised to talk about family business like this."

"I appreciate that." I did. More than she knew. It had been like that in my family growing up too. We never talked about the turmoil inside our home to outsiders. We circled the wagons. Protected each other. But my God, her son's future was at stake!

"Okay, so let's get back to Lauren," I said. "Did you have a chance to get to know her too?"

"A little," she said. "It was sad about what happened to her mother. I've known Gil Rice since we were kids. He loved Julie so much. I went to their house with the church after she passed. Just trying to get him to eat back then ... So much grief. He always seemed lost after that. Which I understand."

"Are you aware of any fights or anything that caused you concern about Cole's relationship with Lauren?"

"Fight?" she said. "Oh, no. I wouldn't think so. Cole's very even-tempered. He's a good boy. I just don't see why they think he had anything to do with what happened to that girl. Do they know for sure it was murder? Maybe she fell."

It was such an odd thing to say. I realized then that Roxanne Mathison seemed to be building a cocoon of denial around herself. It made sense of her demeanor. My being here certainly ran the risk of making her confront reality.

"When did you see Cole next, after that Saturday night?" I asked.

"Um, he had to work at the lumberyard on Sunday. I

First Degree

wake up by eight and I make him breakfast. Yes. We had breakfast together. So maybe it was nine o'clock or so. He came up from downstairs. I remember asking him how his night went. He told me he didn't end up staying out very long. It was just a normal day. A normal conversation."

That was at least consistent with what Cole had said all along. But it left a roughly three-hour block of time unaccounted for. A witness at the party remembered seeing Lauren leave around midnight, a few minutes after Cole said he did. His cell phone data didn't pick back up until almost three in the morning back here.

It was a problem. A big one.

I didn't know how many more ways I could get this information from her. Where the hell was Rudy Mathison in all this?

"I understand," I said. "But this is why I really need to speak with your husband. He could provide an alibi for your son. Why hasn't he?"

"Oh, you'd have to ask Rudy about that," she said.

I curled my fists beneath the table. Talking to this woman was like trying to nail spaghetti to the wall. If she presented this way on the witness stand, it could be devastating.

"Do you have Rudy's cell phone number?" I asked.

"He doesn't like to talk when he's driving," she said.

"Roxanne," I said, barking it more than I should have. "I need to know why your husband hasn't come forward. The police were here too. It's a loose end that needs to be tied up. If Rudy doesn't remember seeing Cole, then he doesn't remember. But if he does, why on earth hasn't he come forward? Cole is his son!"

She blinked rapidly. I was coming at her too hard. I knew it. And yet, I couldn't seem to stop myself. I felt like I cared

71

more about what happened to Cole than his own parents did. It made no sense.

"I'm sure if Rudy thought he could help, he would," she said. "But Rudy does what he thinks is best."

"I need to talk to him," I said. "Preferably today. Can you please either give me a contact number or tell me when the best time to reach or find your husband is?"

"Leave me your card," she said. "I know Rudy wants to help if he can. You're wrong to think he wouldn't."

"I haven't said he wouldn't. I just need to talk to him. That's really all I'm saying. And I need to caution you. You will be called as a witness in this case. I think it's probably for the best if you don't talk to other people about it."

"I want to help my son," she said, tears forming in her eyes. "I'll do the best I can. I wish I'd stayed up and waited for him. I had a bad feeling that day. I don't know why. And maybe I'm just remembering everything wrong. I'll try to do better."

I took a breath. "You're doing fine. You really are. But will you please impress on your husband how important it is that I speak with him? If you want to help your son, that's the single best thing you can do."

She nodded and rose with me. Roxanne Mathison ushered me to the door. We said our goodbyes. I left there feeling less sure about this case than ever before.

Chapter 9

"I DON'T WANT to think about it," I said as I stood at the end of the dock. The last week in October, and we were still near eighty degrees.

Eric came up behind me. Warmth flooded me as he slipped his arms around me and I leaned back, resting my head against his chest where it fit best. Across the lake, the leaves reached their peak fall colors, framing the water in red, gold, and green. A few jet skiers were out, soaking up likely the last day of good weather on the water.

"Joe still planning on taking the dock out tomorrow?" he asked.

"Bright and early," I said.

"I'll bring my waders," he said.

"You don't have to," I said. "Matty's coming out; the two of them can manage."

"I don't mind. And I want to see how they do it."

"Okay." I turned in his arms. "But you might want to leave the waders. They'll call you a sissy."

"Sissy?" He smiled. "It's warm now, but it's been getting down to forty at night. That water is freezing."

Laughing, I took him by the hand. We made our way up to the porch where I had a pitcher of sangria waiting. I made one of two dishes I was decent at: lasagna. It would be ready in a half an hour.

"Great," Eric said. "I get to freeze my balls off to prove to your brothers that I have them."

"Bingo," I said.

Eric shook his head and poured each of us a glass. We sat in silence together for a little while, watching the boats in the distance. Joe had already pulled my pontoon and trailered it into the pole barn.

A pit formed in my stomach as I thought about his original plan to teach Cole how to winterize it.

"So," Eric said after a time. "You going to tell me about your meeting with the governor's office?"

I set my glass down. "Not much to tell. I'm filling out a form."

"Mmm hmm," he said. "And when is said form due?"

"Relax," I said, drawing my knees up. "I'm doing it. At least, I'm going to fill out the form. They're not in a huge hurry, anyway. They said I have until the end of next month to get it in. They aren't looking to install an interim judge until after the New Year."

"Rumor has it Bill Walden is also throwing his hat in," he said.

I sat back up. "Bill? Lord. He's a million years old. There's an age cap. Even if he got elected, he'd only be able to serve out one term."

Eric smiled. "For somebody who's been pretty cavalier about the whole thing, that's a hell of a strong reaction."

I stuck my tongue out at him, realizing too late that he'd been baiting me.

"It would be just like them to stick somebody like Bill in that seat," I said. "Good ol' boy network in full swing."

"So," Eric said. "Put up a fight. Make them realize you are the best and only person good enough for that job. And you know you are."

I finished my drink, feeling it go to my head already. Eric made it strong, but good, just like he was.

"Eric," I said. "If I put my name in, things could get complicated. They pick me, I'm still going to have to run in two years to keep the seat if I want it."

"Put my name at the top of the list for a yard sign," he said.

He stared out at the water, his eyes sparkling. I reached for him, smoothing his hair behind his ears. He needed a trim, but I liked him this way, a little rough and rugged around the edges.

"I'm not exactly squeaky clean," I said. "And I don't know if I'm ready for that kind of scrutiny."

Eric turned to me. "Are you talking about Thorne? Cass, it's been years since you worked for him. As much as I hate the guy, he's never been convicted of anything. You ... well ... you made sure of that."

The comfortable silence between us evaporated, leaving something heavy in its place. I knew what people thought. I knew what Eric thought. He might not be one of them, but most people believed I'd done shady things in my past life as a mob lawyer. I hated that term. But there was truth to it. For years, I'd looked the other way while Killian Thorne, my former client and fiancé, stayed one step ahead of the FBI. Then it all caught up with me. I nearly lost my career and my life because of it.

"Still," I said. "You know I won't run unopposed. It's not

just my professional past I'm worried about. It's my personal one."

"What," he said. "Because you're a Leary? Because once again, your old man was a piece of trash who burned every bridge there is in this town? Sure, there are still idiots and snobs in Delphi. But there are a lot more good and honest people who know who and what you really are. Count me as first in line on that list, Cass. I know for a fact both the Delphi P.D. and the Woodbridge County Sheriff's office will endorse you. Patrol and command. We've never backed a loser yet."

I reached for his hand. My throat felt thick. "Thanks. Wow, Eric. Really. Thank you."

"It's not just my doing," he said. "In fact, it's none of my doing. They respect you. Even if you fight for the other team."

I rolled my eyes. "I fight for the same team, Eric. Somebody just needs to keep you on your toes."

He poured me another drink. If I kept it up, I'd be asleep before the oven went off.

"About that," he said. "If you do get serious about this judicial appointment, what does that mean for the Mathison murder trial?"

"It doesn't mean anything," I said. "At the earliest, even if I get through vetting and selection, I wouldn't take the bench until spring. Or late winter at the earliest. Cole's set for trial the first week of January."

"You *have* been thinking hard about all of this," he said.

"I think hard about everything," I smiled. "Some people say that's my problem."

We were heading into touchy territory. It wasn't appropriate for either of us to talk specifics about the case. But I knew it was the biggest thing going on at the Delphi P.D., just like at my office.

"Well," I said. "I'm just glad you weren't assigned to it."

Eric remained stone-faced. Which was enough to tell me something about it bothered him too. I should have left it alone, I know. But I didn't.

"It's a career maker for Megan Lewis," I said. "I have to say, as much as I see gaping holes in the case, it's good that the higher-ups trusted her with it. Gives me hope for Delphi. We might just be sliding into the twenty-first century yet."

"It wasn't a token assignment," Eric said, surprising me with the sharpness of his tone.

"Eric," I said. "I'm not fishing. I swear. It's just ..."

He turned to me with a smirk on his face. "Just what?"

"It's just that if this were your case, you wouldn't have rushed it through like this. It's not tight."

He gave me a pat answer. "That's prosecutorial discretion, not ours."

"Right," I said. "And we've got a brand-new prosecutor who's also trying to make a name for himself with this case. It's going to blow up in both of their faces."

I hadn't meant to get too far into this. I hadn't meant to get into it at all. I knew it was at least partially the sangria talking. I set the unfinished portion of my second glass down. Better to quit before I stuck my foot in it deeper.

"Anyway," he said, finishing his glass. "It's not my case. I've done my damndest to stay out of it. For you."

"For me?"

"Yes," he said. Eric drew himself closer, bringing me nose to nose. "Wouldn't want you to violate ... what is it ... the appearance of impropriety?"

With his hot breath on my cheek and strong hands around my waist, I had the urge to be decidedly improper.

The oven timer went off. Still touching noses, Eric and I laughed together. Saved by the literal bell.

We walked inside just as the wind picked up and a chill

bit the air. Eric was right. The water would be damn cold tomorrow morning.

As we ate our dinner, we left the shop talk out of it. I was glad Eric had walled himself off from the Mathison case. But, as I cleared our plates, something else nagged at me.

"Eric," I said, as we made our way into the living room. "It's not something I want you to make a habit of doing."

"Which thing?" he asked, holding his arms out for me to snuggle into.

"Passing up cases at work because of me. I know you. You would have loved to sink your teeth into this one. Gil Rice is a friend of yours. I know he probably asked you to help. I know he's probably calling you for updates. He trusts you."

"Which is another reason why it was better if I wasn't directly involved," he said.

"Fair enough. But ... sadly, Lauren won't be the last."

He raised a brow. "Well, see, if you slipped on that robe, think how much easier our lives would be." He grew instantly serious, though. "But Cass, I don't want you to think I have some ulterior motive for wanting you to go after the judgeship. Yes, it drives me nuts that you're a defense lawyer sometimes."

I laughed. "It drives you nuts that I'm an excellent defense lawyer sometimes."

He gave me a sheepish grin. Then, he pulled me against him and gave me a kiss that sent my insides spinning.

He tasted good. He smelled good. He was ... good.

It was getting late. The sunset streaked purple and orange light across the water. Eric kissed me again. Deeper. Better.

"What time are your brothers showing up tomorrow?" he asked. I folded myself against him, heat stirring within me.

This was easy. Natural. And what we both wanted.

Except ...

With Herculean effort, I pulled myself away. Eric's hooded gaze found my eyes. Slowly, he too came up for air.

"Eric," I said. "It's not just my past that could be a problem if I'm being vetted for the district court."

He worked a muscle in his jaw. Slowly, he dropped his head then gave me a nod.

"I know."

There was still a thing between us. Wendy. He'd only recently stopped wearing his wedding ring.

"She's never waking up, Cass," he said. Eric's wife Wendy had been in an irreversible coma for over two years now. He'd done the best he could for her, but he was starting to let her go.

"I know," I said, touching his cheek. "And you know I'm not asking you to do anything for me. But ... this ... you and me. Well, I'm ..."

He smiled. "Just Catholic enough." He leaned in and kissed the tip of my nose, then slowly rose to leave.

"Yeah," I said. "Who'd have thunk, right?"

"I did." He smiled. "And though I hate it sometimes too, it might actually be one of the things I love most about you. Get some rest, kid. I'll see you in the morning."

I rested my chin in my palm and watched him head to the door. "Remember," I called after him one last time. "Waders are for sissies."

Chapter 10

ONLY ONE PERSON dodged my calls more than Rudy Mathison. Kaylin Dwyer. She was the witness who claimed to have seen Cole and Lauren together on the side of the road after he claimed he'd left the party.

Though Kaylin took classes at Michigan State, her brother let it slip on the phone that she'd be home the last weekend in October. I caught up with her in Shamrock Park, where she'd gone for a run.

Living in a small town where everyone knows everyone can have its pros and cons. The con today was Kaylin knew exactly who I was as I approached her while she tied her shoe at an empty park bench. She looked left and right, but there was nobody else close by.

Kaylin dropped her foot to the ground and plopped down on the bench, seemingly resigned to the situation.

"Hi," I said. "I'm Cass Leary, but I guess you already know that."

"I don't have anything to say to you. I don't want anything to do with this at all," she said.

Kaylin, as I recalled, served as one of Lauren Rice's

pallbearers. She had a trim, athletic build and dyed orange hair she pulled back under a purple visor.

"I know Lauren Rice was your friend. You gave a statement to the police. You know you'll be called as a witness at trial. The last thing I want to do is upset you. I just need a few minutes of your time."

She sat with her arms crossed, staring straight ahead. Well, at least she didn't get up and bolt. I took that as an invitation to sit down.

"Kaylin," I said. "I'm so very sorry about what happened to Lauren. You were brave to come forward."

"He's saying he didn't kill her, isn't he?" Kaylin said, still staring straight ahead.

"I'm afraid I can't discuss anything like that with you. I only want to ask you about what you saw the night Lauren disappeared. There are a few things in your statement I'd like to follow up on."

"Do you know how much crap I've gotten since I talked to the police? People think I'm the sole reason Cole Mathison got arrested. Like it's my fault or something," she said.

"How so?" I asked.

"I saw them together. Okay? When I left the Pits, they were both by the side of the road. On Carter Road. Right across from the horse farm."

"What time was that?" I asked.

"You said you read my statement. I said all this before. It was a little before one in the morning. They were standing near Lauren's car. She had her driver's side door open and was kind of standing inside of it. You know, with the door in front of her chest. They were talking. Cole stood a little ways back from her."

"Did you hear what they were saying?" I asked. Kaylin's statement was damaging, no question. Only it didn't track.

Every other witness who noticed when Lauren left said it was closer to midnight. That stretch of Carter Road was only about a two-minute drive from the driving entrance to the Pits. It left about a forty-five-minute gap in the timeline.

"I couldn't hear them, no," she said.

"Did you stop?"

"No," she said. "It was seriously late. I don't have a curfew, but I told my mom I'd be back by one and didn't feel like catching grief."

"Do you remember how fast you were driving? Did you slow down at all when you saw Cole and Lauren?"

"I don't ... I don't know how fast I was driving. Lauren kind of shielded her eyes when I came by. Because of my headlights."

"I see," I said. "So Lauren was facing you. Her car was parked on the south side of the road. You were going east?"

"She ... they were on my left, um ... so yeah. That's east," she answered.

"Which car was parked closest to you ... which one did you pass by first?"

She thought for a moment. "I guess Cole's truck. It was parked like behind Lauren's. Like he'd pulled up behind her."

"Got it," I said, writing a note. At no point in Kaylin's statement did she mention knowing what kind of vehicle Cole drove. I didn't see the question even being asked of her.

I drew a quick sketch on my notepad. I made rudimentary, square cars, just to help orient Kaylin and myself to the scene as she described it. I drew a stick figure and gave it long hair, like Lauren's.

"So Lauren was standing kind of half in her car, facing you, right?" I asked.

"Right," she said.

"So was Cole standing to her side? In front, behind?"

"He was in front of her. Standing in front of the backseat door of her car."

"I see." I nodded, taking the drawing back. I wanted to be careful how far I pushed her. Based on what Kaylin described, Cole would have been standing with his back to her.

"You're sure it was Cole Mathison, though," I asked. "Did you see his face?"

She paused. "I know what Cole Mathison looks like," she said. "We went to school together for twelve years. And I'd just seen him like two hours before that at the party."

"Do you remember what he was wearing?" I asked.

"I don't even remember what I was wearing," she said.

"Do you know what kind of car he drives?" I asked.

"Some kind of Ford," she said.

"A truck? A sedan?"

"It's a ... I don't know, it's a truck."

I put my notepad back in my bag. "I know this is hard. And I know you think maybe I'm the enemy. I'm trying to figure out what happened. That's my job."

"I'm not mad at you," she said. "I don't even know you. I just ... I wish I'd never seen Lauren that night. Or Cole. And I wish I'd never told the police anything. I should have just kept my mouth shut."

"But why?" I asked. "Lauren was your friend. No matter what happens, getting justice for her is the right thing."

"Cole isn't ... nobody thinks ... He's just not the kind of guy who would do something like this. Look, you're right. Lauren was my friend. Most of the time. We had our ups and downs like girls always do. She could be a real pain in the ass. Stubborn. And that night, she pretty much pissed everyone off."

"How?" I asked.

"She was throwing herself at every guy at that party. She

was drunk. She almost seemed ... desperate. It was like she was trying to burn every bridge in town. Everyone knew Cole was with Emma. They're kind of made for each other. And Lauren only started sniffing around Cole again when she found out he was happy. I told her to knock it off. A lot of us did. That night ... it was like it all came to a head for her. I don't know what happened. I don't know what set her off."

"Did you see Cole and Lauren argue?" I asked.

"Not argue," Kaylin said. "But Cole was definitely trying to get away from her. You asked me if I stopped to see what was going on. No. I didn't. But if I had, it wouldn't have been to help Lauren. It would have been to make sure she wasn't driving Cole any more nuts."

"Thank you," I said.

"Don't thank me," she said. "I hate myself for all of this. I know what it makes me sound like. I don't know what happened to Lauren. But it was awful. A nightmare. She didn't deserve it. And if I go up there and testify to all of this, then I sound like I'm blaming her. Or slut-shaming her. She wasn't any of those things. She was just ... going through something. I just ... please don't make me do this. Don't call me as a witness. Don't make me put this crap on record."

I adjusted my shoulder strap and put a hand on Kaylin's knee. "I wish I could promise you that won't need to happen. But you know it will. And all anyone is going to ask you is to tell the truth. I just want to be sure ... there's no doubt in your mind it was Cole you saw on Carter Road?"

"It was Cole," she said. "I know his hair. I know how he stands."

She left it there. Just a tiny opening. But that night on Carter Road, I felt certain Kaylin Dwyer never actually saw Cole's face.

Chapter 11

By the next Monday, I still hadn't heard from Rudy Mathison despite four more voicemails and another drive by his house. Cole had no insight to give me other than to say it wasn't unusual for his dad to take off for weeks at a time when he was on the road. He confirmed what Dave Carver and my brother suspected. Roxanne and Rudy lived apart off and on. It was strange. Evasive. And I was sick and tired of putting up with it.

Once again, I had Miranda clear my morning as I drove up to Lansing to check in with the offices of the small trucking company Rudy Mathison allegedly worked for. Subpoena in hand, I meant to leave with a copy of Rudy's schedule.

I found the warehouse office easily enough. A pretty blonde receptionist sat behind a plexiglass window. By the sour look she gave me, I was pretty sure she'd already pegged me as a lawyer. Her name plate read Veronica.

"Hi," I said. "My name is Cass Leary. I'm looking to find one of your drivers, Rudy Mathison. If he hasn't checked in today, I'd like to talk to someone who can give me some insight into his schedule."

I handed her a copy of my subpoena. Veronica barely even glanced at it.

"You want payroll for wage garnishments," she said. "That's handled off-site." She reached for a business card and slid it beneath the plexiglass.

"I'm not here about a wage garnishment," I said. "I'm not a process server. I mean ... yes. That's a subpoena. But I'm after Rudy's schedule."

"He's not on the hot seat for child support?" she asked.

"Um ... no," I said. "Not from me, anyway. When was the last time you saw him?"

She took the card back. Her jaw dropped a little, and she cast a nervous glance over her shoulder. Two men were talking in the hallway of the offices behind her.

"I haven't seen him in a while," she said. "But you maybe want to talk to Terry. Terry Nelson handles dispatch. He'll know what happened with Rudy."

"What happened?" I asked. What did she mean, *what happened?*

Veronica closed the partition, muffling the sound as she walked back and spoke to who I could only presume was Terry. A big, burly guy with an unkempt moustache, Terry looked over Veronica's shoulder and glared at me. Finally, he patted her on the arm and opened a service door, leading to the warehouse where I stood.

"Can I help you?" he asked. Terry wore a blue shirt with his name embroidered in the center of a white patch.

"Mr. Nelson," I said, extending my hand. He wiped his off on his pant leg and shook mine.

"You want to know about Rudy?" he asked. "What the hell's he got himself into this time?"

"Nothing," I said. "That is, I don't know. I just want to

talk to him about a case I'm working on. It's to do with his son. Are you not aware of that situation?"

Terry screwed up his face. Then he shrugged. "I stay out of domestic issues," he said.

What in the ever-loving hell was going on here?

"Look," I said. "I just want to talk to the guy. If you could help me out with where to find him, that'd be great."

Terry let out a laugh. "Where to find him? Lady, you got no idea. I've been looking for that mother effer myself for weeks."

He jerked his chin toward Veronica. She scurried to the other side of the room and pulled something out of a file drawer. Terry went up to the window and took it from her.

"You said you're working for his kid?" Terry asked.

"I am," I said. "I'm his attorney. My name is Cass Leary."

"Fine," he said. "I don't care. His kid probably needs this more than Rudy does. The hell with him. Rudy doesn't work for me anymore. I've been trying to fire his ass for about a month. He's AWOL. Screwed up my whole supply chain. You have no idea how many chances I've given him."

"I'm sorry to hear that," I said. Adrenaline heated my blood.

I looked at the envelope he'd given me. It was from the payroll department, presumably Rudy Mathison's last check.

"Mr. Nelson," I said. "When's the last time you or anyone here has heard from or seen Rudy Mathison?"

He looked at Veronica again. Even behind her plexiglass, she apparently heard every word we said. She turned and typed something on her computer. I followed Terry as he walked closer to her. Veronica turned the screen toward us.

"He was supposed to show up on Monday, September 2nd," she said. "Never did. Phone log says we've tried to call him something like twenty times. He was last here the morning of Saturday, August 31st."

My throat ran dry. I could barely find the words to say thank you for your time. As I collected myself and walked out of that warehouse, reality sank in.

Rudy Mathison hadn't been seen or heard from since August 31st. The very night Lauren Rice disappeared.

Chapter 12

I'd WANTED to avoid it. The single biggest reason I hesitated getting involved in Cole Mathison's defense descended on my front door.

"Trick or treat!"

My niece Jessa peered up at me through a black silk mask. I perched a giant orange bowl on my hip and had the urge to dump the entire thing right into her pillowcase. She was just that cute.

"I'm a ninja!" she proclaimed.

"I don't think you're supposed to tell people that," Joe said behind her. "It defeats the purpose, Jess." He came up the walk with Katy and Matty trailing behind. Vangie brought up the rear, carrying a second pillowcase full of candy.

"She hit the west end of the lake first," Vangie said.

Emma stood to the side of them, her arms crossed, sulking in the shadows. My sister Vangie caught sight of her and gritted her teeth through a smile.

"Come on, Emma," Vangie said. "Jessa's been looking forward to walking with you. We still have a lot of houses to cover."

Vangie heaved the full pillowcase to Matty. It caught him right in the gut. He made a big show out of doubling over, making Jessa giggle.

"I'll share my reefus cups with you," Jessa said. She started pronouncing it that way last year when she lost her front teeth. It stuck.

Only Jessa could have gotten a smile out of Emma's face, I think. Emma took Jessa by the hand. She and Vangie turned back down the walk and headed to my neighbor's house.

That just left me to deal with the rest of the sullen faces as they brushed past me on their way to the pizzas I'd already ordered. "How bad is he?" I whispered to Katy as my brothers disappeared into the house.

"About an eight and a half," she said. "They had a fight on the way over. A beer would take the edge off, but he's not going to do that around Matty. I don't think we'll stay long tonight."

"Got it," I said. I was about to close the door when a pair of Disney princesses and a Jedi stormed up the walk yelling "trick or treat."

Katy took the candy bowl from me. "I'll take over," she said.

"Traitor," I whispered. "I was born into this family. You actually had a choice."

Laughing, I squeezed her arm and turned to confront my sulking brother.

Matty was just as traitorous. He'd already made his way out the back door toward the water's edge. That left me alone with Joe. I could tell from the set of his jaw that Katy had misjudged. He was well on his way to a nine out of ten.

"You've got to talk some sense into her," Joe said.

"Which her are we talking about? I thought I was the one you normally think needs more sense."

"You do," he said. "But I'm talking about Emma."

I sat at the kitchen table. A beer would have been good for me too, but not with Matty around. His sobriety was far too fragile.

"Cass," he said, instantly deflating. "I need you to be straight with me."

"When have I not been?" I asked.

He plopped down across from me. "Am I wrong about this kid? I don't think I am. It's just ..."

"It's just your daughter is dating a guy who's accused of murdering his last girlfriend," I finished for him.

"She's still seeing him," he said. "I wasn't supposed to tell you. She hasn't come over to the house with him, but I know she's gone to his place."

"Joe, I need to know everything. And I need to talk to you about something."

He lifted his chin, alarm lighting his eyes. "Cass ..."

"I need you to tell me about Rudy Mathison. You've only said you didn't think he was much interested in spending time with his own son. What else do you know about him?"

I hadn't told anyone but Jeanie and Tori about what I'd learned, not even Cole. That was tomorrow's task. In the meantime, I was still waiting for the fruits of a subpoena on Rudy Mathison's phone records.

"I don't know much," he said. "Just ... I don't know. He always came off as a real blowhard. Cole was a pretty good football player. For Delphi, anyway. Too small to play in college. But he tried really hard. I coached him in Pop Warner like ten years ago. He's always just been a hard-working, earnest kid. Coachable. Starved for it, really. And Rudy ... I don't know. I saw something I didn't like."

"Like what?" I asked.

"Like he wasn't happy unless Cole was trying to beat the

crap out of some other kid. He'd lose it if Cole did anything less than run with the ball himself. And if Cole got hurt, well, Rudy didn't have a lot of sympathy for that. It got to a point where the other coaches didn't like having him at practices."

"I see," I said. It fit with the impression I had of Roxanne Mathison. Her fear when talking to me felt like something more than just concern for Cole.

"Do you think he was abusive?" I asked.

"Cass, I can't say that for sure. But I asked Cole about it once. He was helping me replace some rotted wood around one of the windows in my garage. I reached across him to grab a hammer off a hook on the wall. Cole kind of recoiled. Hard. It was totally involuntary."

"Like a conditioned response to an arm coming at him?" I asked.

"Yeah," he said. "And ... I know that feeling."

I cast my eyes downward. Of course Joe would know it. Our own father had laid hands on him when we were growing up.

"What did he say?" I asked.

"He shrugged me off," Joe said. "I didn't press. But I never wanted Emma over there. That's one of the reasons I preferred them hanging out at our house instead of his. I don't like that she's going over there now."

"Understandable," I said.

"Cass," Joe said. "I just want to know. Am I wrong about this kid? I need you to promise me. If you have any reason to start thinking he hurt that girl, you have to tell me."

"Joe ..."

"No!" my brother shouted. He pounded his fist against the table. "Don't you lay any crap on me about attorney-client privilege. This is Emma we're talking about."

"And you're the one who begged me to get involved in the first place, Joe," I said.

"I know!" He was still shouting. Katy poked her head around the corner. She gave me an 'I told you so' look, then disappeared once the doorbell rang.

"I know," he said, quieter. "I'm just worried about Emma. I told you. She's been seeing him. Going over to his house."

"Joe, have you seen Rudy around town lately?"

"I haven't," he said. "I think he's moved out again. He's done that in the past when things get extra tense with Roxanne. That's what Emma has told me. She's just so wrapped up in it all. I never thought, not in a million years, that things would go this far. I thought the cops would figure out they had the wrong kid. That there'd be something ... Cass. He didn't do this. He can't have done this. But what if ..."

He couldn't finish the sentence. I'd never seen my brother this distraught. Well, almost never. We'd lost a lot together. And we'd survived much worse.

"Joe," I said. "I don't think you're wrong about this kid. But I can't make you any promises. You know that. I agree with you. The case against Cole is weak. To be honest, I can't figure out why Rafe Johnson pushed it to trial so fast."

"I've heard things about him," Joe said. "Nothing great. Rafe Johnson's not one of us, Cass."

"Joe, you're a lot of things. Racist isn't one of them," I said sharply.

"No," he said quickly. "I'm not talking about the color of his skin. Christ. You know me better than that. He's not from Delphi. He's just using that job as a stepping stone to something else. He's not like Jack."

"You're right," I said. I believed it in my gut that Jack

LaForge never would have signed off on charges against Cole. But here we were.

"So you'll tell me," Joe said. At that point, Matty came back into the house, probably sensing that Joe had cooled back down.

"I'll tell you what I can," I said. "And you have to believe me. You *both* have to believe me that Emma's on my mind in this too. For her own sake, maybe she needs to pull back and stop seeing Cole for a while."

"No!" Emma's shriek zinged straight through my veins.

"Christ!" Matty said, jumping too.

Breathless, Katy hurried around the corner. "Sorry," she said. "I told her to leave you guys alone to talk."

"No," Emma said. "Aunt Cass, you're Cole's lawyer. You have to be that before you're my aunt. You took an oath."

"Calm down," I said. "I can be both."

"I knew he'd try to get you on his side," Emma said. "I'm not giving up on Cole. You have no idea what all of this is doing to him. I'm worried. Really worried."

"Have a seat," I said. "There were some things I wanted to talk to you about too. Maybe you can help."

I got an admiring glance from Joe. I'd said the exact right thing to calm Emma down. She sat beside me.

"Emma," I said. "What do you know about Cole's dad?"

She folded her hands in her lap. Her skin went a little pale, and it told me far more than her words.

"He's afraid of him," she finally answered. "Mr. Mathison has a temper. I've asked Cole about it. I mean, specifically. He won't talk about it. But ... I've seen bruises."

"On Cole?" I asked.

She nodded. "And on his mom. One time when Cole's car was in the shop, I picked him up to take him to work. Mrs. Mathison answered the door. She had a black eye. I don't think she was expecting me. She tried to cover it real quick. And Mr. Mathison came up behind her. He pretty much slammed the door in my face and told me to wait in the car."

"Dammit, Emma," Joe said. "That's the kind of thing you need to tell me."

"And what?" she asked. "Were you going to fly over there and beat the crap out of him?"

"Maybe!" Joe shouted.

"We don't hang out there usually," she said. "Cole doesn't like being there when his dad's around. And I'm not stupid. I don't like Cole's dad either. Even without all that other stuff."

"Why is that?" I asked.

She bunched her shoulders. Joe being here wasn't helping. I was about to ask him to leave us alone when Emma blurted out the rest of it.

"He's inappropriate," she said.

Joe's face turned red. Katy got to him and whispered something in his ear. He clenched his jaw but stayed quiet.

"How?" I asked.

"It's like he's in a constant pissing contest with Cole. He'd always try to embarrass Cole around me. I didn't like the way Mr. Mathison looked at me either. It was kind of leering, you know? Like he'd look me up and down. Compliment me on my clothes or my looks more than he should. He was just creepy."

"Son of a ..." Joe spat. I put a hand up to silence him.

"When was the last time Cole spoke to his father?" I asked.

Emma looked up. "I don't ... I don't know. Why are you asking me that? Did you ask Cole?"

I pursed my lips. We were getting into territory I wasn't comfortable talking about.

"Did Cole's dad lie? About where Cole was that night? Is that why the cops think Cole did this?"

"Emma," I said.

She jumped out of her seat. "It's a lie. Aunt Cass, if Mr. Mathison said something to make things worse for Cole, it's a lie. He hates him. Even my dad knows that. Did he tell you about when he was coaching? He's a bad guy. I can't even believe it. Poor Cole. I was ..."

Her eyes widened. I didn't like the expression that came over her face.

"I'll tell them he was with me. I swear to God I will!"

"Emma!" Joe, Matty, and I all shouted her name in unison.

"Don't say another word," Joe said.

"What if I did?" she asked, her voice raising an octave.

"Emma," I said, trying to keep my tone even. "I don't want you to finish that sentence, let alone that thought. Whatever you say to me, to anyone ... well, it damn well better be the truth. Do you hear me?"

"If his dad says he didn't see Cole ... if he says anything to jam him up, it's a lie. I don't understand it. I don't know how any parent could think it. But Cole's dad acts like he hates him. Like he's jealous of him or something. And I'm telling you I wouldn't put it past him to try to make things worse for him."

"What the hell?" Matty said. "It's not like we don't have experience with a crappy father. But this would just be a whole other level."

"Yes," I said. "It would. Emma, do we understand each other?"

She tightened her lips into an 'o' that reminded me so much of one of Joe's expressions. Stubborn. But reasonable when pushed.

"Yes," she said, sitting down hard. "I wouldn't. I said I'm not stupid."

"I know," I said, reaching for her. "And I also know how unbelievably hard this has to be for you."

"I just feel so helpless. It's like Cole has nobody in his corner. His mom is checked out. His dad is ... I don't even know what. I feel like it's just me holding him together."

I saw my brother's face darken. That was exactly what he was worried about. I wanted to tell them both that everything would be okay. While it was true the case against Cole was weak, that didn't mean I could make them any promises.

As my niece finally crumpled and fell into her father's arms, I took great comfort in that. If Cole Mathison's father was as bad as I thought he was, at least Emma had one of the good ones.

But it made my need to find and talk to Rudy Mathison just that much more urgent.

Chapter 13

I HADN'T SEEN Cole in almost two weeks. My court schedule on other matters heated up as everyone wanted to get things resolved before the holidays. When I walked into his living room, Cole's appearance shocked me.

He'd lost a lot of weight since his arrest. I noticed bald patches near his ears. Roxanne hovered. She set down a tray of soft drinks and a cheese plate. She gave me a knowing, concerned look that seemed to ask me if I could talk some sense into him. I thanked her and waited for her to leave.

"You look horrible," I said. "You aren't eating."

With an unsteady hand, he reached for a cheese cube and ate it as if trying to prove me wrong.

"I'm fine," he said. "It's just hard."

"I know," I said.

"I know you're worried," he said. "About me, yeah. Sure. But Emma. We had a fight."

"Oh?" I said. "Is that something you want to talk about?"

"Not really," he said. "But you should know. I told her her dad was right. Maybe it's not a good idea for her to be coming around. You know. Maybe after. But if ... Cass, she shouldn't have to be dealing with this crap. I don't want her to get hurt. She's supposed to be enjoying her freshman year in college, not pining over her train wreck of a boyfriend who's probably going to end up dead."

"Cole," I said. "You don't have to handle all of this on your own. If you need to talk to someone ..."

"No," he said. "I don't need my head shrunk. I'm just worried about her too."

"I understand," I said. "But there's something we really need to talk about. And it's not Emma. Cole, it's about your family. Your dad, specifically. I need to know where to find him. I know he's not living here anymore."

Cole had a cracker in his hand. He broke it in half and put the pieces back on the tray.

"I don't know where he is. I don't think he wants to talk to me," he said.

"Cole, if I'm going to help you, I need to know everything about your life. Your father hasn't been seen since the night Lauren disappeared. That's something I should have heard from you."

His gaze didn't waver from the disintegrated cracker on the plate. "I didn't know that," he said.

"How could you not know that?"

"He drives a truck. He leaves for weeks, months at a time. My mom used to joke maybe he had another family. He ... he didn't like that."

"And his son has been charged with first-degree murder," I snapped. "It's been in the news. Delphi is Delphi. There is no way he doesn't know. Your mother won't tell me anything about his whereabouts either. I had to find out from his trucking company that he'd actually been fired. That's how I figured out when he went AWOL too."

Still barely a twitch in Cole's facial expression. He

reminded me of his mother. I had no doubt in my mind they were both hiding something. Perhaps protecting each other. It was becoming more and more clear that they both lived under the specter of abuse.

"He hurt you," I said, trying another tact. "And he's been hurting her too, hasn't he?"

He squeezed his eyes shut. "I can't talk about that."

"You'll have to," I said. "Cole, your father is your alibi. Are you trying to tell me it's a big coincidence your dad disappeared the same night Lauren did?"

"I don't know about that," he snapped. "I swear. My dad takes off all the time. He and my mom get into it. Off he goes. Maybe she's right. Maybe he does have another family. You want to know if he's been mean to me? Yes. My father is a bastard. He's hurt her too. Before Labor Day weekend, I hadn't had a real conversation with him since, like July. I make it a point to avoid him. And I ... I threw him out."

"You threw him out of the house?" I asked.

"Yeah," he said. "That's what happened in July. I came home from work and found my mom in the bathroom. She was bleeding from a cut on her lip. I knew what happened. What always happens. My dad was sleeping. I got some boxes down from the attic, packed a bunch of his clothes and put them in his truck. When he woke up, I confronted him and told him if he didn't get out for good, I'd call the cops. My mom never will. She's too scared of him."

"Did you threaten him with anything else? Besides calling the cops?" I asked.

"You mean did I threaten to kill him? No. I swear. He laughed at me, tried to take a swing at me, but I'm not a little boy anymore. I threw him against the wall. Broke one of my mom's favorite lamps. He got the message."

"I see," I said. "That must have been very hard for you.
But he came back?"

"I think so. I started noticing little things. Like his shorts
in the laundry. So I know she was letting him back in the
house when I wasn't home," Cole said. "My mom said he'd
changed. Cass, I can't save her. I've tried. She always takes
him back. I was getting ready to move out when all of this
happened. But I'm telling you the truth. I didn't know
nobody's seen my dad since September or whatever. I threw
him out of my life."

"Your mother is trying to protect him," I said. "She won't
let me talk to him. I think she's warned him to avoid me. I
don't understand that. I don't understand why she or your
father isn't trying to help in any way they can. No matter
what else happened, they're your parents."

"Because she chooses him!" Cole spat. His eyes reddened.
"Because she always chooses him. This whole thing? My dad,
wherever he is, he probably thinks it'll make things work out
great for him. A good way to get me out of his way."

"By letting you go to prison for a murder you didn't
commit?" I asked.

"Why not?" Cole said.

He wouldn't meet my eyes. I went back to what I knew
about Rudy's schedule. He'd worked the morning of August
31st. Clocked out. Went home.

"Cole, the truth. Did you really see your father the night
of the bonfire?"

"Yes," he said, spitting the word out.

"When?" I asked. "Where?"

"His truck was in the garage when I came back. So I knew
he'd come home. I told all of this to the police. You were
there."

"What happened?" Why was this so damn hard?

"He was in my room when I got there. Waiting for me. It got ugly, Cass. We both said things we didn't mean and worse things that we *did* mean. I told him if I ever saw him around here again, I'd kill him. I threw my phone at him. He ... he picked it up and went through it. He mocked me about how good I had it. How I was pulling the wool over the eyes of all these so-called friends of mine who thought I was a good person."

"Cole, there are things Emma said about your dad. She told me she was uncomfortable around him. I think the word she used was creepy. Were you aware of that?"

He ran a hand over his face. "It wasn't about her. It was about me. My dad ...he liked to belittle me. Show me up. Make me look bad in front of the girls I brought home. So ... I tried to stop bringing them home when he was around. That's one of the reasons Emma and I started spending most of our time at her place instead of mine."

"Okay," I said. "Your father could give you an alibi. And you're telling me you think your father is staying in the wind so he doesn't have to testify to that?"

"Yes," Cole said. "That's exactly what I'm telling you. If nobody can find him, nobody can make him appear in court. Even if it's to help me. He'd rather watch me rot behind bars."

My chest hollowed out. The pain in Cole's eyes tore at me. Through the horror, what Cole said made a certain sick sense.

"Cole," I said. "I'm going to find him. Okay? Your father might hold the key to helping you."

"What difference does it make?" he asked. "If he hates me that much, he'll just lie."

"You let me worry about that," I said. "For now, I just need you to help me. I need you to write down anybody your dad might have communicated with. Friends. Family. Coworkers. Anyone who he might be staying with."

I slid a pad of paper and a pen across the table. Though his hands still shook, Cole wrote down a few names and slid the pad back to me.

"Hang in there," I said. "Cole, this really could be the break we need."

Through tight lips, he nodded. "It's okay, Cass," he said. "I know my dad better than you do. If my future depends on Rudy Mathison, they might as well skip the trial and lock me up for good."

I slid the pad of paper into my bag and hoped like hell Cole was wrong.

Chapter 14

"What have we got?" I asked. Tori stood in the doorway of the conference room. Cole Mathison's murder trial materials took up every available space.

"Maybe an early Christmas present," Tori said. She held two thick manilla envelopes in her hand. "Well ... two."

Jeanie walked in, bearing a pot of coffee and a stack of Styrofoam mugs. It was four o'clock in the afternoon.

"The World-Tell subpoena request," Tori said, handing me one of the envelopes. I could see the World-Tell globe logo on the outside of the package, and my heart did a little jump. Rudy Mathison's long-awaited cell phone records. Just like Christmas morning.

Jeanie poured me a cup. She took hers black. I liked cream and enough sweetener to make it taste as little like coffee as possible.

"We pulling an all-nighter?" Jeanie asked.

"Maybe," I said as I took the package from Tori and tore it open.

"Cripe," Jeanie said as she sat down next to me. "I'm going to need my glasses. Tori?"

"On it," Tori said. Jeanie was always losing her readers. She refused to wear them on a chain. Tori and Miranda had taken to keeping spares in just about every room in the office. Jeanie bellowed for them anyway.

She took the little pink eyewear case from Tori and slid her glasses on. Tori started handing out highlighter pens.

"How are we doing this?" Jeanie asked.

"Heck if I know," I said.

"What are we doing?" Tori asked. She left a few highlighters for herself and took the seat on the other end of the table.

"Rudy Mathison's cell phone data," I said. "Guy goes off the grid the same night Lauren disappears. Cole thinks maybe his dad likes the idea of Cole spending the rest of his life in prison. Gets him out of the way so he can keep the status quo tormenting his mother. And ... my own niece tells me he's giving her a lecherous vibe."

"Lovely," Jeanie said. "I hate to say it, but Cole might have a point. Never had a good vibe from Rudy. I've seen the Mathisons around town. He's rough with Roxanne. Doesn't like when she talks to other men. Even Lou, the butcher down at Hanlon's Meats."

"Lou?" Tori asked. "He's eighty-seven years old or something."

"Well, that's the kind of guy Rudy is," Jeanie said.

She licked a finger and started running it down a line of texts from a stack I'd handed her. My eyes immediately went to dates. I'd asked for records for the two weeks before Lauren's disappearance to the present.

It only took us five minutes to see the first glaring problem.

"He's gone," Tori said, looking over my shoulder. I had August 31st's entries in front of me.

When I flipped the page, a single line glared up at me. September 1st, 2:27 a.m. End of Report.

"What does this mean?" Jeanie said. She flipped through a few of her pages. She had data from the week leading up to Lauren's disappearance.

"He's gone," I said. "His phone goes off the grid at 2:27 a.m. the night Lauren goes missing."

Tori plopped back down in her chair. "Cass, that's within the exact timeframe everyone says Lauren was likely murdered. The M.E. says she likely died between the hours of one a.m. and four a.m. of the 1st."

"Son of a bitch," Jeanie said.

"Where was he?" Tori asked.

"I'm not sure," I said. "Show me the records from Cole and Lauren's phones at that time."

Tori had already made a blow-up of the relevant timeframe. I planned to possibly use it as a trial exhibit.

"Here's the thing that hurts us," Tori said. "Cole and Lauren's phones get shut off around the same time. Half past midnight. Lauren's never goes back online. They find it in her car the next day. Cole's phone goes back online at just after one a.m. and hits the tower closest to his house."

"Right," I said, chewing on the end of my highlighter. "What tower is Rudy's hitting at 2:27 a.m.?"

Jeanie squinted as she read the line. "Manley Court," she said.

I rose from my chair. On one side of the room, I had an easel set up with a 25 X 30 pad of paper. I flipped through it until I found what I was looking for.

Tori had made me a map of the local cell phone towers. I knew Rafe Johnson planned to introduce all of this. He would use the cell phone data to track Cole and Lauren's movements, correlating them to each other. He could try to say whatever he wanted about the time gap when Lauren and Cole's phones were apparently shut off and not submitting data.

"Manley Court," I said. It took me a second to find it. The towers themselves covered roughly a triangular area. A user would pass through one zone, then get picked up by the next tower.

I had pinpoints on the map showing the location of the bonfire, Cole's house. Lauren's house, Cole's workplace, and the location where Lauren's body was found on Lumley Road.

"Cass," Tori said, her voice rising with alarm as she tracked the path of my finger.

"This can't be," I said. "I mean, it *can't*. Can it?"

"The hell you two on about?" Jeanie asked. She repositioned her glasses further up her nose and came around the table to stand beside us.

"I'll be damned," she said.

"2:27 a.m.," I said. "Cole was back home by then. His phone is hitting the tower that serves his address."

"And this is after Cole said he had his confrontation with his dad," Tori said, her tone picking up the excitement I felt.

I tried not to breathe. I was afraid I might blink and the triangular area before me would vanish. A loose thread, ready to blow away in the wind.

I went back to the records.

"Dobbins Street," Jeanie said, catching up with my train of thought. "That's the tower closest to Cole's house. The old man's phone hits there at 12:45. Just like Cole said."

"Then it moves," Tori said. She still held the other manilla envelope in her hand. As Jeanie and I zoned in on the cell data, Tori sat on a chair in the corner and ripped the envelope open.

I went back to the easel and tracked forward from the Dobbins triangle to Manley Court. It went northeast, about six miles from Cole's house.

"Where's he going?" Jeanie asked.

My finger stopped on one of the pinpoints. I waited for her to make the same connection. Rudy Mathison's phone is all over the timeline. It goes from Carver out to Lumley.

"Holy hell!" she shouted when she finally did. "Lauren's car was facing the wrong way if she was heading home. But the right way if she was heading to Cole's. Rudy leaves after he has his confrontation with Cole. He could have run into her. Stopped her. Then ... he leaves ... he goes to ..."

"Manley Court," I said. "Jeanie, that's the tower closest to where Lauren Rice's body was found. Rudy Mathison was there. He was right there at 2:27 a.m."

"Cass," Tori said. Her mouth hung open as she looked at two sheets of paper.

"What is it?" I asked.

"Your second Christmas present, I think," she said. She handed me the paper. In addition to the cell phone records, I'd filed subpoenas on Rudy Mathison's bank and credit card records.

"His savings account?" I asked, trying to make sense of the dates and numbers.

"He drained it," Tori said. "Eleven thousand dollars. Cass, look at the date."

I did. She was right. There was a large withdrawal coming out at 9:13 a.m. on September 2nd. The first Monday after Lauren disappeared.

"He took the money and ran," Jeanie said. "Son of a bitch. Rudy took the money and ran."

Chapter 15

I HADN'T MEANT to lose my temper. I hadn't meant to show any emotion at all, but as Rafe Johnson stared at me stone-faced behind his desk, I unleashed.

"What do you mean you're not going to do anything about this?" I asked. He had copies of Rudy Mathison's cell phone records and the bank records. They were part of discovery. I'd left him three voicemails and wrote a detailed letter outlining my concerns. He'd responded to none of them.

"This doesn't change anything," he said.

"It changes everything," I said. "Rafe, you're not being reasonable. Is this really the hill you want to die on? The first case you want to be known for? You'll lose. You rushed this thing to trial. I have reasonable doubt. You have to see that."

He sat with one ankle crossed over the opposite knee. Infuriatingly calm.

"Rudy Mathison's whereabouts have no bearing on this case," he said. "I appreciate you bringing all of this to my attention, but we're not considering dropping charges. Is your client ready to discuss a plea deal?"

"He is not," I said. "And I'd like to know what's being done to find Rudy Mathison."

"You'll have to take that matter up with his wife. She doesn't seem to think he's missing. There's no crime where he's concerned."

"He's a material witness," I said. "His cell phone data puts him near the scene where your victim's body was found."

"None of this proves he was at the scene. This grid is a two-mile radius, Cass. And those are all things you're welcome to try to explore at trial. But surely you didn't come here expecting me to give you trial preparation advice?" His snide tone made me want to rip his face off.

"He's a kid, Rafe," I said. "An innocent kid. And you have rushed this thing from the get-go. You're going to lose. I think you know that. What I don't know is why you don't care."

He paused for a moment. I let the heat drain from my head and dissipate a bit. In all honesty, I just never thought I'd hit this particular brick wall with him. It was pure insanity.

"We'll look into it," he said. "I just don't think it's as solid as you do. But then, maybe you're not looking at any of this objectively. Have you considered that maybe you're too personally close to it?"

There was movement behind me. Rafe's secretary poked his head in. "I'm sorry to interrupt," he said. "But you told me to let you know when your one o'clock got here."

I glanced over my shoulder. Rafe Johnson's one o'clock paced nervously across the hallway.

"Great," I said, rising. "By all means, please don't let me keep you. Detective Lewis, maybe you should join us!"

Megan Lewis's face had drained of color. She looked like she wanted the floor to open up and swallow her. Part of me, a part I'm not proud of, wished for the same thing.

"Cass," Rafe said. "Let's all just be civil. I'm sorry you don't like your case ... but I'm not sorry I like mine."

"Oh, I like my case just fine," I said. "This has been shoddy detective work from the very beginning, too. You want to tell me why you never pursued any other leads?"

Megan opened her mouth to answer, then clamped it shut. I knew it was me who needed to do the same. Rafe was right about one thing: if he wasn't going to budge, these were the kind of questions I'd need to save for cross-examinations and closing argument. If a kid's life weren't hanging in the balance, I could almost get excited about it.

"Have you reviewed the cell phone records I sent over?" I asked her, trying to keep my cool. "And he drains his savings account first thing Monday morning after Lauren goes missing. Nobody sees him after that. You should have been sitting on his house!"

"Yes," she said. "You can think what you want, but we've pursued all leads, Cass."

"Look again," I said, jabbing my finger on the stack of phone records Rafe now had at his desk. "You need to find Rudy Mathison. Today."

"Is there anything else you want to bring to my attention?" Rafe asked.

"I want to know that you're making diligent efforts to find and question Rudy Mathison," I said to Detective Lewis. "And I want to be notified the minute you get him. Don't stand there and tell me you're not already trying."

"Of course we're trying," she said. "Believe me, I want to talk to him too. I'm going to talk to the wife again tomorrow, actually. If anything turns up, you'll be one of the first to know."

I dared her to challenge me. At the same time, I was

already writing my cross with her. I hoped she gave me the exact same stunned expression.

"If there is anything new that comes up," Rafe said. "I'm fully aware of my duties under the law, Cass. Besides, from what I hear, you may not even be around to try this case."

"What are you talking about?" I asked.

"Oh," he said. "I still have plenty of friends in Lansing. I hear you've impressed a lot of the governor's people. You might be sitting on the bench."

I couldn't tell whether he was trying to flatter me or tick me off. Maybe both.

"We're in trial in four weeks," I said. "I'm not planning on going anywhere before then. So, I'm sorry to disappoint you if you thought you'd be sitting across from someone else at the Mathison trial."

Rafe reached across the desk and extended his hand. "Well then, I look forward to sparring with you for the first time."

It was petty of me not to take his hand. But the hell with it. I was feeling just that petty.

I stopped in front of Megan Lewis. "You know I've got a subpoena out for Rudy Mathison."

"Good for you," she said, finding her courage. "I'm just as interested to talk to him. But of course you know serving it will fall on the deputy sheriff's desk. My badge says Delphi P.D. Detective, Cass."

"You'll both be lucky to walk away from this one without having misconduct investigations launched against you," I said.

"Have a good one, Cass," Rafe said. I managed to leave his office without slamming the door.

Chapter 16

ERIC AND I MADE A DEAL. During work hours, I was Cass Leary, defense lawyer. He was Detective Eric Wray. For months, the arrangement had been working. But Friday night when he walked up the drive bearing wine, he took one look at me and knew he might be in for it.

"Should I have brought a white flag instead?" he quipped.

"No," I said. "But maybe you didn't bring enough wine."

I wanted to bitch. I wanted to unload on all the reasons his bureau had done the wrong things by Cole Mathison and Lauren Rice. But Eric had a way of disarming me with that smile of his and thawed my heart.

"Come here," I said. I took the wine he did bring and let him come inside.

"Thanks," he said. "It's damn cold out here. I think the lake's already frozen."

"Winter is coming," I said.

"Two more weeks according to the Farmer's Almanac," he joked.

"You becoming a farmer now?" I asked. "Because I wouldn't hate that. It would make my life easier."

We took our wine to the couch. I already had a fire going. Eric managed to warm me more than it could. I curled up beside him, tucking my bare feet beneath me.

"I thought I already made your life easier," he said.

I considered his words. "Well," I said after a pause. "You're handy with that corkscrew. And my brother said you're not completely hopeless with a hammer."

"Not completely hopeless?" he said, clearly offended. "I built that new entertainment center at my place all by myself."

"From IKEA," I teased. "Joe and Matty would never be caught dead in that place."

Eric grumbled, but let the statement stand. He was teasing anyway, and so was I. It felt good. It was more than just Eric's charming smirk that disarmed me.

"You know," he said after a while. "There's still that one other thing that would make our lives together easier."

I held my breath, not knowing where his thoughts were about to land.

"Cass," he said. "Be honest. Where's your head with this judicial appointment?"

"Oh," I sighed. "That. I don't suppose that's up to me anymore. I filled out the paperwork. They're doing whatever they do to figure out if I'm worth the risk."

Eric poured each of us another glass of wine. "Yeah. I've been interviewed."

"What?" I said, sitting up straight. I turned to face him. "When? What about?"

"A few days ago," he said. "You knew they were reaching out to your closest friends and family."

"I know," I said. "But I never disclosed that you ... that we ..."

"Clearly someone else did," he said. "Does that bother you?"

"What? No," I said, though it did a little. Not that I had anything to hide. I just hated that Eric or anyone else had to be scrutinized.

"Well," he said. "I only told them the good parts."

I laughed. "You want to enlighten me on what the bad parts are?"

"Well," Eric said. "You're kind of a slob. And I'll never get over the way you like to put ketchup on your eggs. That's just gross. And weird."

I lobbed a pillow at him, which he neatly caught. "And you can barely boil water, let alone cook a decent meal. Though I can't yet speak from experience, I'd bet good money your morning breath is something else."

"Fine," I said, grabbing another pillow. I settled back on the couch further away from him.

"In all seriousness though, it wasn't bad."

"Good," I said. "But did they ... did they ask if we were dating? Eric, that could be complicated. With Wendy ..."

"Wendy isn't anything you have to worry about," he said. "And there's nothing you and I have ever done that either of us should be ashamed of. But if that's the thing somebody in Lansing thinks should keep you from ..."

"No," I said. "Don't even finish that thought. You're right. I'm not ashamed of my life or how I live it. They approached me. I didn't seek this out."

"But now that they have," he said. "Cass ... you really want it, don't you?"

I reached for my wine. "Yeah," I said. "I kind of think I do. I know it would make things easier for us. Like maybe I wouldn't have the urge to throw things at you as much. For being so pigheaded and all."

"Me? Pigheaded? You might want to look in the mirror there, Porky."

I threw a second pillow. He caught that one and slipped it behind his head. Now I had no pillows.

"It's just ..." I traced a circle around the rim of my wine glass.

"Spit it out," he said. "You've been wanting to the second I walked up."

"Detective Lewis," I said. "She's ... Eric, she's in over her head. If you were lead on this case, I know you wouldn't have sent it on to Rafe's desk. Not without tracking down Rudy Mathison. Not with the state of the evidence the way it is."

He set his glass down. "Cass, Megan knows what she's doing. And you know we can't get too far into this particular conversation."

"I know," I said. "But it would bother you. You can't tell me this thing with Rudy Mathison's whereabouts wouldn't bother you. It's more than a loose end."

"Maybe," he said. "But like you said. It's not my case. Megan's good. She's damn good. She's had to deal with a lot of shit from command in my department. There are unfortunately still a lot of people with old-fashioned ideas about what a real detective is supposed to look like."

"I get that," I said. "Hell, I've lived it. It's just, I know this kid ... I ..."

Eric's phone rang. The way he screwed up his face, I had a feeling it was a call he had to take. Not two seconds later, my phone rang too.

Anytime we got synchronous calls like that, it meant something serious was happening in Delphi. We exchanged a glance and went to our neutral corners.

In my case, Rafe Johnson's cell phone flashed on my caller ID. I heard Eric answer and call his lieutenant by name.

"Rafe?" I said.

"Hey, Cass," he said. "I wanted you to hear this first from me. We've had a development in the Lauren Rice case. Some physical evidence has been discovered."

"What physical evidence?" I said. On the other end of the room, I heard Eric tell his caller that he'd be right there. And I heard him ask what the crime scene unit had to say.

"Rafe?" I asked.

"Cass," he said. "We've found some of Lauren's missing clothing. Her, uh ... underwear. It was thrown under a bush not that far from the ditch where she was found. We've got the preliminary report back on the DNA."

"A DNA sample?" I asked. "Rafe? When did this whole thing go down?"

"A few days ago," he said. "It took a while for them to figure out what it was and who it belonged to. I needed to be sure. But it's Lauren's. You'll, of course, have all the science."

"Of course," I said, feeling sick to my stomach.

I hung up with Rafe around the same time Eric ended his call. He looked grim as he walked back to me.

"Cass," he said.

"Tell me what it is," I said. "I know you already know. And you know Rafe's going to have to disclose what you have, anyway. He said they found Lauren's underwear."

"Yeah," he said, hanging his head. "Cass, I'm sorry. They found traces of semen. Waiting on the official labs, but the preliminary report is saying it's a hit. It's Cole Mathison's DNA."

Chapter 17

"WE GOT TO HIM IN TIME," Maxine Carver said. "Cass, I'm sorry. That's all I can say."

I sank into a chair in the hallway just outside the emergency room. Maxine sat beside me. She'd taken a panicked call from Roxanne Mathison, who had been afraid to call the police or an ambulance. Maxine and Dave had no such fear and raced over.

"Hell of a twenty-four hours, yeah?" she said.

I couldn't even answer. Instead, I found myself assuming an airplane crash position with my face in my hands and my head between my knees.

Thirty minutes after I called to break the news to Cole about the new evidence against him, he'd tried to off himself by swallowing half a bottle of his mother's antidepressants.

Roxanne couldn't look up when I came to her. She sat with her head on her cousin, Dave Carver's shoulder. "He's okay," she whispered. "He's gotta be okay."

"We're here, Rox," he said. "He's getting the best care."

Heavy footsteps drew my attention. One of the nurses gestured to Maxine.

"That's you," Maxine said, patting my shoulder. "Kid said he'd only talk to you."

Roxanne looked up. "Will you tell him I'm here? Tell him I love him."

"Of course," I said, leaning down to meet her eyes. "It's going to be okay." I should have grabbed a coffee before I headed over. It was going to be a long night.

The kid I saw in that hospital bed bore no resemblance to the one I'd known all summer. It was as if every drop of blood had drained from his body. He became a wax figure with white lips and sharp-boned cheeks.

"Cole," I said. I pulled up a stool and sat beside him. I felt my phone vibrate in my pocket. That would be Joe. Or Emma. Or both.

At first, I didn't think he heard me. Then, a flicker of movement. He turned his head and met my eyes.

"Why is this happening?" he asked.

I felt cold. Detached. I had questions to ask but knew if I pushed too hard, the kid might break for good.

"They found your DNA on Lauren's underwear, Cole," I said. "That's what's happening. I know you feel like the walls are closing in, but this isn't the answer."

He sat up. The hospital gown hung off of him. "I couldn't do it," he said. "Didn't they tell you that? I only swallowed three pills. They brought me here as a precaution, Maxine said. I wanted to do it. Or I thought I did."

"How do you feel now?" I asked.

He lifted his shoulders. "Like no one will ever believe me."

"What do you want them to believe?" I asked.

He stared at me. "Not they. You. I want you to believe me. I didn't ... whatever they found, it wasn't me. It can't have been me."

"Semen," I said. "That's what they found. In her underwear. They have your DNA. It matched."

He shook his head. "Cass, I didn't ... I didn't rape Lauren."

I snapped. "You don't have to have raped her. Cole, I need you to tell me. Right here. Right now. What really happened that night?"

"I've already told you!" he shouted. "God. I feel like I've woken up in hell. Lauren and I weren't having sex. Not that night. Not since months and months before that. I don't know how they found what they found. Are you sure? Could there be some kind of mistake? Like a bad test?"

I folded my hands in my lap. My heart and head warred with each other. I'd been around hardened criminals before. Murderers. Hitmen. The worst kind of evil. Cole Mathison still seemed like nothing more than a scared kid.

But no, the DNA didn't lie.

"I don't think so," I said. "It can be challenged. But a match is a match. So, I'm going to ask you again. What happened?"

He threw his head back against the pillow and stared up at the ceiling. "Nothing happened. I've told you everything. I saw Lauren at that stupid party. I didn't like the way she was acting. Everyone wants to say it was a fight. It wasn't. I was just kind of sad. I told her I didn't think it was a good idea for us to even be friends anymore. But that was the end of it. Cass, I didn't have sex with her."

"Cole ..."

He lifted his head. "I'm telling you the truth. Hook me up to a lie detector. I'll do anything."

Part of me wanted to do just that. Though it wouldn't be admissible in court, they were far more accurate than people gave them credit for.

"We're just weeks from trial ..." I started.

"We?" he asked, desperation making his voice crack. "Are we still a we? You're not going to give up on me?"

I slapped my hands to my knees. "I don't know," I snapped. It kind of poured out of me. "I'll be honest. I don't even know what the hell to think right now. I have more questions than answers. That's not really the place I want to be this close to a first-degree murder trial, Cole."

"I know," he said, barely above a whisper. "I know. There are so many things I wished I'd done differently. But I swear to you. I swear to God, this wasn't me. I wasn't with Lauren like that that night. It's got to be a mistake. It *has* to be."

"It isn't," I said.

"Did you find my dad?" he asked. "Maybe ..."

"Maybe what?" I asked.

"My dad," he said. "I think you have it right. I think he's staying off the grid because of all of this. I thought it was just because he didn't want to get asked to help me. He would do that. He hates me that much. The fight we had in July was really bad. I already told you that. I didn't want to believe it, but I think he would do everything he could to ruin my life."

"Cole, his cell phone data is very disturbing. What Emma has said is very disturbing. It paints a picture that you have to confront. I've never asked you this point blank. Could he have killed that girl?" I asked.

"I don't know," he said. "I've been running it through my head over and over."

"Cole," I said. "I want to believe you. I really do. But DNA doesn't lie."

"No," he said. "I know. But ... do you think ... someone is setting me up. I don't know who. I don't know why. I just know that whatever they found, I did *not* have sex with Lauren Rice that night. I just didn't."

My head throbbed. It got hard to focus under the harsh glare of the fluorescents in this room. I needed a good night's sleep. I needed a stiff drink. I needed ... something.

"Cole," I said. "I have a lot to think about."

"Will you stick with me?" he asked.

I couldn't answer. That's the honest truth.

"Give me some time," I said.

"Right," he said. "No. I know. But could you tell Emma ..."

"No," I said. "That I can be pretty clear about. I'm not going to be your go-between. I've blurred enough family and professional lines as it is."

"Okay," he said. "I'm sorry. Gosh. I'm just so sorry for everything."

"Cole," I said. "I need to know. Are you planning on doing anything like this again?"

He let out a breath. "No," he said. "I told you. I wasn't ... in the end I couldn't even go through with it. I just ... I panicked."

"Okay," I said. "Well, you're in here for the next seventy-two hours. Dave and Maxine had to file a report. It's their job. So, I think you need to take this time. Get your head straight. Maybe take the advice of the good doctors that work here. Then, I don't know. I'll figure out what I'm going to do."

He nodded. "That's fair. I get it. Thank you. For everything. No matter what you decide or what happens. You're a good person."

"All right," I said. "So get some rest. Actually, that's good advice for both of us."

Just as I rose, the nurse came back to take Cole's vitals. I said goodbye and headed back down the hall.

My phone buzzed again. I reached in and turned it off.

Maxine and Dave were still in the waiting room with Roxanne. I went to her.

"He's okay," I said. "But he's fragile. They'll keep him here a little while, then he'll be able to come back home."

She sniffled. "Thank you. I want to see him. Can I see my baby?"

I caught Maxine's eyes above Roxanne's shoulder. "I'll let you work all of that out with the doctor."

I rose. Dave rose with me. We stepped down the hall, out of earshot.

"You deserve a gold star," I said. "Thanks for being there for them."

"Third cousins or not," he said. "We're still family. I'm just glad Roxanne's *letting* us be here for her. If Rudy were around, he wouldn't have it."

"Do you have *any* idea where he might be? I'm getting desperate, Dave."

"I don't know," he said, his tone going flat. "I don't understand it any more than you do. I promise I'll keep an ear out, but Rudy won't have anything to do with any of us. If anything, I'm a repellant where he's concerned."

"I appreciate it just the same," I said. Just then, my sister Vangie appeared at the other end of the hall. I said my goodbyes to Dave.

"Hey," I said, nodding toward Vangie.

She put her hands up in a gesture of surrender. "Joe and Emma are losing their minds," she said. "Me coming instead was the best I could come up with for keeping them at bay."

I filled her in on what I could so she could relay it to my brother. "He's okay," I said. "And I'm exhausted."

"Come on," Vangie said. "You want to grab a cup of coffee?"

I checked my smartwatch. It was after midnight.

"No," I said. "But we can walk each other back to our cars."

"Sounds good," she said. Then my little sister put her arm around me.

"Who's with Jessa?" I asked.

"I dropped her off at Joe's. That was another one of my brilliant ideas. Watching her might be a welcome distraction."

"Good thinking," I said. "What's the temperature over there?" Though I had a pretty good guess.

"Joe's ready to send Emma off to a convent," she said. "And he wants to know what you're planning to do. There are rumors on the internet that the cops found new evidence."

"What?" I said. I stopped walking. Had Rafe Johnson leaked this?

"Some neighbor tipped off a reporter that there were cops searching near that ditch where Lauren Rice's body was found."

I let out a sigh. Citizen journalists. The last thing I needed in this case.

"It's complicated," I said.

"It always is." Vangie laughed. "So you didn't answer my question. Are you going to stick with this kid?"

"Vangie, he's my client. He's set for trial in a couple weeks. Even if I wanted to withdraw, Judge Niedermayer likely wouldn't allow it. Not without the prosecution agreeing to postpone the case. Which they won't."

"They can do that?" she said. "They can force you to stay on a case?"

"They can," I said.

"Wow," Vangie said. "Glad I don't have your job."

"Thanks," I said, giving her side eye.

We'd reached our cars. Vangie had managed to find a spot just a few over from mine.

"I'll handle Joe and Emma for tonight," she said. "He's just worried about her. And he's worried about you too. We all are."

"Hey." I smiled. "That's supposed to be my job. I'm the one that worries about the lot of you."

"What, us?" she teased. "We're perfect angels. The most well-adjusted, functional family in Delphi."

I rolled my eyes. "Right."

"Listen," she said, getting serious. "Just ... if you need anything, just let us know."

I went to her with my arms out. My little sister let me fold her in them. I missed this. From the time she was about thirteen on, Vangie had been the prickly one. It was Matty who was my hugger.

"Don't get used to this," Vangie said, sensing my thoughts. I kissed her forehead as she pulled away.

"Thanks," I said. "I really mean that. I don't know what's going to happen over the next few weeks, but it helps to know you all have my back."

"Always," she said, saluting. "Now go get some sleep. You look terrible."

I gave her a different kind of salute as I climbed behind the wheel. I waited for my sister to pull out before I put my car in gear.

Part of me wanted to just crash my head against the steering wheel and let my blaring horn match my insides.

I had believed Cole was innocent. I needed to. Even though I knew it objectively didn't matter. Now this.

As I approached the security gate, doubt swirled around my heart. Doubt, and the nagging sensation that Cole might be right. Something was off. The timing of this new evidence just didn't sit right. I had to know for sure. But someone, somewhere might have set Cole Mathison up. My theory as to who started to take shape but that's all it was. A theory. Not enough to delay the trial. Not enough to get him acquitted if I couldn't get past that DNA. I said a prayer as the red and white security gate went up and I drove on through.

Chapter 18

MONDAY, January 8th, I sat at Cole Mathison's side as he faced a jury of his peers for the very first time.

Peers.

They could hardly be called that, but it was the closest Woodbridge County could come to it. Seven men ranging from twenty-seven to seventy-four in age. Five women ranging from thirty-one to sixty-three. Each of them wore their best poker faces as Judge Niedermayer called us to order.

It was time.

Cole sat beside me, expressionless. Well-shaven in a new suit, he looked closer to fourteen years old than his nearly twenty-one. Stress and weight loss thinned his hair. Red splotches appeared on his cheeks as Judge Niedermayer got settled in.

With the ousting of Judge Tucker in district court, Greta Niedermayer was the newest judge on the Woodbridge County bench, having been elected ten years ago. Generally, once given the gavel, judges around here were almost impossible to unseat. It was something to think about as I whispered a word of encouragement to Cole. I knew it wouldn't help. He was counting on me to save him from a lifetime behind bars.

"Mr. Johnson?" Judge Niedermayer said. She was in her early sixties with steel-gray hair she wore in a neat bob. I'd heard rumors it was a wig. If so, it was one of the best I'd ever seen. Greta Niedermayer had cool green eyes that she trained on Rafe Johnson as he buttoned his jacket and stepped up to the lectern.

"Ladies and gentlemen of the jury," he said. "I'm a new face to most of you. I know my being here might serve as a reminder of a tragedy this town suffered with the untimely passing of my predecessor, Jack LaForge. I have big shoes to fill. I hope I can make him proud."

Rafe gave the jury a big, genuine smile. He paused for a moment, gave Cole one last look, then turned to the jury.

"We're here to talk about an even bigger tragedy that befell our little town last fall. The killing of Lauren Rice.

"Nineteen," he continued. "She was just nineteen years old. A good kid. Great student. But she was more than that. Lauren was an only child. A girl who had been forced to grow up way too fast when she lost her mother to cancer when she was only thirteen. Since then, it has been Lauren and her father Gil against the world. Lauren passed up the chance to go off to college out of state on a scholarship. She didn't want to leave her dad alone. She looked out for him. Took care of him. In a lot of ways, she almost assumed the role of a parent. A nurturer.

"Now, Gil Rice has to bear the rest of his life without her. She was the most precious person in the world to him. A treasure. He'll tell you how he doesn't think he could have gone on living if it weren't for Lauren.

"She was a good friend. A mentor to younger girls. You'll

hear about how she was a leader on her cheerleading squad. A scholar-athlete.

"Ladies and gentlemen, Lauren Rice mattered. She was important to so many people. But on the night of August 31st, this man, the defendant, treated her as if she were worse than garbage.

"Lauren Rice's great flaw was that she loved too much. Trusted the wrong people. Because of it, she was abducted, murdered, and thrown into a ditch by the boy she loved.

"That man." Rafe pointed to Cole. "The defendant, Cole Mathison. You'll hear how he used her. Strung her along. Abused her feelings for him. Her trust. She tried to move on after their break-up. But Cole wouldn't allow it. He tormented her. Played mind games. Wouldn't let her go.

"Then finally, on that final, fateful night, you'll hear how Cole Mathison lured Lauren away from her friends. How he brutalized her, smothered her, then dumped her body by the side of the road. How he's been lying ever since.

"Lauren Rice no longer has a voice. But she still has stories to tell. With her body that Cole so callously cast aside. Her final texts. She cried out for help in so many ways. No one was there for her. The one person she trusted above all is the one who betrayed her. Who murdered her.

"It's all here, ladies and gentlemen. Though it will be hard to hear. And I wish I didn't have to put you through the agony of seeing this evidence. Of reliving Lauren Rice's last, horrific moments on earth. But you must. We all must. We must give her back her voice and bring her killer to justice.

"Ladies and gentlemen, Cole Mathison is a master manipulator. He's charming. Good-looking. An all-American boy. You'll hear about that too. Don't believe it. Don't be fooled by the lies and misdirection you might hear."

Rafe paused. He pursed his lips as if weighing his words.

Pure theatrics. I knew he had planned every word he meant to say.

"He cast her aside," he said. "When Lauren Rice became a bother to him. When her very existence threatened Cole's future plans, he got rid of her. Tossed her away. He did what was convenient for him. Every moment since that day, he's done what is convenient for him. Lies. Obfuscation. Misdirection. That's all he has. But we have something else. We have the truth. We have incontrovertible evidence. The weight of it will astound you. Eyewitnesses. Mr. Mathison's own words and Lauren's via text. There are no coincidences. And above all else, we have the physical evidence. Though it will be difficult to hear, the conclusion you draw—that you *must* draw—will be very simple. Cole Mathison murdered Lauren Rice in cold blood, with malice aforethought, then he dumped her body like yesterday's garbage.

"But he won't get away with it. We won't let him. Lauren Rice mattered. She had immeasurable worth. She was a vibrant force in so many people's lives. You'll get to know her. You'll understand her. You'll grieve for her. Then, you'll have the power to bring her killer to justice and give her the final rest she deserves. Thank you."

Rafe put his hands in his pants pockets and walked over to his table. Once again, he hesitated as if he meant to say one final thing. Then he sat down and folded his hands in front of him.

"Is the defense ready to proceed?" Judge Niedermayer asked.

"We are," I said.

I didn't pace. Didn't move around or posture. I simply stood at the lectern with my hands folded as I addressed the jury.

"Good morning," I said. "Thank you for your time. I know

136

this is a tough job for you. For all of us. My colleague, Mr. Johnson, is right about something. Lauren Rice mattered. She had worth. She was valued. And what happened to her is unspeakable. Unforgivable.

"But," I said, pausing. "Cole Mathison didn't kill her. He made many mistakes where she was concerned. I imagine there are things he wishes he would have handled differently about their break-up. But that doesn't mean he murdered her. Because ... he didn't.

"When the state brings murder charges against someone, they must prove each and every element of the crime beyond a reasonable doubt. The defendant is entitled to the benefit of the doubt. He is entitled to the benefit of any reasonable inference of innocence when you weigh the facts.

"We don't want Lauren Rice's killer to walk free. We want justice for her just as much as you do. We want to be able to rest easy at night knowing the good guys win and the bad guys get caught. But Cole Mathison isn't the monster the prosecution would have you believe.

"Is he flawed? Of course. But he's not a murderer. He did not kill that girl. The prosecution has crafted a story. But that's all they have. A story. They do not have facts. They have witnesses who can tell you Ms. Rice and Mr. Mathison argued. Nothing more. They have no proof that Mr. Mathison was anywhere near where Lauren Rice disappeared. They cannot even prove to you how she died.

"Think about that," I said. "Because you'll want that answer. They have no murder weapon. They have no conclusive evidence as to what killed her. There are gaping holes in their timeline.

"You will come away from the state's presentation with far more questions than answers. How did she die? When did Lauren die? Those are just the two most basic. But there's another one. Something so disturbing it might haunt you as much as the fact of Lauren's death.

"They stopped," I said. "The police and the prosecution gave up. When presented with solid leads about other potential witnesses, they didn't pursue them. They were the ones who lied and obfuscated. Why? Why would they do that? What would they have to gain?

"I'll tell you," I said, entering the thin ice portion of my opening. But my objective was only to get some of these questions in the jury's mind as they began to hear Rafe's evidence.

"You have a brand-new prosecutor. You have a new detective assigned to the case. They must win at all costs. A young girl is dead. The whole county is watching. The whole state. But it's no excuse. I want Lauren Rice's killer off the streets as much as anyone else. I am horrified with how she was found and what her final moments might have been like. The only thing we know for sure is that she was found alone. Unprotected. We cannot go back in time and save her. We cannot comfort her anymore. But we can strive to ensure the system works for her. We can put the police and the prosecution to the test. They failed Lauren Rice. We won't.

"When you hear Mr. Johnson's evidence, you will find it lacking. And when you do, you will have no choice but to enter the only just verdict. Not guilty."

I thanked the jury and took my seat next to Cole. He stared straight ahead. I warned him to. I wanted no thanks from him. No pat on the back. Nothing that might be construed as gloating or satisfaction, even if I scored a point or two.

They needed to see his grief. His pain for losing Lauren. It's what I saw in him since the moment I learned she was dead.

"Mr. Johnson?" Judge Niedermayer said. "Are you ready to call your first witness?"

Rafe cleared his throat. "I am, Judge. The state would like to call Gilbert Rice to the stand, if you so please."

Judge Niedermayer nodded and gestured to her bailiff. He opened the courtroom door and motioned for Lauren Rice's father to enter.

Gil Rice wore his grief as he walked into the room. The weight of it bent his back. His hand trembled as he grabbed the side of the witness box and slowly climbed in.

Chapter 19

"Mr. Rice," Rafe started. "Thank you for being here today. I can't even begin to imagine how difficult this is for you. I'll try to keep my questioning brief."

"I don't mind," Gil said. He repeated himself when his voice broke on the first go-around. He cleared his throat and pulled the microphone closer.

"I'll do anything for Lauren," he said.

"Of course," Rafe said. "Mr. Rice, what can you tell us about your daughter?"

"She was ... she was. I know she wasn't perfect. I say that because you have to. But she really was. To me. She was a good kid. Smart. She taught herself how to read when she was four or five. Julie, that's my wife. She was always the one who helped Lauren with her homework. I wasn't as good at that. I'm better with my hands. Books weren't my thing. They were Julie's though. She would read to her all the time. For hours. Chapter books too, from the time she was real little. She always got straight As, Lauren. Honor roll. All of that. We were older when we had her. Julie and me, we tried for a long time. Went to different doctors and such. We were even thinking about trying to adopt. Had a meeting with a lawyer. Then, two days before we went to it, Julie found out she was pregnant."

"That must have been something," Rafe said.

"Sure was," Gil said. "I stopped believing it would happen, you know? I was forty-two years old. I'd kind of given up on having kids of my own. I was happy enough with it just being me and Julie. But when her belly started growing, when I started feeling those little kicks ... boy ... it was like my whole world opened up. I tell people, you never really know what true joy is until you have a kid."

He paused. Gil shut his eyes tightly. When he opened them, he had tears in them. "But you never really know what true terror is either."

Rafe paused. I knew if Gil Rice never said another thing, the impact of his testimony had already set in. Beside me, Cole hung his head.

"Mr. Rice," Rafe continued. "I'd like to talk about the past year, year and a half with Lauren. Can you tell the jury what was going on in her life?"

Gil got quiet for a moment. Then he straightened and started again. "Lauren was all set to go to Valparaiso. She had a partial scholarship on account of how she did on her SATs and track. I told you she was smart. Then ... at the last minute, she decided not to go."

"Do you know why?"

"Not at the time, no," he said. "I suppose I should have. I should have pushed her. Hell, I should have put my foot down and made her go. But I was a little selfish. I liked having her around. We lost Julie when Lauren was thirteen. She died of cancer. Lauren helped me take care of her in the end. God. She was thirteen! What thirteen-year-old kid should have to deal with that? She did, though. Like a trooper. She took care of us both. I don't know how I would have got through that without Lauren."

"I understand," Rafe said. "That must have been devastating for you both."

"Anyway," Gil said. "I found out later ... after she passed. Lauren stayed home and went to community college here because she was afraid to leave me all by myself. She was going to take her common classes, then transfer later. If I'd have pushed her, I don't know. Maybe she'd still be alive."

Rafe moved around the lectern. He leaned against it with one elbow.

"Mr. Rice," he said. "About this last year. Can you tell me what else Lauren was doing besides taking classes at the community college?"

"Well," he said. "She worked here and there. Had a part-time job at the Bait Bucket. That's a bait store here in town on Finn Lake. I went to school with Randy Richmond, who owns it. Lauren would work early mornings making donuts there. She liked it because she was usually done for the day by ten, then could get to class. She did that three or four days a week."

"Was she doing well in school?" Rafe asked.

"She was. She had something like a 3.8 after her first year. She was still trying to figure out what she wanted to do when she graduated. And she had a boyfriend."

"Who was that?" Rafe asked.

Gil lifted a finger and pointed at Cole. "She was dating Cole Mathison."

"Do you know when that started?" Rafe asked.

"I got the impression it was an off-and-on thing. Lauren didn't like to talk about it a lot. They seemed to be getting along in the beginning. She smiled. Blushed when she talked about him, that kind of thing."

"I see," Rafe said. "Did she ever express any problems they were having?"

"Objection," I said. "Calls for hearsay."

"Sustained, Mr. Johnson," Judge Niedermayer said.

Rafe looked down at his notes. "Did you ever observe any problems between Lauren and the defendant?"

Gil scratched his chin. "Observed? Like, did I see them fighting? No. But I know Lauren wasn't happy as things went on."

"How did you know that?" Rafe asked.

"I caught her crying in her room a lot. I heard her talking on the phone to one of her friends about him. She said ..."

"Objection," I said again. "I'm sorry, Mr. Rice. Your Honor, I'd ask for an instruction to the witness that he may not testify as to anything he claims his daughter said regarding the defendant."

"Mr. Rice," Judge Niedermayer said. "It's improper for you to repeat statements your daughter may have made if you're offering them to prove they are true. Does that make sense?"

"Yeah," Gil said. "Mr. Johnson told me that."

My ears perked up. Rafe Johnson's face dropped. I made a quick note for cross.

"Mr. Rice," Rafe said. "Let's try to confine your testimony to what you actually observed, not statements that were made. You said you heard Lauren crying. Is there anything else you can point to that caused you concern about her relationship with Cole?"

"Just that she seemed kind of mopey around the house. Lauren wasn't generally like that. I got off easy with her. I've heard horror stories about what it's like raising teenage girls. I never had that. She was pretty even keel and happy. But this last summer, that changed. She never seemed to smile. She was checking her phone all the time. When that boy would call, or text, she'd light up. When he didn't, she was agitated. I didn't like that one bit. I told her no boy was worth all of that."

"Okay," Rafe said. "So let's focus on Labor Day weekend of last year. When was the last time you saw your daughter?"

Gil took an unsteady breath. "I saw her at about five o'clock on Saturday August 31st."

"How can you remember that so specifically?" Rafe asked.

"Because it's like you said. That was the last time I ever saw or spoke to my daughter. I'd just come home from work. I kind of rushed because she'd told me earlier she was going out. So, I stopped at the Wendy's to buy her dinner. She hadn't had much of an appetite that I saw. She likes their chili. So I was in a rush to get home with it so I could catch her before she went out."

"And you did catch her?" Rafe asked.

"I did. But only just. She already had her keys in her hand. We almost ran into each other in passing through the garage door. I tried to get her to come inside and eat. That way I'd know she had some food in her before she went out."

"Of course," Rafe said. "What happened next?"

"She didn't eat," he said. "She said she'd eat when she was out. Can I say that? Anyway, I put the Wendy's in the fridge and told her not to stay out too late. It was touchy, though. She was nineteen years old. Too old for a curfew in my mind. Hell, when I was her age, I was already in the service. I left home when I was seventeen and never looked back."

"Do you remember approximately when it was that she left?" Rafe asked.

"It was a little before six," he said. "My sister, Linny ... Linda. She calls me every day at six to check up on me. She's been doing that since Julie died. I think she promised her. Linny lives in Arizona, so there's a time difference. It's a joke between us. Linny seems to always call when I'm about to have my dinner. Anyway, she hadn't called me yet that night. I had just enough time to finish my own food before my sister called. I checked my phone and her call came in at 6:08 that night."

"Thank you," Rafe said. "So just to be clear, you're saying you think Lauren left roughly fifteen to twenty minutes before Linny's phone call?"

"Yes," Gil said.

"Okay, so then what happened?"

"I did a little work on a table I'm fixing out in the garage. I came in and watched a couple episodes of this reality show I like. They restore cars. Then, by eleven or so, I went to bed. Right before I did, I texted Lauren to remind her not to stay out too late and to call me if she needed anything. That was at 11:15. I fell asleep right after."

"When did you wake up?" Rafe asked.

"I slept right on through until my alarm went off at seven thirty. I got up, and that's when I realized Lauren wasn't in her room. And she never answered my text. I started calling her, but it went right to voicemail."

"What did you do then?" Rafe asked.

"I ran outside. Her car wasn't there. That's when I started to panic. I called a few of her friends that I knew. They told me they saw her out at the Pits, but that she left."

"What did you do then?" Rafe asked.

"I called every place I could think of. I called Randy at the Bait Bucket. She wasn't scheduled to work. I called Cole. He told me the same thing as everyone else. That he'd seen her and talked to her at the party, but that he left before she did. Then ... I called the cops. I just knew. From that moment on, I just knew something bad happened."

Gil Rice broke then. Sobbing, he buried his face in his hands.

"Thank you, Mr. Rice," Rafe said. "I don't have any more questions for you."

"Ms. Leary?" the judge said.

Great. Poor Gil was a wreck. He'd done what Rafe had called him for. He had established the beginning of the timeline for Lauren's last hours on earth. He was solid. Believable. Sympathetic. I would do more harm than good if I poked too hard.

I waited a moment, taking my time walking up to the lectern. By the time I got there, Gil had more or less composed himself again.

"Good morning, Mr. Rice," I said. "Are you okay to continue? Would you like a break?"

"No, ma'am," he said. "I can do this. Lauren would do it for me."

"Of course," I said. "I just have a few follow-up questions. When you said you called everyone you could think of when you realized Lauren was missing ... you mentioned Mr. Mathison. But he's not the only person you called, right?"

"No, ma'am," he said.

"Who else did you call? Can you give me their names?"

"I called her friend Maggie Jarvis. I called Savannah Hill, another friend. I called Ben Sharpton."

I had Gil Rice's phone records in front of me, ready to refresh his recollection if I needed it. But he was spot on.

"What was her relationship with Ben Sharpton?" I asked.

"Ben? Oh, they went out a time or two."

"Went out," I said. "As in a date?"

"He took her to prom her senior year," he said.

"Was that before or after she started dating Cole Mathison?"

Gil paused. "It was after. I think. As I said, she and Cole were on and off again. Ben was in between."

"Senior prom is a pretty important event in a teenage girl's life, isn't it?" I asked.

"Yeah. I guess so."

"And she went with Ben, not Cole?" I asked.

"Yeah."

"And that wasn't the only date she ever went on with Ben, was it? In fact, they dated for several months after her break-up with Cole Mathison, isn't that right?"

"I think," he said. "I couldn't give you exact dates."

"Isn't it possible that the boy trouble you thought she was having could just have easily related to Ben as to Cole?"

Gil paused. "I don't ... she was upset about Cole."

"When was she upset about Cole?" I asked.

"After they broke up," he said.

"But to be clear, she started dating Ben well after that, right?"

Gil looked at Rafe. From the corner of my eye, I could see Rafe look away.

"I guess so," Gil answered.

"Mr. Rice," I said. "How many times did you meet with Mr. Johnson to go over your testimony here today?"

"I think, three or four," he said. To be honest, that number surprised even me.

"You said in your direct testimony that Mr. Johnson told you you couldn't testify as to things Lauren might have said to you. In other words, Mr. Johnson told you what you could and couldn't say."

"Yeah," Gil said.

"Objection!" Rafe popped up. "Now Ms. Leary is eliciting hearsay testimony."

"Your Honor," I said. "I am not offering these statements

for truth. I'm exploring the extent to which this witness was prepped prior to coming here today."

"Overruled, Mr. Johnson," Judge Niedermayer said.

I turned toward the lectern, then remembered one of the most basic rules of cross examination. Quit while you're ahead.

"I have nothing further," I said.

"Mr. Johnson? Any redirect from you?" Judge Niedermayer said.

"Just one thing," Rafe said, brushing past me.

"Mr. Rice," he said. "Did I coach you in what to say today?"

"Objection," I said. "Counsel is leading the witness."

"Sustained," Judge Niedermayer said, surprising me.

"Mr. Rice," Rafe said. Then he stopped. Floundered.

Gil leaned forward. "Nobody told me what to say. I came here to tell the truth and help my girl."

Rafe pursed his lips. "Thank you. I have nothing further for this witness."

Gil slowly rose and left the witness chair. I got in some hits. It would remain to be seen how much of an impact they had. But at the moment, I felt like crap.

Chapter 20

Through the next morning, Rafe Johnson called a parade of Lauren Rice's friends. The strategy puzzled me. For the most part, they all testified along a similar theme. Lauren was studious, responsible. They knew she had an on again/off again dating relationship with Cole.

I got in the hits that I could. None of them could testify to ever witnessing a major fight between Cole and Lauren. They all admitted she had dated other guys more recently. So far, Judge Niedermayer upheld all my hearsay objections when Rafe tried to get any of these girls to testify to things Lauren might have said about Cole.

Lacy Carter established that Lauren arrived at the Pits a little after nine o'clock and that she'd driven herself there after a group of them had dinner at a local diner. All of this was consistent with her cell phone records from earlier in the evening.

After the lunch break, Kaylin Dwyer took the stand.

Rafe asked his foundational questions. He'd used the exact same ones for each of Lauren's five friends he'd called throughout the day.

"How long did you know Lauren?" he asked.

"I'd known her since elementary school," Kaylin said. "We've always been friends. But she wasn't part of my core group of friends until high school."

"I see," Rafe said. "Who was in that core group of friends?"

"Well, besides Lauren and me. There's Lacy Carter, Miranda Bernecki, Elizabeth Thompson."

"Okay," Rafe said. "We've heard testimony from those girls earlier today. Can you tell me what you know about Lauren's relationship with Cole Mathison?"

"They dated for a while," Kaylin confirmed.

"Was it serious, to your knowledge?"

"It was," she said. "Lauren thought they'd be together forever at one point."

"Objection," I said. "Calls for hearsay and speculation."

"Sustained, Mr. Johnson," Judge Niedermayer said, becoming exasperated with the dance.

"Ms. Dwyer, are you familiar with the circumstances surrounding Cole and Lauren's first break-up?" he asked.

"I know they stopped dating by Christmas our senior year," she answered. "Cole had already graduated by then. Lauren was getting ready to go away to school. It just got hard for them to maintain a relationship. And Lauren was worried Cole was starting to see other people."

"Do you know who initiated the break-up?" Rafe asked.

"Honestly, I had the impression it was mutual. That's definitely what Cole told me."

"You talked to the defendant about that first break-up?" Rafe asked.

"Objection," I said. "Mr. Johnson is framing his questions in such a way that he's testifying, Your Honor."

"Mr. Johnson?" the judge said. "Reframe your questions."

"Yes, ma'am," Rafe said. "Ms. Dwyer. How would you characterize Ms. Rice's and the defendant's relationship in the last year of her life?"

"I don't ... they were friends," she said. "Lauren never ended up going away to school. I think everyone already knows that. So, I know she had some regrets about letting things fade out with Cole. She really did care about him. But early this year he started seriously dating someone else," she said.

"Who was that?" Rafe asked.

"Emma Leary," Kaylin answered, her eyes darting to me.

"Emma Leary," he said. "Are you aware of any relationship she might have with defense counsel?"

I bristled. I could object, but it would serve to underscore the point Rafe would eventually try to make. It made no difference, but juries are fickle. Rafe wanted to show that I was biased. That strategy could also backfire on him.

"Her dad is Ms. Leary's brother, I think," Kaylin said.

"Small world," Rafe said.

"Just a small town," Kaylin answered, surprising me. I hid a smile.

"All right," Rafe continued. "Let's get back to the night of August 31st of last year. Where were you?"

"A group of us got together at my house. Lacy, Lauren, Miranda, Elizabeth. We hung out for a while. Then we went to LaPlant's Diner. We ate burgers there. Somebody mentioned there was a party at the Pits in Shamrock Park. I wasn't really in the mood, but everyone else wanted to go. So, we did."

"Do you know what time that was?" Rafe asked.

"We left LaPlant's around nine. I called my mom to tell her I wasn't coming straight home. She asked me when she could expect me. I said probably by midnight or one, I didn't want to stay out very late. I was tired and had to work the next day."

"Okay," Rafe said. "So what time did you arrive at the Pits?"

"I think by nine thirty," she said.

"Did you see Lauren with the defendant?" Rafe asked.

"Yes," she answered. "Lauren was ... well ... she'd been drinking. I didn't realize that at first. I wasn't. Like I said, I had to work the next morning."

"How would you characterize the exchanges between Lauren and the defendant?" he asked.

"Lauren was agitated. She'd been talking about Cole a lot at dinner. She was definitely still hung up on him. Anyway, she kind of made a pass at him at the party."

"What do you mean by that?" Rafe asked.

"She was hanging off of Cole," Kaylin said.

"What do you mean by that?" Rafe asked.

"Just what I said. She threw her arms around him. They kissed."

Cole leaned in and whispered in my ear. "That's a lie. She kissed me. I was trying to get away from her the whole time."

I put a steadying hand on his arm but stared straight ahead. I hoped my message was clear. No reaction. Give them nothing.

"They kissed," Rafe asked.

"That's what I saw," she said.

"Okay," Rafe said. "Did you know when Lauren left the party?"

"Before me," she said. "I'd offered to drive her home. I was concerned about her drinking. I never saw her actually consuming alcohol, but she was acting drunk. Slurring her words. Stumbling. And she was overly friendly and laughing a lot. She just wasn't acting herself. Lauren wasn't a partier. But that night, she was really blowing off some steam. I don't know. I should have stayed with her. We got into an argument when I tried to insist that she let me take her home. She said I wasn't her babysitter, and she was over eighteen. I was just so tired. I didn't feel like getting into it. I went to go talk to another friend of mine, Grant Paulsen. I lost track of Lauren after that."

"Then what happened?" Rafe asked.

"I'd been talking to Grant for a while. Longer than I meant to, actually. I checked my phone, and it was twelve thirty-two. We'd been talking for over an hour and I didn't even realize it. So, I told Grant I had to get home. We said goodbye, and I left."

"Then what happened?" Rafe asked.

"I got in my car and left. That's when I saw Lauren again. She was standing in the door of her car talking to Cole."

"Did you hear what they were saying?" Rafe asked.

"No," she said. "But Lauren looked upset. Like she'd been crying."

"What did you do, if anything?"

"Well, I slowed down my car and rolled down the window. Lauren caught my eye, and she looked just as annoyed as she'd been when we had our argument earlier. She waved me off. I kept on going."

"Approximately what time was that?" Rafe asked.

"Probably a quarter of one," she said. "After I checked my phone, I told Grant I had to leave. Said some goodbyes, walked to my car. I saw Lauren and Cole about a mile down the road from where everyone parks near the Pits. So I'm guessing that all took about ten to fifteen minutes. I was home by one in the morning and it's no more than a fifteen-minute drive to my house from the Pits."

"Thank you," Rafe said. "I have nothing further."

"Ms. Leary?" Judge Niedermayer said.

"Thank you," I said, rising from the table. Admittedly, I felt my nerves as I walked up to the lectern. Rafe's questioning left out large chunks of what Kaylin had told me during our interview. If she changed her story now, I wasn't sure what I could salvage.

"Ms. Dwyer," I said. "You and I had the opportunity to speak at length a few months ago. Do you remember?"

"Of course," she said.

"Do you also remember what else you told me about what you saw the night of August 31st?"

"Objection," Rafe said. "Ms. Leary's favorite objection so far seems to be hearsay. She's eliciting it now."

"Ms. Leary?"

"I am not," I said. "I asked the witness if she remembers our conversation. I have not asked her what she said to me."

"She's right, counsel," Niedermayer said. "Overruled. Proceed."

"Okay," I said. "Ms. Dwyer. You said in your direct testimony that Lauren wasn't like herself, in your opinion. You said she was hanging off the defendant. But he wasn't the only one, was he?"

Kaylin bit her lip. I knew she hated having to say this. Part of me hated having to make her. But the facts were the facts.

"Lauren was kind of manic that night. Maybe it was the alcohol. I don't know. But she made a lot of people angry that night. She was flirting with just about every guy there."

"What do you mean flirting?" I asked.

"At one point, I saw her climb on Grant Paulsen's lap while he was sitting on the log at the bonfire. It made him uncomfortable, and he kind of squirmed away. She moved off and then sat on Tony Barker's lap. Tony's girlfriend Shayla was standing with her back to him and when she turned around, her face just dropped. It was ... it was all for show. She kept looking over at Cole, like she was trying to make sure he saw it all. I think she was trying to make him jealous."

"But Cole didn't react, did he?" I asked.

"Not that I saw," she said. "He just sort of moved away. Then he left. I thought he left. By the time I had my words with Lauren, I didn't think he was there anymore."

"And you stated previously that you had your words, as you described them, with Lauren around eleven thirty, right?"

"That's right," she said.

"So Cole had left the party, in your recollection, by eleven thirty."

"I didn't see him leave. I just didn't see him there anymore," she said.

"Now," I said. "You claim you saw Lauren speaking with Cole on the road about an hour later, correct?"

"That's what I saw, yes," she said.

"But you never saw Cole's face," I said. "Whoever was talking to her had their back turned to you, correct?"

Kaylin screwed up her face. "I mean ... yeah. They were on my right on the side of the road as I drove by. Lauren was facing me."

"In fact," I said. "Isn't it true your headlights hit her in the eyes?"

"That's true," she said. "Lauren held her hands up to shield them."

"Did the person she was speaking to ever turn to face you?" I asked.

"I don't. I don't think so, no," she answered.

"What kind of car does Cole Mathison drive?"

"Some kind of Ford truck," she said.

"What color?"

"Um ... maybe black or brown?" she answered.

"Or dark blue?" I asked.

"Maybe."

"Did you catch the license plate of the truck you claim was Cole's?" I asked.

"Um, no."

"How tall is Cole Mathison?" I asked.

"I don't know. Taller than me. Six feet, maybe?"

I went back to my table and pulled out a thin file I'd saved for Kaylin's testimony. It contained five blown-up photographs.

I held up the first and marked it for identification.

"Ms. Dwyer?" I said. "How far away were you from Lauren and the person you believe was Cole at approximately twelve forty-five on the early morning of September 1st?"

"I'm not sure. Maybe fifteen, twenty feet?"

"If you'll indulge me, Your Honor," I said. I took out a tape measure and walked off fifteen feet from the edge of the witness box to a point in the center of the courtroom. I picked up my file of photographs again.

"Ms. Dwyer," I said, holding up Cole Mathison's mugshot. "Do you recognize the person in this photograph?"

"That's Cole," she said.

I picked up the second photograph. This was Cole's senior yearbook photo. "And do you recognize this person?"

"That's also Cole," she said.

I held up a third photograph. This was one found on Lauren's phone, taken about a year ago.

"That's Cole too," she said.

I held up the fourth photograph. In this one, the subject was standing against a gray wall, smiling. It was a work identification photo taken just six months ago.

"That's also Cole," Kaylin said, exasperated.

"Are you sure?" I asked. I took two steps closer.

"It's Cole," she said. "I know what he looks like."

"May I approach?" I asked.

"You may," Judge Niedermayer said. "But before Mr. Johnson says it, allow me. Get to your point, Ms. Leary. The witness has already established she's qualified to identify Cole Mathison. She's known him for years."

I handed the photograph to Kaylin. She took it. Her eyes widened a bit when she got a closer look.

"Wow," she said. "No. That's not Cole. Who is that? Is that his dad? I can read the ID badge. It says Rudy Mathison."

A rumble went through the jury.

"Your Honor!" Rafe finally jumped up. He'd gotten lazy. Fatigued, maybe. "This entire line of questioning is irrelevant."

"Judge," I said. "This witness's ability to identify the defendant is perhaps the most relevant point about her testimony."

"Overruled Mr. Johnson," Judge Niedermayer said. "But I hope you're done with this, Ms. Leary."

"I am, Your Honor," I said. "I have no further questions for Ms. Dwyer at this time."

Kaylin still clutched Rudy Mathison's photo, her eyes wide as dinner plates as the judge dismissed her from the stand.

Chapter 21

R AFE CALLED A MELIA T RAINOR, M.E. to the stand first
thing the next morning. As Woodbridge County's medical
examiner, I'd faced her in court plenty of times. Juries tended
to love her. She looked like what they thought a coroner
should. Thin. Pale. Immaculate down to her polished,
sensible shoes, rod-straight posture, and slicked-back blonde
hair. In the dead of winter, Amelia's skin was nearly
translucent.

If somebody wrote a paranormal version of Delphi, Dr.
Trainor would definitely get reimagined as a vampire. An
unfair characterization, but Amelia was fully aware of and
relished it. I'd known her to have a biting sense of humor in
private, though she rarely cracked a smile.

Rafe made quick work of her impressive credentials.
Then, he got to the most devastating part of her testimony, the
crime scene and autopsy photos.

"Dr. Trainor," he said. "Can you tell me what we're
looking at in State's Exhibit, photograph number twenty-
two?"

Amelia turned to the overhead projector. "That is a

photograph I took on the morning of September 4th last year. Those are Ms. Rice's remains as they were found on the side of Lumley Road."

"Objection as to foundation," I said. "This witness is not qualified to testify about how the victim's remains were found."

"Mr. Johnson?" the judge asked.

"Your Honor," Rafe said. "Ms. Leary will have ample opportunity to cross examine this witness, but I'm ..."

"Sustained," Judge Niedermayer said.

I actually winced at that one. Rafe Johnson was getting the "new-kid-in-town" treatment full bore this morning.

"Let me clarify," Dr. Trainor said. "That is a photograph I took that represents the condition in which I found the victim's remains that morning."

"Fair enough," Rafe said. "And what condition was that?"

"The victim was found on the south side of the road, lying supine in a ditch, facing east. That is, her feet were pointed toward the east."

The next few minutes would represent the most memorable point in the trial for many of the jurors. I watched their faces go through the natural stages of shock and horror as they looked at Lauren Rice's lifeless body. Her opaque eyes remained fixed, staring sightlessly up at the sky. Color had drained from her frozen face. She appeared white, waxen, her lips disappeared. Leaves tangled in her hair.

"Were you able to determine a time of death?" Rafe asked.

"I was. Within a reasonable degree of medical certainty, the victim likely expired no more than seventy-two hours prior to the discovery of her body."

"I see," Rafe said. "And how were you able to determine that?"

"It was based on a number of factors," Dr. Trainor said.

"Primarily, the state of rigor mortis had passed. But based on
the state of decomposition, discoloration of the body, and
other common factors, that is my estimation."

"Do you have a theory about where Ms. Rice may have
been killed?" Rafe asked.

"Objection," I said. "Once again, improper foundation
and assuming facts not in evidence. There has been no
showing that Ms. Rice was killed at all."

This got a reaction out of a few of the jurors. Shock,
maybe.

"I'll rephrase," Rafe said. "Do you know whether Ms.
Rice died in that ditch?"

"Well, we look at any number of factors. One is lividity.
When a body expires and the heart is no longer pumping
blood through it, gravity sets in. Blood begins to pool at the
lowest point with relation to how the body is positioned. In
other words, if a victim dies in a supine position, you would
expect to find lividity patterns along the back, the back of the
legs, etc. It appears as bruising, to put it in layman's terms."

"I see," Rafe said. "And what, if anything, did you notice
about the lividity patterns on the victim's body?"

"Ms. Rice showed signs of lividity along the right side of
her body, which would indicate that she was positioned on
her side, her right side, for a period of time after she expired.
She was found, however, in this supine position in the ditch.
This would indicate that she was likely moved."

"She was dumped there after she died," Rafe said.

"Objection!"

"Sustained, Mr. Johnson," the judge said. "Save your
arguments for closing."

"Understood," Rafe said. "Dr. Trainor, what other
observations did you make when conducting your autopsy?"

"I noted bruising on her upper arms that suggested she'd

been gripped there. She had a contusion on her right cheek. Those injuries were sustained prior to her death. A few capillaries in her right eye had burst."

"Were there any signs of sexual assault?" Rafe asked.

"There were signs of recent sexual penetration," Dr. Trainor said. Rafe pulled up a page of the autopsy report. It showed a genderless drawing of a human body. Dr. Trainor's notes marked the areas of bruising she described.

"Can you explain that?" Rafe asked.

"Well," Dr. Trainor said. "There was obvious chafing around the victim's labia. I also noted bruising in that same area, a hand-print pattern along her left thigh. As if her leg had been held open."

"Thank you," Rafe said. "Can you tell the jury what you concluded about the victim's manner of death?"

"Based on the location of the body, the bruising patterns, etc., it is my theory that this individual died of asphyxiation. As such, I ruled her death a homicide."

"She was killed," Rafe said, staring straight at me.

"Correct," Amelia answered.

"Doctor, did you perform a pregnancy test on the victim?"

"Yes," she said. "The victim was not pregnant at the time of her death."

"Is it possible she could have been pregnant before?" he asked.

"You mean at some other time in her life?" Dr. Trainor said. "That isn't something I was able to determine during the autopsy."

"But she could have been," he asked.

"Objection, calls for speculation and assumes facts not in evidence."

"Sustained," the judge said.

"Thank you," Rafe said. "I have nothing further."

I passed him on the way to the lectern. "Would you mind?" I asked him under my breath.

He looked puzzled for a moment. "Oh, of course," he said. Rafe had strategically left Lauren Rice's giant death photo up on the projector. I knew it wasn't an oversight. He clicked his remote, and the screen went dark.

"Dr. Trainor," I said. "Mr. Johnson was very precise in the way he worded one of his questions to you. And frankly, your answer was pretty precise. I'd like to explore that, if I may. You were asked, what you were able to conclude about the manner of Ms. Rice's death? In your answer, you said you theorized her manner of death was asphyxiation. But in fact, I have your official autopsy report in front of me. Can you read what you wrote in your conclusion for the cause of death?"

Amelia didn't need to read from her notes. I knew she had her report memorized word for word.

"The official cause of death was indeterminate," she said.

"Indeterminate," I repeated. "So asphyxiation is merely a theory, correct?"

"That's correct."

"Her actual cause of death was inconclusive," I said.

"That's correct."

"But you've ruled her death a homicide, anyway. So that, in turn, is also just a theory."

"Well, yes."

"Was she strangled?" I asked.

"I couldn't determine that, no."

"Because isn't it true in a strangling, you'd tend to see bruising around the neck? Injury to the larynx?"

"Very often, yes," Dr. Trainor answered.

"You saw no such injuries to the neck or throat on Lauren Rice, did you?"

"No," she said. "I did not."

"You said you saw what you believed to be bruising around Ms. Rice's arms and her thigh. But those were inflicted while she was alive, yes?"

"Yes," Dr. Trainor answered.

"So none of those wounds were fatal, correct? In fact, they were superficial, at best."

"That's correct," she said.

"You indicated there was evidence of sexual penetration," I said. "But you found no evidence of assault, did you?"

"Beyond the bruising we just discussed, no," she said.

"Chafing to the labia," I said. "Is that dispositive of rape, Dr. Trainor?"

"No," she said. "Not at all. It's evidence of sexual penetration. I determined within a reasonable degree of medical certainty that Ms. Rice had sexual intercourse within twenty-four hours of her death. Likely within a few hours."

"Okay," I said. "Fluid and tissue samples were taken, were they not?"

"Of course."

"You didn't find any skin under her fingernails, did you?"

"I did not."

"In fact, you found no injury that would have been consistent with so-called defensive wounds, did you?"

"I did not," she said.

"You found no foreign DNA on Ms. Rice at all, did you?"

"I did not, no," she said.

"No one else's blood," I said.

"No."

"No one else's semen on her body."

"No."

"I see," I said. "And none on the clothing you removed from her body?"

"No," she said. "But I should point out that Ms. Rice was

found partially nude. She was wearing the tee shirt you saw in the photo. She had on a pink bra. That's been catalogued. But her pants, underwear, shoes and socks ... those had all been removed. She wasn't wearing any of that when she was found in that ditch."

"Was removed?" I said. "But you don't know that. Ms. Rice could have removed them herself."

"I don't obviously know how or when those articles of clothing were removed, no."

"Thank you," I said. "I have nothing further."

"Mr. Johnson?" the judge said.

Rafe charged back to the lectern.

"Dr. Trainor," he started. "You ruled Ms. Rice's death was a homicide, even though her exact cause of death was indeterminate. How is that possible?"

"Very often cause of death conclusions must be drawn from inference. Or the ruling out of any other major causes. This victim did not suffer a heart attack. She was not shot or stabbed. She was probably not strangled for the reasons Ms. Leary just underscored. I found no evidence of any underlying pathology that would have resulted in her death. She didn't have a stroke. She didn't drown. She had broken capillaries in her right eye that would be consistent with asphyxiation or smothering. Her body was most definitely moved after death, from at least one location to where she was discovered in that ditch. Based on all of those factors, it is my learned opinion that Ms. Rice was the victim of a homicide."

"Thank you," Rafe said. "That's all I have."

"Recross, Ms. Leary?" the judge asked.

"Yes," I said, rising, though I didn't step back up to the lectern.

"Doctor," I said. "These broken capillaries you've described. Were they substantial?"

"I'm sorry?"

"Well, were they consistent with the kind of injury you've seen with other asphyxiation deaths?"

"I'm not sure if I follow," she said.

"Okay," I said. "Isn't it true that a person can suffer broken capillaries in their eye for any number of reasons? For example, if you cough. If you sneeze."

"You can," she said.

"Thank you," I said.

"And you mentioned the term smothering," I said. "You didn't find any evidence of synthetic fibers in Ms. Rice's nose or on her face, did you? Like from a pillow. Or a plastic bag?"

"I did not, no," she said.

"Thank you," I said. "I have no further questions."

Dr. Trainor stayed expressionless as she left the witness box. I hoped I'd thrown real doubt into her testimony. But I knew we had far bigger hurdles to overcome.

As she looked at the clock, Judge Niedemayer called the lunch recess.

"Back to my office," I whispered to Cole. "We have a lot to talk about."

Chapter 22

O<small>UTSIDE</small>, Cole's supporters had gathered in full force. Emma told me a #freecole hashtag had started to trend locally. I couldn't concern myself with that. The worst was yet to come.

Jeanie, Miranda, and Tori waited for us in the conference room. We had two and a half hours before Judge Niedermayer called us back in session.

Once we shut the doors and Cole took a seat, his demeanor changed. He gave me a bright smile.

"It went good, didn't it?" he asked. "They can't prove how Lauren died. How can they say I killed her ... or that anyone killed her if they can't say for sure how she died?"

Jeanie gave me a look as she took a seat across from him. I needed to pace a little. Miranda would serve as sentry, fielding any incoming calls or keeping my brother at bay if he showed up. Tori took our lunch orders and headed down the street to the bagel shop to fill them.

"We scored a point or two," I said. "But in the end, I don't think a single member of that jury is going to believe Lauren's death was anything but a homicide. Dr. Trainor makes a good witness. She proved Lauren's body was moved. That alone is probably enough to put that question to bed."

"Still," Cole said. "I just don't understand any of it. I'm telling you, they're setting me up. I never should have agreed to that DNA test."

"It wouldn't have mattered, son," Jeanie answered. "They could have gotten a subpoena for it. The fact that you voluntarily submitted to it helps you."

"You have to let me tell them," Cole said. "I can't stand just sitting there letting these people say all that stuff about me. It's like Kaylin said. Lauren was off that night. Everyone saw it. Maybe she was trying to make me jealous. I swear, I didn't get that. I was just trying to get away from her."

"Have you decided what you're going to do about that?" Jeanie asked, nodding toward Cole.

"I don't know," I said. "Cole, there are substantial risks in putting you on the stand. Rafe is getting his footing. He's a good prosecutor. He'll try to kill you on the cross. He's got the skills to do it and there's only so much I can do to protect you."

"I can handle it," Cole said. "I just want to tell what happened. They'll believe me. Somebody has to believe me. I didn't kill Lauren. I didn't rape her. We weren't ... we weren't together like that that night."

"Cole," I said. "The fact is, your DNA was found in her underwear. I'll fight like hell, but that evidence is likely going to come in."

"Someone planted it!" he shouted.

"We have to give the jury a plausible reason as to who, Cole," I said. We'd been round and round on this for weeks. Every lead I chased led me nowhere. I had the same instincts as Cole. It was too damned convenient how and when that evidence was found.

"My dad could have done that too," he said. "It's sick ... but ... we weren't talking. He still came and went as he pleased in that house. And sometimes ... ugh. I can't even say it. It's embarrassing. But ... we lived in the same house and I'm human, okay. He could have ... I mean from the laundry or the garbage or ..."

Jeanie pulled a face. I tried my level best not to. But yes, the thought had crossed my mind that Rudy Mathison could have had access to a sample of Cole's DNA. The level of planning that would have taken made me heartsick.

"We're not there yet," I said. "Rafe won't be calling any more witnesses today. We've got some routine evidentiary motions to get through outside the jury's presence. But tomorrow morning he's calling Detective Lewis. Between her direct testimony and my cross, I expect her to be on the stand all day and heading into Friday. Then, we'll have the weekend to regroup."

"Who else will he call?" Jeanie asked.

"After Lewis?" I said. "He's got his DNA guy. I think I can get in what I need without having to call a counter expert, but I've got one ready to go."

"You run a risk with that," Jeanie said. "Juries get bogged down in science. Less is more."

"Right," I said. "But I expect Rafe will probably rest by Monday or Tuesday at the latest."

"Then you'll put me on the stand?" Cole asked.

"Let's just see where we are after this weekend."

"That detective is lying," Cole said. "She has to be. Why are they doing this? She has to see how obvious all this stuff with my dad is. Why doesn't she want to go after him? Why me?"

He buried his face in his hands. At that moment, he looked like a little kid. I felt for him. I did. Never mind whatever was going on with his father. His mother's behavior bothered me as much as anything else about this case.

"Cole," I said. "I need to talk to your mother again."

"No," he said. "You need to leave her alone. She's been through enough."

"She's protecting your dad. Why?" I asked.

"Because she always does," Cole said, his voice dropping. "She's just ... she's just trying to survive."

"You're her son. Her only child. She should worry about protecting you," Jeanie said.

"She has!" Cole snapped. "At least, she's tried. But I'm an adult now. It was me who should have done more to protect her sooner. I tried. I thought if I could draw his anger away from her, he'd leave her alone. I thought I could take it. Physically I could. It's just, it never helped. Nothing ever made it better until the day I thought I got him to leave."

"Then she let him back in behind your back," I said.

"I don't want to talk about it," he said.

"You'll have to," I said. "If we're even going to entertain the idea of putting you on the stand, I need to make that crystal clear. If you didn't do this, someone else did. Right now, your father is the biggest question mark. He skipped town right when Lauren disappeared with their savings. You're right. If someone framed you for this, he had the means. Awful as that would have been. But the jury needs to understand why."

"My dad was ... complicated. He hated me. In the sense he saw me as competition once I started getting older. At the same time ... well ... he's not exactly a fan of women. She's never said it, but I know my parents had to get married. He got her pregnant. I used to hear him say that all the time. If it wasn't for me ..."

"That's awful," Jeanie said. "And your parents' choices aren't on you."

Lord. Jeanie had said those exact same words to me at least a hundred times in my life. In a lot of ways, she'd been more of a parent to me than my own. She'd come into our lives when the state tried to separate us after my mom died. She'd been appointed guardian ad litem for my younger siblings, Vangie and Matty. They would have gone into foster care without her. I also knew my family was nothing close to the worst she'd seen in her career.

"Yeah," Cole said. "I know. Like in my head, I know it. It's just ... You've seen her texts. You know what was going on with Lauren and me. I swear to you. I didn't get her pregnant. We weren't having sex. Not since like a year before she died."

"I know," I said. "I mean about the pregnancy, anyway. The autopsy would have shown that."

"I just keep thinking. It's like you said. I think Kaylin saw my dad talking to Lauren, not me. What if she told him she was pregnant? By me?"

"You think it would have triggered him?" I asked.

"Maybe," Cole said. "I can tell you that man resented me every single day of my life. I don't think he would have done something like that to Lauren out of some need to save me from the same fate. But I think, if he was drunk or angry enough, and here's this girl saying she's going to trap some guy. Whether it was me or someone else. Yeah. I think maybe that might have triggered him."

On the surface, Jeanie stayed calm. But her eyes flashed as she met my gaze. I knew her. Her blood pressure kicked up. So did mine.

It was as good a theory as to motive as any. But it underscored my need to find Rudy Mathison, and fast.

As Cole dropped his head and rested it in on his arms, Tori came in with our lunch. I welcomed the break. We would have the small respite, I said, but Megan Lewis's testimony could make or break Cole's future in the coming days.

Chapter 23

COURT ENDED JUST AFTER FIVE. We'd tied up the last of the evidentiary motions and would start bright and early at eight the next morning. When I pulled up my drive, my heart sank. Joe's truck was parked beside the barn.

I didn't want a fight. I didn't want anything but a cold glass of wine. As my tires crunched through the snow and I pulled into my garage, Joe came out the side door holding the latter. I smiled.

"A peace offering?" I asked.

"I didn't know we were at war? Are we? It's so hard to keep track."

This got a laugh out of me as I tossed my leather bag on the hall table and took the wineglass from him. Kicking off my boots, we made our way into the living room.

The lake wasn't yet fully frozen. That didn't stop a few idiots on the north end from trying to set up their ice fishing gear near the shore. We went through this every year. Joe and Matty would stand at the shoreline spouting off about natural selection.

"Don't ask me how it went," I said as I plopped onto my

couch. Joe took one of the new recliners I bought. There were two. I hated the things, but promised my brothers they could each have one. They spent about as much time here as I did when I was in trial.

Marbury, one of my two mutts, jumped on the couch beside me and curled himself into a perfect ball. Within about thirty seconds, he'd worked up a doggie snore. His mother, Madison, took a spot on the floor at Joe's feet.

"I let 'em out when I got here," he said. "Marby took a big dump right outside the back door. Careful if you go out that way. I'll shovel them a path later."

"Thanks," I said. For all his bluster, Joe was a big softie when it came to the animals. They knew it.

"How's Emma holding up?" I asked.

Joe sipped a beer he had nestled in a Yeti cup. "She asked me the same thing about Cole."

"About as well as he can," I said. "We've got a rough couple of days ahead. And that's really all I want to say about it."

"I have to ask," he said. "Are you going to call her as a witness?"

I drank my wine. "I don't know yet," I said. "She wasn't with him the night Lauren went missing. She didn't go to that party. Thank God."

"Do you think Johnson will call her?" Joe asked.

"Not if he's smart," I said. "She's been consistent in her defense of him. Rafe would have no reason to give her an opportunity to do that. For my part, she can't offer admissible testimony as to Cole's character. There really isn't anything legally relevant she could say on that score."

"Good," Joe said. "I don't want her to have to go through that."

I let the silence settle between us. "Joe," I said. "If I can find a way to get my theory about Rudy in ...I may have no choice. I may have to put her up there."

He grimaced. "I thought she knew better," he said. "Why the hell didn't she tell me how uncomfortable he made her?"

"Because she was worried you'd overreact," I said. "Women ... girls stay silent a lot of the times not just because they don't think they'll be believed, Joe. Sometimes it's because they know the alpha men in their lives might decide to do something about it that could land them in trouble."

"It's my fault?" he said, raising his voice.

"Of course not. I'm just saying, it's not always as simple as you want it to be."

"Now you sound like Vangie," he said. He went hollow on me. I could almost feel his guilt washing over him. It was a guilt we shared. Years ago, our baby sister had been sexually abused by a teacher. She hadn't told us until recently. My niece had been the product of it. For almost ten years, Vangie kept her secret and ran away from Delphi. I knew Joe was having a hard time with that still. So was I.

"I just want to protect them," he whispered, clenching his fists. "Cass, you have to tell me if you think for a second that ..."

We'd had this conversation before. Joe wanted me to promise that I'd tell him if he had anything to worry about with Cole. And I'd tell him it was far too late for that.

"They broke up," he said abruptly. My pulse quickened.

I set my glass on the side table. "Excuse me?"

"They broke up. Emma and Cole. I thought you should know."

I didn't know how to react. I'll admit. The lawyer side of my brain kicked in before the aunt side.

"I see," I said, letting the aunt side win. "Is she okay?"

Joe shrugged. "We don't talk a lot anymore. She doesn't exactly respond well to my opinions."

I smiled. I knew the feeling. Joe could say the same about me.

"I think she still loves him," he said.

"Do you want to tell me what happened?" I asked. "If you know?"

"She said it was a mutual thing. But I think it wasn't. I think Cole pulled the plug. Dammit, if I don't like the kid more for that. I think he told her while this trial is going on, he wanted to give her space. With the way Emma's been crying, I don't think it's what she wants. But ... she's trying. You know?"

"Lord," I sighed. "What a mess."

"Yep," Joe said. He got up and poured me more wine. When he sat back down, he got silent. It was then I noticed the duffle bag in the corner of the kitchen.

"Joe?" I said. "You're staying?"

"If you don't mind," he said.

I tried to suppress a smile as I lifted my glass to take another drink.

"Don't say it," he said.

"Let me guess," I said. "You were a little too forceful about your opinions with Emma."

Joe rolled his eyes.

"You got kicked out of your own house?" I raised a brow.

"Not kicked out," he said. "It was voluntary. Katy and I ... we just figured it was a good idea if Emma and I went to our neutral corners for a day. Plus, someone's got to make sure you're eating. I know how you get during trials."

I shook my head. I had a feeling Jeanie might be behind some of this. I didn't have the energy to argue.

Joe got up and headed into the kitchen. He pulled a

brown paper bag out of the fridge and the smell of delicious Italian food hit me, making my stomach growl loud enough for Joe to hear.

"I thought so," he said. "Grab a plate. I'll heat this up."

Gently pushing Marbury off of me, I headed to the kitchen to join my brother. In spite of his opinions, he was good to have around.

Chapter 24

"WE'LL SEE how far we get today," Judge Niedermayer said. "If the courthouse has to close due to the weather, it'll be out of my hands."

All the weather models pointed to a wallop of snow headed our way, starting at lunchtime and continuing until midnight. They predicted ten to twelve inches and blizzard conditions.

"Your Honor," I said. "I would like the opportunity to begin my cross of Detective Lewis immediately after her direct."

"I'd like that too," the judge said. "But as I just said, we'll see how far we get. Mr. Johnson, is your witness ready?"

"Yes, Your Honor," Rafe said.

Judge Niedermayer gestured to her bailiff. He led the jury in. Once they were seated, Rafe called Megan Lewis up to the stand.

Her size was always the first thing anyone noticed. Megan was tiny. Five feet one in heels. She weighed one ten at most. But people were wise not to underestimate her on that basis alone. She was an athlete. The only female high school wrestler Delphi had so far produced. These days, she competed in Tough Mudder contests and generally blew everyone in her age group away.

"Detective," Rafe started. "Will you state your name for the jury and describe your relationship to this case?"

"Of course," Megan said. "Megan Lewis. I'm a detective with the Delphi Police Department, serving in the violent crimes division. I was assigned lead investigator for Lauren Rice's case."

"Thank you," Rafe said. "So can you tell us how you first became involved in this case?"

"In the afternoon of September 1st of last year, Sergeant Lapan dispatched me to investigate a missing persons case. Lauren's father, Gil Rice, was concerned that his daughter was unreachable."

"So what investigative steps did you take at first?" Rafe asked.

"I went to the Rice residence. I took Mr. Rice's statement. He reported that he'd never heard his daughter return home from a party the night before. I sent a crew out to the Pits, the location of the party. On the way, they found Lauren Rice's car parked along the road. It is still registered to Mr. Rice, so he gave me permission to search it."

"What did you find incident to that search?"

"The keys were still in the vehicle, lying on the passenger seat. Ms. Rice's purse, containing her wallet and ID, was on the floor of the passenger seat. Her cell phone was underneath that."

"What did you do next?" Rafe asked.

"At that point," she said, "I shared Mr. Rice's concerns that time was of the essence."

"Why was that?"

"Well," Megan said. "The way the car was found, abandoned, was suspicious. Mr. Rice reported that it wasn't his daughter's habit to leave her cell phone and purse behind like that. In my investigative experience involving teenagers, I've also found that to be true. Mr. Rice also reported that he'd already called several of his daughter's closest friends. Those that he understood to have been with her the night before. They all reported that she'd left a party at what they call the Pits a little before midnight and no one had reported seeing her since."

"What did you do then?" Rafe asked.

"I began contacting this group of friends myself. I spoke to Lacy Carter, Kaylin Dwyer, Elizabeth Thompson. A picture began to emerge that this core group of girls had met at Lacy's house a little after six p.m. They then traveled in separate vehicles to a diner where they stayed for over two hours. At that point, they left, again in separate vehicles, and attended a party at the Pits in Shamrock Park. After speaking with Ms. Rice's friends and coworkers at the Bait Bucket, it became clear, in my professional opinion, that I was likely dealing with a disappearance by virtue of foul play or an accident, rather than a runaway."

"Why was that?" Rafe asked.

"The victim's father and friends were unanimous in their opinions that Lauren wasn't one to just take off without leaving word. No one had heard from her since she was last seen after the party by Kaylin Dwyer."

"So then what did you do?"

Megan cleared her throat and took a sip of water. "At that point, I contacted her cell phone carrier and called our cell phone forensics team to do a phone dump ... er ... to provide me with rapid data about where her phone may have traveled that evening. I was trying to track Ms. Rice's movements in the immediate timeframe before she went missing."

"What, if anything, were you able to determine from that data?" Rafe asked. At that point, he introduced the cell phone forensic reports. He pulled up a grid map showing the local towers so Megan could refer to them.

"Well," Megan said, taking her pointer. "The tower hits for Lauren's phone were entirely consistent with the witness reports about her movements that evening. She leaves home just before six p.m. as her father indicated. The phone then pings the Northwood tower here. This one serves the area closest to Lacy's house. From there, at approximately seven p.m., the phone travels east where it finally pings the Woodmont tower, which is the one closest to the diner. Finally, a little after nine p.m., she travels north. The closest tower to the so-called Pits area is the Lakeland tower. That's where the phone stays until 12:13 a.m. the morning of September 1st."

"What happens at 12:13 a.m.?" Rafe asked.

"Objection," I said. "Improper foundation."

"I'll rephrase," Rafe answered.

"Detective Lewis, with regard to the phone forensics, what is significant about 12:13 a.m.?"

"At that point, Ms. Rice's phone is no longer trackable. Upon examination of the phone, as it was found in her vehicle the next day, her phone was set in airplane mode at that time."

"Just so I'm clear," Rafe said. "What is the impact of airplane mode on Ms. Rice's phone?"

"It's like turning it off as far as the data usage. It's no longer sending signals to the data towers. It goes dark."

"I see," Rafe said. "We'll come back to that. So, can you tell me what your next investigative step was?"

"There were several," she said. "I had the crime scene unit out combing for any physical evidence from Ms. Rice's car. Any blood patterns, foreign DNA, that sort of thing. At the same time, I continued to gather witness statements. I was looking to speak with every person who attended that party at the Pits. I interviewed about a dozen. Some were reluctant to speak with me as most were underage and it was well reported there had been alcohol consumption at the party."

"I see," Rafe said. "At what point did your investigation begin to focus on the defendant?"

"He was a person of interest from the beginning," she said. "One of the first questions I asked of Lauren's friends was whether she was dating anyone. Whether she had a boyfriend. Who they'd seen her spending her time with at the party. Their statements were consistent. Lauren had had a recent break-up with Cole Mathison. He was seen with her at the party. Additionally, there were a variety of texts from Lauren to the defendant that raised alarm bells for me."

"At this point, I'd like to move for admission of exhibits 41 through 57."

"Any objections, Ms. Leary?" the judge asked.

"No," I said. Rafe was entering the transcripts of Lauren's texts. Though damning, I had no legal basis for objecting to their admission and in fact had already stipulated to this pretrial.

"Detective," Rafe said. "I'd like to draw your attention to a series of text exchanges between the victim and the defendant beginning on August 17th. Would you please read those into the record?"

"She texted the following. Lauren: I came by your house. I know you were home. Either pick up your phone or meet me somewhere. I miss you."

"And then on August 27th, four days before the murder,

she texts: You're not going to get away with ghosting me, asshole. This little problem of yours isn't going to go away. I've been more than patient. I'm not trying to ruin your life. I'm trying to get you to do the right thing."

I watched the jury. They sat at attention. No slouching, no drooping, tired eyes. They were riveted. Beside me, Cole was starting to sweat. I put a hand on his arm under the table.

Steady. Look straight ahead.

In response, he scribbled a quick note on the pad I'd put in front of him.

"You have to let me tell them what was really going on!"

"What did you do next, Detective?" Rafe asked.

"I had a brief interview with the defendant. His story was at that time consistent with what I'd been told by the other witnesses. He said he'd left the party just before Lauren and hadn't seen her since. At that point, we were also focusing on search efforts. A group of volunteers had been combing the woods near the party and other areas around town. On Thursday, September 4th, two of those citizen volunteers, Jacob and Mitchell Bradley, discovered a body in a ditch alongside Lumley Road matching Lauren Rice's general description. The boys knew her personally and identified her. I met the crime scene unit and Dr. Trainor at the site and a positive ID was made."

"What happened next?"

"Over the next few days, I continued to gather witness statements. I awaited autopsy results. Those took a few days. When they came in, it became clear that Ms. Rice was in fact the victim of a homicide. Additionally, there was evidence in Dr. Trainor's report that Ms. Rice had engaged in sexual activity within a few hours of her death. I re-interviewed a few of Ms. Rice's closest friends. Kaylin Dwyer provided the additional details that she'd seen Lauren with Cole Mathison arguing by the side of the road as she was leaving the party. The timing of this was inconsistent with what the defendant had reported to me in our brief interview. I asked Kaylin if she knew Cole Mathison's cell phone number. She did. So, I subpoenaed cell phone data from his carrier and awaited those results."

"Then what happened?" Rafe asked.

"I felt with the information I had, a second, more detailed interview with Mr. Mathison was warranted. I went to his home and was told by his mother that he'd gone to the lake to attend a gathering at Ms. Leary's home. So, I went there to see if I could talk to him. He came willingly and he along with Ms. Leary met me back down at the police station."

"How did that go?"

"The defendant made no mention of this argument he had on the side of the road. I asked him to submit a DNA sample, which he did. He indicated that he and Ms. Rice were no longer dating, but that it was amicable. He said they were just friends. I found his story wildly inconsistent with what the remainder of the party witnesses and Lauren's friends had to say."

"What did you do then?"

"At that time, I told the defendant he was free to go. Within a few days, I received the cell phone reports from his phone. One detail in particular jumped out at me."

"What was that?" Rafe asked.

"Well, Lauren Rice's phone went into airplane mode at 12:13 a.m. just after pinging the Lakeland tower, as I said. The defendant's phone also went offline, approximately thirty seconds later. And stayed offline until just before four a.m."

"I see," Rafe said. "So what did you do next?"

"At that point, based on Mr. Mathison's deception in my interview, the increasingly contentious nature of their relationship as evidenced by their text exchanges, witness statements regarding his behavior the night Lauren disappeared, plus Ms. Dwyer's statements about seeing them together by the side of the road, I felt I had enough probable cause and I secured a warrant for the defendant's arrest."

"Objection! It is improper for this witness to characterize any statements allegedly made by the defendant as deceptive."

"Your Honor," Rafe responded. "Detective Lewis, in her capacity as lead investigator of this case, can absolutely make a decision based on her perception of the defendant's truthfulness."

"Ms. Leary?" the judge said.

"Counsel has argued my point. This detective's perception is one thing. But claiming there was deception as a matter of fact is another."

"I agree in part," the judge said. "The jury should disregard the detective's conclusion that the defendant's statement was deceptive."

"Thank you," Rafe said. "Detective Lewis. Was that the conclusion of your investigation into this case?"

"It wasn't," she said. "As indicated by Dr. Trainor and in my report, the victim's body was found partially nude. And we had reason to believe she'd been moved from the location of her killing to that ditch. Her body was dumped. As such, we continued to search for clues as to the site of her killing and recovery of any further physical evidence in this matter."

"Did that search bear fruit?"

"It did," she said. "Roughly six weeks ago, I received an anonymous tip from a hiker near the woods on Lumley Road.

This person had spotted an article of clothing that they were concerned might be of relevance."

"What did you do then?" Rafe asked.

"I called the crime scene unit at the entrance to what's called the Haney Trail. It's just off the corner of Lumley and Culpepper. It's a popular spot for hikers and nature watchers. About thirty yards off the trail, we did in fact see what appeared to be a pair of undergarments tangled in some branches in the underbrush. Then the crime scene unit stepped in and retrieved them."

"I'd like to mark state's exhibit fifty-eight for identification," Rafe said.

He held up a plastic evidence bag containing a pair of pale-pink lace underwear.

"Detective, can you identify this item?"

"I can," she said. Lewis identified the evidence tag on the bag. "This is the underwear C.S.U. found in early December of last year. I sent it off for DNA and fiber testing."

"Can you describe the results of that testing?" Rafe asked.

"Yes," she said. "DNA from two individuals was found on the ... uh ... crotch area of the underwear. One was a positive match for the victim, Lauren Rice. The lab found traces of skin and cervical mucosa. The second profile came from a semen stain in the same area. It was a positive match for the defendant's DNA."

"Detective," Rafe said. "Can you orient this item of clothing to the location in which Lauren Rice's body was found?"

"Yes," she said. "Her underwear was found approximately twenty feet uphill in the brush from where Lauren's body was found."

"Thank you," Rafe said. "I have nothing further for this witness."

The judge and I looked out the high windows on the east wall of the room. The sky was white, but the snow had yet to fall.

"Ms. Leary," she said. "We're in luck. The storm's not here yet."

"Thank you, Your Honor," I said as I stepped up to the lectern. It was my plan to become the storm.

Chapter 25

"Good afternoon, Detective," I said. I didn't make eye contact with Megan Lewis. Instead, I kept my gaze centered on the notes in front of me. Or rather, what she and the jury thought were my notes. Instead, I was staring at a blank page.

"Can you tell me, how long have you been a detective?"

"I had my third anniversary with the bureau just last week," she said.

"Congratulations," I said. "Before that, what was your role with the Delphi P.D.?"

"I worked my way up," she said. "I was a civilian clerk during college. I worked in the public relations department. I stayed in that position for two years after college. I entered the police academy eight years ago. From there, I worked in field ops, what some people call a beat cop, for five years before I was brought in to the detective bureau."

"In the three years ... strike that. So in the roughly two and a half years from the time you joined the bureau to when you caught the Lauren Rice case, how many homicide cases have you served as lead detective on?"

"I ... Lauren Rice was actually the first case that I served as the official lead on," she said.

"So," I said. "Wouldn't it be fair to say that until Lauren Rice's tragedy, you always served in a subordinate role on any of the homicide cases you had involvement with?"

"I suppose that's technically true," she said. "But very often, the lead detective status is merely a label for administrative purposes. I was actively involved and helped secure convictions in almost three dozen homicide cases in Delphi since I made detective."

"I see," I said. "But isn't it true the lead detective is actually responsible for the path of an investigation?"

"I'm sorry?"

"Well, as lead detective, isn't it true you're the one who decides which witnesses to interview?"

"That's true, yes," she said. "Though it is often a collaborative process among several detectives."

"But you didn't really collaborate on this case, did you? You didn't work with a partner on the Rice case, did you?"

"No," she said. "I didn't. But that doesn't mean I didn't work with other detectives. There are the computer forensics team, the crime scene unit, etc."

"Right," I said. "How many witness interviews did the cell forensics team conduct at your behest?"

"None," she said. "Their role was to run forensics on Lauren's phone and computer, as well as the phone or computer of other potential witnesses or suspects."

"Got it," I said. "On the topic of suspects, how many other persons of interest did you pursue in this case?"

"I followed a number of leads," she answered.

"Do you know who Ben Sharpton is?" I asked.

"Yes," she said. "Several of Lauren's friends indicated that she briefly dated him."

"I see," I said. "But you never actually brought Ben Sharpton in for questioning, did you?"

"Brought him in? No. We spoke over the phone and I think on email."

"Interesting, I said. "You knew Ben Sharpton was Lauren Rice's most recent romantic interest, and yet you never felt the need to formally interview him."

"There was no need," she said. "Mr. Sharpton was attending college at Ferris State. He wasn't in town the weekend Lauren Rice disappeared."

"I see," I said. "I want to go back to your experience as a detective before catching Lauren Rice's case. Isn't it true that you were originally partnered with a Detective Tim Bowman?"

"Yes," she said. "Detective Bowman was my original partner."

"And isn't it also true that within the Delphi detective bureau, partners are generally reserved for rookie detectives? You train with a partner for a period of time, and then you work solo, is that right?"

"Yes," she said. "That's true."

"Detective, how long did you train with Detective Bowman?"

"I believe it was close to a year."

"I see," I said. "And even that's unusual, isn't it? Generally, a detective's training period with the bureau is more like two years, isn't that right?"

"Well, there's no set rule."

"But that's standard," I said. "Two years."

"I suppose so," she said.

"And isn't it also true that the reason you didn't train with Detective Bowman for the full two years was because he took a leave of absence, didn't he?"

"Yes," she said. Megan began to squirm in her seat. She knew where this was headed.

"He was subsequently suspended and then terminated, isn't that right?" I asked.

"Objection," Rafe said. "This line of questioning is irrelevant."

"Ms. Leary?"

"Your Honor," I said. "The witness has admitted Lauren Rice's case was the first she handled on her own. It is entirely proper for me to explore the nature of the training she received."

"Overruled, Mr. Johnson," Judge Niedermayer said. "But make your point, Ms. Leary."

"Shall I repeat ..."

"No," Megan said. "Yes. Detective Bowman was ultimately terminated from his position."

"For misconduct," I said. "In fact, Detective Bowman was terminated after a lengthy investigation of his handling of another murder case. He was found negligent in the handling of evidence, wasn't he? In fact, Detective Bowman was accused of suppressing witness testimony that would have exonerated another defendant in a murder case, wasn't he?"

"Yes," she said. "I believe that's correct, though I was never privy to the exact nature and evidence in his internal investigation and disciplinary hearings."

"All right," I said. "So I'm clear. I'd like to focus on the evidence you used to establish probable cause to arrest Cole Mathison in this case."

"All right," she said.

I picked up my copy of the arrest warrant. "You based your warrant on the cell phone data. As you said on direct, you believed both Ms. Rice's and Mr. Mathison's phones were set in airplane mode at roughly the same time on the early morning of September 1st."

"Not roughly," she said. "Within thirty seconds of each other."

"But you don't know how those phones were put in that status, right? In other words, Lauren could have done it herself?"

"She could have," Megan said. "I was more concerned with the coincidental event of it, rather than the mechanics of it."

"Sure," I said. "And you also based your arrest warrant on the nature of a handful of texts between Mr. Mathison and Ms. Rice."

"That's right. They showed a pattern of escalating conflict between them."

"In your opinion," I said.

"In my opinion," she said.

"This little problem of yours isn't going to go away. She texted that. Right? But you don't know what that statement means. You just inferred."

"It sounded like blackmail," she said.

"Sounded like," I said. "And you had Dr. Trainor's autopsy report by the time you wrote your arrest warrant. You knew Lauren Rice wasn't pregnant at the time of her death."

"At the time of her death," she said. "But that doesn't mean she couldn't have been earlier."

"Could have been. So you spoke to her doctor? Because I don't see that in your report, Detective. And I don't see any mention of a prior pregnancy from any of the other witnesses ... friends of Lauren's that you spoke to."

"Objection," Rafe said. "Is counsel questioning or arguing?"

"Sustained, Ms. Leary. You know how this goes."

ROBIN JAMES

"Of course," I said. "And you based your warrant on the fact that Kaylin Dwyer believes she saw Ms. Rice speaking to Cole Mathison just before one a.m. on the night she disappeared."

"He was the last one seen with her before she went missing, yes," Megan said.

"You never asked her if she could see Cole Mathison's face though, did you?"

"She knows the defendant. She knows what he looks like," Megan said.

"You never asked her whether the person Lauren was speaking to was facing toward or away from her, did you?" I asked.

"I don't recall."

"Kaylin Dwyer couldn't hear what was being said though, correct?" I asked.

"Correct."

"Did you determine what kind of vehicle Cole Mathison drives?"

"Of course," she said. "As I indicated on direct, we searched it."

"Searched it and found no traces of Lauren Rice ever having been in it, correct?"

"We found no physical evidence, no," she said.

"What kind of truck does Cole drive?" I asked.

"It's a 2003 Ford F-150. It's a pickup truck."

"What color?" I asked.

"It's black," she said.

"And you performed a search warrant at Cole's home, correct?"

"I said that, yes."

"What kind of vehicle was found in the garage at Cole's home?"

196

"Another Ford F-150. A newer model, though. I think it was a 2006."

"What color?" I asked.

"I'll have to check my report," she said.

"Please do," I said.

Megan looked through the paperwork in front of her. "There were two other vehicles found at the Mathison home when we searched it on September 15th incident to his arrest. A white Mercury Milan registered to Rudy Mathison. I learned his mother, Roxanne Mathison principally drove that one. And there was a dark-blue Ford F-150 parked in the garage registered to Rudy Mathison."

"Another dark-colored Ford F-150?" I asked.

"Yes," she said.

"Okay, let's get back to your witness interview with Kaylin Dwyer. Neither she nor any of the other witnesses you interviewed claimed Mr. Mathison was ever violent with Ms. Rice, isn't that right?"

"They didn't report that, no," Megan said.

"In fact, nowhere in your report do you have a shred of evidence that any of Ms. Rice's friends was concerned for her safety with Cole," I said.

"Well, no, I mean, other than after she turned up dead," Megan snapped.

I bit the inside of my cheek. That was sloppy of me. I'd left her that opening.

"Finally, your warrant indicates your belief that Mr. Mathison was deceptive in his answers about where he was the night Lauren went missing, right?"

"That's correct," she said.

"You indicated that Mr. Mathison said he went home after midnight and went to bed," I said.

"That's what he said, yes," Megan said. "I didn't find that

credible."

"Not credible," I said. "You determined who else was in the home that night?"

"Mr. Mathison lived with both of his parents," she said.

"Both of them," I said. "You interviewed Mrs. Mathison?"

"I did. She could not confirm her son's alibi. He came in after she'd already gone to sleep."

"What about Rudy Mathison?" I asked. "Cole's father. What did he have to say?"

"I didn't interview Cole's father," she said.

"Didn't interview him. But you knew he lived in the home with Cole. You included a statement from Mrs. Mathison in your report where she stated her husband could have been up during the timeframe Cole would have come home."

"She said that, yes," Megan said.

"And you knew Cole Mathison reported speaking with his father when he came home from the party. But you never saw fit to confirm Cole's alibi with his father. Why is that?"

"Objection," Rafe said. "To the extent counsel is asking for hearsay."

"Your Honor, I am not eliciting testimony from this witness about what Rudy Mathison said or didn't say. I'm merely trying to establish whether the detective made the effort to contact a potentially corroborating witness in this matter."

"Overruled. You may answer."

"I didn't speak to Rudy Mathison," she said. "I followed up with his employer, who told me Rudy hadn't come in to work that day. Despite repeated attempts on my part, Rudy Mathison would not respond to my calls or messages. His wife reported that he left town."

"Left town," I said. "So did you ever follow up with his employer when he got back?"

"No," she said.

"You never asked them to call you if he showed up?"

"I asked them that," she said.

"You asked them to call you when he showed up for work again. So why didn't they?"

"Because as I understand it, Rudy Mathison quit his job and left no forwarding information."

"Quit his job," I said. "Did he give a two-week or any other kind of notice, to your knowledge?"

"Not to my knowledge, no."

"What other efforts did you make to track Rudy Mathison down?"

"What do you mean?" she asked.

"Did you check his cell phone records?"

"Not at that time."

"Check his credit cards?"

"Yes," she said. "There was no activity after mid-August of last year," she answered.

"Did you check his bank records?" I asked.

"Not at that time," she said.

"But you've had the opportunity to review both Rudy Mathison's cell phone records and his bank records since you arrested Cole Mathison, haven't you?"

"I've seen them, yes," she said.

"Did you find them interesting?" I asked.

"Objection," Rafe said. "This is getting out of line."

"Ms. Leary," the judge said. "Let's stick to properly formatted questions, shall we?"

"Fine," I said. "Detective, what did Rudy Mathison's cell phone records reveal about his whereabouts on the night of August 31st and through September 2nd of last year?"

"Objection!" Rafe barked. "Those records are not part of this detective's report. She is not a proper authenticating witness. Those records are, in any case, irrelevant. Rudy Mathison is not on trial."

"Sustained Ms. Leary," the judge said. "You'll have to try to get at it another way. Move on."

I felt momentum building behind me. I gripped the lectern and launched into my final attack. "Detective, to this day, isn't it true that you've never bothered to track down Rudy Mathison to discuss what knowledge he has about the events of August 31st to September 1st of last year?"

"I wouldn't characterize it as never bothered. Mr. Mathison is just gone. No one seems to know where he is."

"Just gone," I said. "Interesting. You *are* aware of a subpoena that was served on Mr. Rudy Mathison's phone carrier?"

"I was given a copy of a subpoena that you filed," she said.

"And when was that subpoena filed?"

"I think it was in late November," she said.

"And you were given a copy of the fruits of that subpoena, weren't you?"

"I was," she said.

"Did you add it to your investigative file?" I asked.

"I didn't," she said.

"Objection," Rafe said. "Once again, Mr. Rudy Mathison's cell phone records aren't at issue. We just covered this!"

"Sustained, Ms. Leary!" the judge shouted. "Confine your questions to the matters within the scope of this detective's investigation."

"Understood," I said. "I'll move on. Detective, you testified that you became aware of and were given a copy of a subpoena my office served on Rudy Mathison's cell phone carrier. At that point, on November 29th, what was the status of your investigation into Lauren Rice's death?"

"The status?" she asked. "At that point, the charges had been filed. The case was in the prosecution's hands."

"I see," I said. "Except that changed, didn't it? You found what you claim is new evidence."

"Yes," she said. "On December 6th, I received the tip about the possible article of clothing near the site where Ms. Rice's body was discovered."

"Hmm," I said. "Conveniently just a few days after you received the fruit of the subpoena my office procured."

"Objection!" Rafe said. "Once again, counsel is arguing, not cross-examining."

"Sustained," she said.

Lord. It wasn't enough. But it was all I had.

"An anonymous tip," I said. "Detective, who was in charge of searching the area around where Lauren Rice's body was found?"

"It was my case," she said. "I was in charge of that scene."

"Of course," I said. "As lead detective. So you want us to believe that you missed this important article of clothing the first time around, right?"

"Lauren's body was found in early September," she said. "There was a significant amount of foliage there. Underbrush. The panties were discovered in the first week of December after the leaves had already fallen."

"Please answer my question," I said. "I'll remind you. I asked you, isn't it true you want us to believe you just happened to miss that article of clothing the first time around?"

She took a breath. "Yes," she said. "It's fair to say that my search team did not find that pair of underwear during the initial processing of the scene where Lauren's body was found."

"You said on direct that this area of the woods near

Lumley is well trafficked. Did you question any of the hikers or people who routinely use that trail?"

"I questioned one or two," she said.

"One or two. That's all?"

"Yes. It's in my supplemental report."

"Detective, you never took a detailed inventory of the items of clothing remaining in Lauren Rice's bedroom, did you?" I asked.

"We took photographs of her bedroom," she said.

"But sitting here today, you have no record of how many pairs of underwear were in Lauren's room after she went missing," I said.

"How many pairs? No," she said.

"And you were in Lauren's bedroom multiple times, weren't you?" I asked.

"I mean, yes. We searched Lauren's bedroom."

"We," I repeated. "So, many people had access to that bedroom."

"I wouldn't say that."

"You looked in her drawers, you went through her things, didn't you?" I asked.

"Yes," Lewis said, her tone sober.

"Detective, you had a search warrant for Cole Mathison's home and truck, correct?" I asked.

"Yes," she said.

"But that didn't end your search of the area around his house, did it?" I asked.

"What do you mean?" she said.

"What I mean is … you searched more than just his house and truck, right? More than what your search warrant indicated."

"Objection, foundation," Rafe said.

"I'll rephrase. Detective, it's standard practice to search a suspect's garbage, isn't it?"

"In a murder case?" she said. "Very often, yes."

"In fact, you *did* search the trash put out at the Mathison home, didn't you?"

"I did," she said.

"More than once?"

"I believe so, yes," she said. "I can't say for sure."

"You can find all sorts of things in someone's trash, can't you?" I asked.

"Of course."

"And you don't need a warrant to pick through someone's garbage, do you?" I asked.

"Generally, no," she said.

"You could search Cole Mathison's trash this afternoon if you wanted to, couldn't you?"

"If it was put out at the curb, yes," she said.

"I don't see any evidence from the Mathison's garbage catalogued in your report; why is that?" I asked.

"Because I didn't find any," she said.

"As far as we know," I snapped. It wasn't like me. But it got a final statement out of Megan that gave me gold.

"But if you're suggesting I planted evidence from that garbage or anywhere else, you are mistaken."

No. I hadn't suggested that. I'd implied it. And Detective Lewis spoke it out loud.

"Thank you," I said. "I have nothing further for this witness today but reserve the right to call her on rebuttal."

As Megan Lewis stepped down, I prayed. I prayed I'd planted a seed. And I prayed it would be enough.

The snow began to fall in earnest and Judge Niedermayer adjourned us for the day.

Chapter 26

THE BLIZZARD RAGED Wednesday night and into the early hours of Thursday morning. The courthouse shut down. Everything shut down until the plows could come through Thursday night. The Woodbridge County Road Commission never saw the area around Finn Lake as essential. Luckily for me, I had a younger brother with a big truck and a plow. Matty dug me out and blinked his headlights when he was ready for me.

I let the dogs out one last time (Matty plowed that little path for them too), slipped into my snow boots and carried my heels in a grocery bag.

"I can make it in my Jeep, Matty," I said as I climbed into his truck.

"Joe would kill me if I let you drive in this," he said. "So would Eric, come to think of it. Though I wouldn't mind if he threw the first punch."

"Zip it," I said. But Matty had a smile on his face. As brothers, Joe and Matty would forever give men I dated a hard time. But I knew Eric had worn them both down over the last year. He had that effect on people.

"Are you working today?" I asked.

"Nah," he said. "The shop's shut down because of all of this. I go back in on Monday. So just shoot me a text when you're ready to get picked up."

"Okay," I said. "But I'll probably walk to the office once court's over. It's a block and a half. Don't even start."

I added the last bit when Matty gave me a brotherly scowl. He also knew he could only push me so far.

Matty's plow ripped through another foot of snow. I shared a private drive with two other neighbors up on the hill. I knew they'd both be grateful for Matty's efforts today. He got me to the courthouse just before eight.

"You sure they're open?" he asked. "Parking lot's almost empty."

"They're open," I said. "But no member of the public in their right mind would bother coming down here today."

"Just a bunch of lunatic lawyers, cops, and judges," he said. "My favorite people."

"Hey," I said. "Your sister might just be two out of three and she's dating the third."

Matty winked at me. "Good luck. Break a leg. Whatever the heck you're supposed to say."

"Thanks," I said as I climbed out of the truck. I got a few feet away before Matty whistled through his open window. I'd forgotten my shoes. He tied off the bag and tossed them to me. I caught them against my chest like a football, then waved him off as I headed into the courthouse.

David Carver also owned a truck with a plow. He got Cole here in one piece, and I was grateful for that. I took my seat beside him in the courtroom.

Rafe called his DNA expert, Dr. John Tobias, to the stand. Dr. Tobias worked out of a crime lab based in Detroit. He had Tom Cruise good looks and some of the same charm.

He went through his analysis in bite-sized chunks the jury could understand.

He was good. Potentially devastating. I got in a few good swipes on direct aimed mostly at interrupting his flow. But I saved my best ammo for cross.

"Dr. Tobias," I said as I stepped up to the lectern. "You stated in your direct testimony that the samples you tested were collected from an article of clothing, correct?"

"That's correct," Tobias said. "Swabs were taken from a pair of underwear."

"With regard to the sample you positively identified as belonging to Lauren Rice, isn't it true that you can't say with certainty how old that sample was?"

"I cannot."

"So, for example, you can't tell this jury whether the sample you say belonged to Lauren Rice was present on that clothing for days, weeks, months, or hours prior to its deposit. Correct?"

"That's correct."

"And you can't say for certain how it got there, correct?" I asked.

"Well, I'm not sure if that's entirely accurate. As I testified, it was a fluid sample. Most likely cervical mucosa."

"I see," I said. "And you didn't find evidence of blood DNA belonging to Lauren Rice, correct?"

"No. I did not," he said.

"And it's also impossible for you to tell us whether that sample was deposited on that clothing with consent, correct?"

"No," he said. "Of course not."

"Okay," I said. "I'd like to ask you some follow-up questions about the results of the semen analysis you conducted. The sample allegedly matching Mr. Mathison ...

once again, there is no way for you to know how long that sample was present on that article of clothing, correct?"

"That's correct," he said.

"It could have been days. Or weeks. Or months. Possibly even years?"

"Well, in theory, yes," Dr. Tobias said. "But samples such as this, in the location where it was found, exposed to the elements, would tend to degrade over time. So, I would think the most plausible timeframe we're talking about would not include years or many, many months."

"I see," I said. "Doctor, isn't it true that you found *no* evidence of environmental degradation on this sample correct?"

"Nothing significant, no," he said.

"It's almost as if it were *just* put there, right?" I said.

"Objection!" Rafe said.

"Sustained."

"Doctor," I said. "Would you agree that it's possible, from your inspection of this clothing sample and its condition, that it could have been placed there within a day or two of its discovery?"

"It's possible," he said.

"But in any case, or in other words, it is impossible to determine whether that sample was deposited on the night or days following Lauren Rice's disappearance on August 31st, isn't that true?"

"It's impossible to determine whether the sample was deposited on August 31st exactly. That's true."

"Isn't it also true that you have no way to determine whether those samples were deposited in the commission of a crime?"

"No," he said. "I don't know that. The scope of my

analysis is to determine if the defendant's DNA matched the samples found."

"In fact," I said. "It would be equally likely that DNA samples originating from mucosa and semen, as you've described, might have been deposited through a consensual act, correct?"

"Sure, it could have been," he said.

"Your analysis can't even determine whether Ms. Rice had ever actually worn the underwear where your samples came from, can it?" I asked.

"Well, no," he said. "Not specifically. Though you can generally infer ..."

"I'm not asking you to generally infer," I cut him off. "I'm trying to establish the scope of your specific results. As such, you are not qualified to offer an opinion as to the method or manner in which those DNA samples came to be on that article of clothing, are you?"

"No," he said. "I can't dispositively tell you that. Not a hundred percent."

"Thank you," I said. I walked back to the lectern and quickly scanned my notes.

Tobias couldn't tell the jury how long the underwear had been hanging in the brush. He couldn't tell them how the samples got there. He could only tell them that Cole and Lauren's DNA were found in a pair of underwear that at least circumstantially seemed to belong to her.

It should be more than enough for reasonable doubt. I hoped.

"Thank you, Doctor," I said. "I have nothing further."

"Mr. Johnson?" the judge said.

"Dr. Tobias," Rafe said. "To clarify, what kind of environmental factors might compromise the condition of a

DNA sample such as what you were asked to analyze in this case?"

"Well, water submersion is one of the biggest destroyers. But exposure to wind, rain, sun, insects, animals, all of that can wreak havoc with a DNA sample."

"Did you find any evidence of compromising environmental factors?" Rafe asked.

"Nothing that interfered with the integrity of the analysis, no. Fortunately, this garment came to rest on dry land in a grove of trees. As such, there was some natural protection against the elements."

"Would a period of ten weeks from the time of deposit to collection be within the realm of possible age for this sample?"

"Objection," I said. "The witness has already established that he cannot conclusively establish the age of the sample."

"Your Honor," Rafe said. "As a qualified expert, this witness is able to offer his best estimation of the timeframe in question."

"Overruled, Ms. Leary," Judge Niedermayer answered. "The witness may answer."

"I would say ten weeks is certainly within the window of time this sample could have been out there. The underwear looked fairly new in the sense the elastic wasn't degraded. It wasn't ripped or frayed."

"Objection!" I shouted. "Your Honor, Dr. Tobias is qualified as a DNA expert. He's not a fabric expert."

"Sustained, Mr. Johnson," Judge Niedermayer said.

"Noted," Rafe said. He chewed the side of his cheek.

"Thank you," he said. "That's all for me, Dr. Tobias."

"Recross, Ms. Leary?"

"No, Your Honor," I said. "As always, we reserve the right to call this witness on rebuttal."

"You may," she said. "Dr. Tobias, you may step down."

The wind howled outside, rattling the windows. It was three o'clock.

"We're going to stop here and let the jury drive home while it's still light out and before the snow starts up again. Bailiff?"

Within a matter of minutes, he had the jury scuttled out of the room.

"Counsel, we're still on the record. Let's have you both approach."

I made a "sit tight" gesture with the down sweep of my hand to Cole. His cheeks flushed with nerves as I approached the bench with Rafe.

"Okay," Niedemeyer said. "What's the agenda for tomorrow, Mr. Johnson?"

"Your Honor, the state is prepared to rest."

My pulse skipped. I kept my face neutral.

"Good enough," she said.

"Then I'd like to move for directed verdict," I said. I looked back at Tori, sitting in the gallery. She was getting quite good at reading my mind.

"If I may," I said. I quickly stepped to the table and reached across it. Tori handed me three copies of a ten-page motion and brief. I walked it back to the bench and handed Rafe his copy.

"Your Honor, if we're still on the record?"

"We are," she said, nodding to her court reporter.

"I won't belabor the points in my written motion, but the State has failed to meet the elements of first-degree murder as a matter of law. He has not established how the victim died. He has offered no evidence on the defendant's intent. He simply doesn't have it."

"Mr. Johnson," the judge said. "You prepared to argue this

now or would you like until morning to submit a written response?"

"I'll respond now," he said. "Directed verdict is improper when there are facts in dispute. There are ample. Dr. Trainor's esteemed testimony as to the cause and manner of death. We have eyewitnesses statements regarding the defendant's animosity toward the victim. Her fears of him. We've conclusively established he lied to the police. We have physical evidence ..."

Judge Niedemeyer raised her hand. "I agree. I'm sorry, Ms. Leary, you don't have it on this one. This isn't a legal question, it's a factual one. This is for the jury. Your motion is denied. I'll have Mr. Johnson formally rest in front of the jury Monday morning, then you need to be prepared to call your first witness. Are you?"

I looked back at Cole. I knew exactly who he wanted that to be. I wasn't as sure. We had the weekend to fight it out.

Chapter 27

"I DUNNO," Jeanie said. "I'm just not impressed. This kid came down from Detroit. He's not green."

Kid. Of course Jeanie would think of Rafe Johnson that way. I think he was thirty-nine.

"The DNA kills you," Tori said. She sat at the head of the conference room table. Jeanie paced in front of the whiteboard. I stayed in the corner, surveying it all.

"Homicide is a non-starter," I said. "I threw as much smoke as I could. I'll argue in closing there's some doubt about whether Lauren was murdered."

"But it won't go anywhere," Jeanie finished for me. "Nineteen-year-old girls don't just turn up dead like that. And he proved her body's been moved."

"Still doesn't mean she was murdered," Tori said.

"No," I said. "But I think the jury can get there. And that damn DNA on her underwear. Tori, I need something. Anything. Where are we on figuring out who Lewis's informant was?"

She gave me a hopeless look. Great.

"If he or she had come into the station, that would be one thing," I said. "But an anonymous caller? Oy."

"I think you're winning," Tori said. "I really do. I've been watching the jury. They didn't like Megan's testimony. That line about going through Cole's garbage landed. I'm sure of it."

"I hope so," I said.

"You can dance around it all you want," Jeanie said. "But you've got to figure out what the hell you're going to do about Cole. You puttin' him on?"

I sat down in one of the chairs against the wall. "Tell me what you'd do. Honestly."

Jeanie heaved a great sigh. "I don't know. That's the truth. There's all the standard pitfalls about putting a defendant on the stand. I said I wasn't that impressed with Rafe Johnson. That doesn't mean he can't draw blood on cross. You know he will."

"Can you get Rudy Mathison's phone records in?" Tori asked.

"I think so," I said. "It just won't be pretty. I'm going to have to call Roxanne Mathison."

"Christ," Jeanie said. "That woman is just plain weird. I'm sorry. That could backfire, Cass."

"I know," I said.

"And she's going to say she didn't hear Cole coming or going. She can't corroborate his alibi."

"I know," I said again. "But she can at least corroborate that her husband was home when Cole said he was. That's how I backdoor the phone records. And I can show that Rudy was near the site of where Lauren's body was dumped."

"But it doesn't mean anything without Cole up there giving it context."

My head hurt. My feet hurt. My soul hurt.

Jeanie came to me and put a soft hand on my shoulder. "You know what you have to do, kiddo."

"Yeah," I said. "I think I do. But I can't shake the feeling it'll sink this case."

"I'll clear my schedule," Tori said. After a year working for us, she'd gotten pretty good at reading my signals and my mind.

"Yeah," I said. "I need a night. Let me sleep on it one more time. Then, tomorrow, we get Cole in here for more prep. I'm going to have to put him on the stand."

"What about Emma?" Jeanie asked. "You gonna call her?"

"I really don't know," I said. "I'm going to have to see how it goes with my other witnesses. If I can get the phone and bank records in, that might be enough without her. I just don't know how well she'd stand up to cross. She's been a wreck. And anyway, Joe says they broke up a little while ago. Sounds like Cole initiated that."

"It's gotta be for the best," Jeanie said. "I think the kid's being railroaded. I honestly do. But I want Emma clear of all of this."

"Me too," I said.

"She sure is getting a rough entry into adulthood," Jeanie said.

"Yeah."

"Well," Tori said. "At least the snow's letting up."

"Oh crap," I said. "I was supposed to call my brother. I don't even have a car here. He pretty much plowed me out to get me here. We've gotten at least another six inches since this morning. Tori, how are you getting home?"

"I've got four-wheel drive," she said.

"That's my girl," Jeanie said. She'd actually gone car shopping with Tori. Jeanie had talked her into getting a Rav 4 like Jeanie's.

I was just about to reach for my phone when the back door downstairs opened. Miranda had already left for the day.

"Anybody home?" a deep male voice called up. It was Eric.

"Well," Jeanie said. She moved away from me and put her hands on Tori's shoulders. "That's our cue, kid. Just enough daylight to make it home. They're expecting another four to six inches tonight. I think maybe you'd better plan on getting Matty to plow a path to Dave and Maxine's house if you want to do witness prep with Cole over there. Probably better not to have him around his mom when you do."

"Good thinking," I said. "I'll give them a call later."

Eric bounded up the stairs. His smile widened when he saw the group of us.

"Sorry to interrupt the pow wow," he said. "I figured you'd need a ride home."

"I was supposed to call Matty," I said.

"He called me," Eric answered. "He picked up a side job plowing out Deerwood Estates on the other side of town. Said Joe's not answering his phone so you're stuck with me."

I narrowed my eyes. That didn't quite sound like either of my brothers. I suspected the truth might be the other way around. Eric had probably called Matty and told him he wanted the honor of taking me home. It meant he was up to something. It meant he probably wanted to corner me.

"Well, we need to scoot," Jeanie said. She gave Eric a formidable slug in the shoulder as she passed him. He winced from it and waited until she was out of the room before he brought his hand up and rubbed the spot.

"Ya big baby," I teased.

"You ready to go or do you still have some things you want to tie up here?" he asked.

"I can be ready," she said. "If I can make a clean getaway, that is."

"Coast is clear out there," he said. "No protestors. No press. No one trying to ruin your life for the clients you take."

Eric's grin seemed a little hollow. We walked downstairs. I grabbed my coat off the hook, slipped my heels off and slid my feet into my snow boots.

Wind and snow blasted me in the face as I opened the door. Eric came up behind me and worked the latch, locking it. He hit his key fob, unlocking his car door. I climbed into the passenger seat and waited for him.

He was still pensive when he slid behind the wheel and pulled out.

"So," I said as we made the turn away from the downtown area and toward the lake. "You want to tell me what this is really about?"

"What do you mean?"

"You've got something on your mind. Might as well get it out."

He set his teeth on edge. "How do you do that?"

"Do what?"

"Always seem to know what I'm thinking," he answered.

"Oh, you're easy to read."

This got the first genuine smile out of him. "And you are literally the only person who's ever said that about me."

"Well?"

"It's just ... dammit, Cass. You can't really think Megan Lewis set that kid up. You're winding up to say she planted evidence. Aren't you?"

"Wow," I answered. "So who fed you that one?"

"Everyone," he said. "In case you haven't noticed, the Mathison kid's trial is pretty much the only thing interesting going on in town right now."

"Well, like you said, at least nobody's throwing rocks through my window over it this time. I've finally got a client people want me to defend," I said.

"I just ... I don't want to see Megan's career get blown up because of it," he said.

"This is how it works, Eric," I said. "And you of all people know it. It's in the Constitution. I have a right to explore how this investigation was conducted. Megan's conduct is fair game. You want to tell me you've never been questioned like that in any of your cases? Give me a break."

"She didn't plant evidence," Eric barked.

"Do you think he's guilty? Come on. Give me your honest opinion. You know ... you *know* the case against him was weak at best until that semen evidence just happened to show up. The timing doesn't bother you? Not even a little? It was just days after I got the cell records back on Rudy Mathison. Don't tell me you don't know what they showed. It's too convenient."

"It's Cole Mathison's DNA!" Eric snapped. "You're not even trying to deny that. For God's sake, Cass. That kid ... at a minimum he was sleeping with Lauren Rice while he was dating your niece."

"That makes him a crappy boyfriend," I said. "It doesn't make him a murderer."

He made the turn toward the lake. The plows still hadn't been through. At this late in the day, it wouldn't be until maybe sometime tomorrow. By then, there would be more accumulation. I'd need Matty to dig me back out.

"She's a good cop," Eric said as he came up my driveway.

"I never said she wasn't," I said. "I'm doing my job. If she was thorough when doing hers, she's got nothing to worry about. You mind telling me what's really bugging you? Come on, Eric. You know how this works. You know, as lead detective, Megan's work goes under the microscope. That's just how it is."

He put the car in park and turned to me. "Yeah. I know how it is. It's just ... why haven't you made a decision about the judicial appointment yet?"

Ah. So that's what this was about. "I've been a little busy," I said.

"I just ... I wanted to make sure it wasn't because of me. Whatever decision you do end up making."

"They've talked to you again," I said. "The governor's people?"

He pursed his lips. It was an answer.

"Great," I said. "They don't like that I'm dating a married man."

"They didn't say that," he said. "They just ... dammit. I don't want to be the reason you say no. And I don't want to be the reason you say yes, either. I don't know. It's just hard. It's always so damn hard."

I smiled. "Yeah. It is. And you're a loyal friend. I get that. I also know that if Detective Lewis knew you were out here trying to plead her case, she'd probably box your ears. It's noble. Chivalrous, even. But you're not helping her."

He shook his head. "Yeah. I suppose she would do exactly that. I just ... damn. This is how rumors get started."

"Eric," I said. "You never answered my question."

"Which one?"

"The DNA sample. You know it doesn't pass the smell test. I think Lewis even knows that. This case is so important to her ... Eric, I know what happens to her if I get an acquittal. I'm sorry about that. I really am. But no, I'm not going to pull a single punch."

"I'm not asking you to," he said quickly. "God. I don't want you to think that."

"Good," I said. "Because you're right. She should be prepared. Things might get rough for Megan before I'm through. I'm not into dirty tricks. But I'm also not going to sit by while any of them are played on my client. And ... if it were you. If this were your case, or Jack's. We wouldn't be here. Tell me that's not true."

He went stone silent. That, too, was an answer.

After a moment, I touched his face. "Cheer up," I said. "Rafe's good. It's just ... well ... I'm better."

Eric took my hand in his. "I know. That's the problem. That's always been the damn problem. And you're impossible."

He kissed my palm. At the back door, Marbury and Madison started to bark and scratch at the glass.

"I better get inside," I said. "They're liable to bust through to get to you."

I dropped off the rest of my sentence, the part where I was going to ask him to stay. If things were different, I would have invited him inside. But they weren't. I had a trial to prepare for. One that might very likely destroy his friend's career. There was still the small matter of my possible judicial appointment and appearances we had to maintain.

Eric leaned in and kissed me just before I slid out of the passenger seat. The wind howled behind me, as if in protest. Easy. For once, I just wanted things to be easy. Something told me they probably never would.

Chapter 28

MONDAY MORNING, at nine a.m., I did what I knew would either be the smartest thing I'd done in my career, or the dumbest. I called Cole Mathison to the stand.

For his part, Cole looked like he'd shed another ten pounds over the weekend. He'd gotten a haircut, but it was still too long. He wore it slicked back. With skin so pale, his blond hair blended into it, making him look a little like a cotton swab as he climbed into the witness box and shakily adjusted the microphone.

"Will you state your name for the record?" I asked him after the bailiff swore him in.

Behind me, the courtroom was packed. The snow had finally stopped, but it melted, leaving Delphi encased in a dangerous sheet of ice. Still, everyone in town who could came to see the show.

"Mr. Mathison," I started. "I'd like you to tell me a little about yourself. Where did you grow up?"

"Um, here in Delphi," he said. "I've lived here my whole life. Graduated from Delphi High School three years ago now. I've never lived anywhere else."

"Do you go to school?" I asked.

"I'm ... not since all of this started. I was about to start my last year at Jackson College. I was working on getting a business degree and then transferring to Eastern. But after Lauren died, I withdrew."

"I see," I said. "Who are you currently living with?"

"My mom," he said. "I've always lived at home. I was working on maybe renting a house of my own before all of this. But ... well ... a lot of things are put on hold."

"Where were you living in August of last year?" I asked.

"With my mom," he said. "Our house is 1421 McGrath Street. I was born there."

"What are your parents' names?" I asked.

"My dad is Rudy Mathison. My mom is Roxanne Mathison."

"I see," I said. "You just live with your mom?"

"Well," he said. "No. My dad, too. Technically."

"Technically," I repeated. "What do you mean by that?"

"I ... my dad is a trucker. He ... uh ... he's always been in and out of my life. McGrath Street is his primary residence, you know, for taxes and mail. But he takes off for weeks at a time."

"Has it always been like that?" I asked.

"Yeah. As far back as I can remember," he said.

I introduced a recent photograph of Rudy. Cole identified it. As we'd established in Kaylin Dwyer's direct testimony, the resemblance between them was striking. Even more so now that the last few months had hardened Cole's appearance.

"Cole," I said. "When was the last time you saw your father?"

Cole gritted his teeth. "I saw him the night of ... well, technically Sunday morning, September 1st of last year."

"How can you be so sure of the date?"

Cole looked down. "Because it was the last night I saw Lauren too. And he wasn't supposed to be there."

"What happened?" I asked.

Cole took a breath. "I was home. Playing on my PlayStation. I'd heard from some friends that there was a party out at the Pits that night. I wasn't going to go, but I did. I didn't stay long. Got there around ten, I was home after midnight. My dad's truck was in the driveway when I came back. And like I said, it wasn't supposed to be."

"Why not?" I asked.

"He wasn't supposed to be there at all. He ... a few weeks before that, we got into a fight. I told him ... well ... we came to an understanding. My dad packed some things, and he left the house. I thought it was for good."

I paused, stepping to the side of the lectern. Cole was doing well. So far.

"Cole," I said. "Why did you want your father to leave the house?"

He pressed his hand to his forehead, gathering himself. "Because my father wasn't a good man. He was ... he hurt my mom. And he hurt me too."

"Hurt you how?" I asked.

"My dad liked to resolve conflicts with his fists, and other things."

"What other things, Cole?" I asked.

Cole was shaking so badly, you could hear his shoes knocking against the wooden sides of the witness box.

"You name it," he said. "Belts, flashlights, electrical cords, whatever he could get his hands on. My whole life. My first memories. He broke my mom's arm. All the fingers in her left hand. Maybe more. She tried to hide a lot of it. And when I was about nine, after I hit a growth spurt, he started to break things on me."

Cole's voice dropped so low in his last sentence, it got hard to hear. He cleared his throat and spoke up before I could remind him.

"Cole," I asked. "What things did your father break on you?"

"My eardrum," he said, pointing to his right ear. "He backhanded me so hard one night when I knocked over a jar on the counter. Spaghetti sauce. It got everywhere. He was careful, though. He didn't break any bones like he did with my mom. Because ..."

Cole tripped over his words. He let out a sob.

"Because why, Cole?" I asked.

"Because he wanted to make sure I could still play football. Baseball. It's the only time my dad was ever in a good mood. Or at least ... the only time he took an interest in something I was doing. But even that got hard. There were incidents on the field when I played in little kid leagues. He got thrown out of a couple of games."

"Why was that?" I asked.

"He used rough language. Threatened an umpire once. Once, he grabbed me so hard after I missed a pass ... he left bruises on my arms and the other coaches saw."

"Did you ever see a doctor about the physical injuries you suffered after these incidents?" I asked.

"My mom took me to our family doctor after the incident with my eardrum. After a week or two, when I couldn't hear out of it. She ... I told the doctor I fell out of a tree," he said.

"You told the doctor. Did someone ask you to do that?"

"No," he said. "It's just ... I knew we weren't supposed to say anything. My mother never said anything. She was afraid."

"Objection," Rafe said. "It's not proper for the defendant to speculate about what his mother was or wasn't afraid of."

"Sustained," the judge said. "Mr. Mathison, you'll need to confine your testimony to your own personal experience and what you observed."

"I never *observed* my mother telling the cops or a teacher or the doctor about the stuff that was going on at home," Cole snapped.

I shot him a look aimed at reminding him to keep his cool. Any show of anger could kill him in the eyes of the jury.

"Cole," I said. "Let's go back to your statement about the fight you had with your father. The one where you said he packed his things and left. What was so special about that night in particular?"

"He was ... I don't even remember what the fight was about. Between him and my mom. Probably money. That was the usual way things started. We needed money for groceries. Basic day-to-day stuff. He would get angry. He would ... call her names. He'd say ... if you want money like a wh... I can't even say it. I won't repeat the name he called her. Oh God. And then it would escalate. And he would start to beat the crap out of her again. I walked in on that. My father had my mother up against the kitchen counter. Bent over it. He was going to ... she was crying. Screaming. And I couldn't let it happen again. So, I just lost it. I grabbed him by the back of his collar and threw him off of her. I stood over him and told him to get out. That I was never going to let him touch my mother again. And then, he did. He dusted himself off. He pushed past me, and my mother. He threw some clothes into a bag and he left. That was early July, I think. And I didn't see him or hear from him for weeks. Not until Labor Day weekend."

"Okay," I said. "Let's back up a bit. Tell me how you knew Lauren Rice."

Cole reached for a sip of water. "I knew Lauren for years.

We went to junior high, and high school together. We were friends. She was always a cheerleader. I was always a football player. Though she was a year younger than me grade-wise, our friend groups overlapped because of football."

"I see," I said. "Was there ever a time when you became more than friends?"

"Yes," he said. "Yes. Lauren was always ... well, she was a flirt. Nothing overt. She was just always so bright and bubbly and kind of touchy-feely, you know? Liked to hug. Liked to put her arms around you. I was used to that. But then ... I think it was sometime in the beginning of my senior year, her junior year, I noticed her kind of focusing that kind of attention even more on me. She was always around. We started texting a lot. Then, finally, homecoming my senior year, I asked her if she wanted to go with me. I think she said something like it's about damn time you figured it out."

"Figured what out?" I asked.

"That she was into me in that way. I felt like an idiot, to tell you the truth. Like I missed all the signals. I was so into my own head. It was nice. We had a lot of fun. Because we were such good friends to start out with. I'd never dated anybody like that before. You know. Someone I was close friends with beforehand. It was easy with Lauren. We were already comfortable with each other. It felt very natural."

"Okay," I said. "Was that your first date? The homecoming dance?"

"Yeah," he said. "We had a really good time. So, we started dating seriously ... um ... exclusively, after that."

"How serious were you?" I asked.

Cole's eyes darted from the jury back to me. "Um ... serious. She was my girlfriend. I considered her my girlfriend. And I was her boyfriend."

"Were you intimate?" I asked.

Cole nodded, then immediately leaned toward the microphone. "Um ... yes. We were ... um ... we were having sex."

"When did that start?" I asked.

"I don't know exactly. Not right away. Maybe a few months into it. I think by Christmas my senior year for sure. And we were still together by the time prom rolled around in May. She was my date for my senior prom."

"Okay," I said. "What happened after that?"

"Well," he said. "Not long after prom, I graduated. We started to grow apart that summer. And it was me. I take the blame for that. I was starting to really focus on what my life would be outside of high school. I'll admit, it bothered me that Lauren was still in high school. When I graduated ... I just felt ... I don't know. I wanted to be done with that place. I wanted to move on."

"Did you break up?" I asked.

"Eventually, yeah. We did. I can't tell you exactly when. I took her to homecoming her senior year. I didn't want to be the jerk who broke up with her right before that. So, it was maybe a couple of weeks after that. And it wasn't like some big scene. Lauren was kind of moving on too. She didn't call or text me as much. We weren't fighting. I know I was cold. That's probably what she would have complained about. I know at one point she accused me of ghosting her. It wasn't that. I was just getting really busy with school. Anyway, we went out to dinner one weekend, after that homecoming dance, like I said. I can't even remember who said what. One of us said maybe we should just go back to being friends. And that was it. Really. If she was angry with me, she didn't say so. And I still talked to her. We still texted after that. I'd check in with her. She'd check in with me. But by Christmas, she was already dating other people."

"How did you know that?" I asked.

"Well, I'd see her out with other guys. And we still had mutual friends. I told you, our friend groups overlapped. And I saw her on social media. Pictures of her with another guy we went to school with, Jason Montel. And then, that next spring, she went to her senior prom with this other guy, Ben Sharpton. I heard through the grapevine they were exclusive for a while."

"How did that make you feel?" I asked.

"I was happy for her. And I heard she got a scholarship to go to Valparaiso; I was really happy for her about that. I texted her and told her. It was a good conversation. No drama."

"Were you ever romantically involved with Lauren after that?"

He looked down. "I don't know that I would describe it as romantic, really. But, a little over a year ago, I started getting worried about Lauren. She seemed down whenever I saw her. She started texting me again after she and Ben broke up. I want to say it was right after Christmas. I think she started regretting not going to Valparaiso. I don't know. But we spent some time together for a couple of weeks early last year. We ... we had sex. Once. Lauren was really depressed. She told me ... I think she tried to kill herself. I went to her house. She'd swallowed some pills. I got her to throw up. She was okay. She wouldn't let me call a doctor. I should have. Looking back, I know that now. It's just, I was so used to not getting outsiders involved in stuff like that because of the way I was raised. Anyway, we hooked up just that once. Then, I knew I had to move on. That I wasn't doing right by Lauren if I strung her along."

"Was she upset?"

"She was down," he said. "But I didn't get the impression it was about me. She went on some dates with other people.

At least, I saw pictures of her online with other guys again. Then, eventually, I started dating someone else too. Emma Leary."

He let that sit for a moment. The jury was already well aware of my family connection to Cole's romantic life.

"When was that?" I asked.

"I started seeing Emma in the spring. It would have been a year ago this upcoming March."

"What about your relationship with Lauren?" I asked. "Did she know you were dating Emma?"

"She did," he said. "Eventually. That summer, there were a few times that I ran into Lauren while I was with Emma. The two of them were friends too. Emma was a year younger grade-wise from Lauren. She's two years younger than me. But Emma and Lauren were friends. It's Delphi. Everybody knows everybody."

"Understood," I said. "Cole, moving into the fall and early last year. Did your relationship with Lauren change at all?"

"Not for me," he said. "I was getting more serious with Emma. We were happy. Things at home for me weren't great. I've already said how things came to a head for me and my dad last summer. Emma was with me through all of that. I spent most of my time at her place. Anyway, late last spring, Lauren started texting me again. Asking me how things were with Emma. Her texts were positive at first. She said how happy she was for me. That we were a cute couple. That kind of thing."

Rafe had already introduced Cole and Lauren's text messages from the summer last year all the way through the night she disappeared. I pulled them up on the overhead projector now.

Cole went through them. The early texts followed right along with what he claimed. On April 7th, Lauren called him and Emma a cute couple. It was June 17th where things started to turn.

"Cole," I said. "What happened on June 17th?"

"That was the night after Emma's graduation party. She had it in the pavilion at Shamrock Park. Lauren came to it. I don't know if she was specifically invited or not. It didn't really matter. Once again, it's Delphi. Pretty much everyone goes to everyone else's grad parties. Anyway, Lauren was acting weird. I thought she was angry with me. She just seemed colder, not as friendly. And I saw her drinking beer. I'd never seen her do that before."

"Did you ask her about it?" I asked.

"No," he said. "I just kind of assumed maybe she was still trying to come to terms with some choices she made."

"What do you mean?" I asked.

"Well, her decision to stay home to be with her dad. I told her that was a mistake. Anyway, she just didn't seem like the same Lauren that night. That's when she started sending me these other texts throughout that summer."

I highlighted a series of texts Lauren sent to Cole that went unanswered. He read them into the record again.

August 17: I came by your house. I know you were home. Either pick up your phone or meet me somewhere. I miss you.

August 27: You're not going to get away with ghosting me, asshole. This little problem of yours isn't going to go away. I've been more than patient. I'm not trying to ruin your life. I'm trying to get you to do the right thing.

"Cole," I asked. "What was Lauren referring to when she said, this little problem?"

"Honestly," Cole said. "I have no idea. I really don't."

"But you know what it might sound like to other people," I said. "How do you explain that?"

"Lauren told me she was pregnant," he said.

"When?" I asked.

"Well, it was a little before that August 17th text. That same week I think."

"How did you respond?" I asked.

"I couldn't believe it. We weren't involved anymore. I hadn't had sex with her in months."

"Not since January that year?"

"Right," he said. "I honestly don't remember exactly. But it was just that one weekend. And it was well before I started dating Emma. And if she was pregnant, Lauren wasn't showing at all. It wasn't mine. I knew she was lying."

"Objection," Rafe said. "The witness is speculating."

"Sustained," Judge Niedermayer said.

The remainder of Lauren's texts to Cole went unanswered through August until the fateful night when she disappeared.

"Cole," I said. "Let's turn your attention to Labor Day weekend, last year. Tell me what happened with Lauren when you saw her."

"I didn't know she'd be at the party that night," he said. "Like I said before, I hadn't even planned on going myself until the last minute. When I got there, I regretted it pretty much right away. It was just the same, immature crowd from high school. And as soon as Lauren saw me, she was all over me."

"What do you mean?" I asked.

"She'd been drinking. I saw her flirting with just about every guy there. When she saw me, she threw her arms around me. She tried to kiss me. When I sat down on a log by the bonfire, she tried crawling into my lap."

"What did you do?" I asked.

"I peeled her off. I tried to be as nice as I could. But she wouldn't stop. I felt like ... like she was trying to get as many people to see her with me until one of them either took a picture or went back to Emma."

"Did you argue?" I asked.

"Yeah," he said. "We did. Lauren was ... I got a text. It was just some spam. You can see it there in the transcripts. I don't even remember what it was. Some car stereo place or something. Anyway, Lauren got jealous. She tried to look and see who it was. I handed it to her to show her. I told her it was none of her business, anyway. It was just ... by that point I realized nothing good was going to come from me talking to her anymore."

"She took your phone," I said. "Did she look through it?"

"For a second, yes," he said. "Then I took it back from her. Then she took her phone and was trying to take a picture with me. She was laughing. Stumbling. I pulled myself away from her."

"Where were you when this argument was taking place?" I asked.

"We'd walked away a little from the bonfire. We were at the edge of the woods."

"Was anyone else around you?" I asked.

"Not right around us, no. But there were people everywhere. We were still within the party group. Still in the clearing, just off to the side."

"What happened next?" I asked.

"I stayed for a little while, but it just kept getting worse and worse. I told Lauren to knock it off. And she kind of did. I turned my attention away from her. I was going to offer to get her home. I was worried she'd get behind the wheel like that. But I'll regret this forever. I was afraid if I got involved with her, she'd turn it against me somehow or get the wrong idea. So I let it go. I just let it go. And that was it. I left the party around midnight, I think it was."

"Did you see Lauren when you left the party?"

"She was still by the bonfire. I think she was sitting on Grant Paulsen's lap. She had a drink in her hand and was laughing."

"Then what happened?" I asked.

"Then, I went home. I saw my dad's truck in the driveway. I was livid over it. Like I said, he wasn't supposed to be there."

"Did you confront him?" I asked.

"I didn't want to. My mom and dad's bedroom door was shut. I was still kind of, well, unsettled about the party. I just ... I didn't feel like getting into it. I knew what would happen if I did. So, I tried to just go to bed."

"Cole," I said. "What were you afraid of?"

"That it would get physical again if I confronted my dad," he said.

"What happened?"

"When I went downstairs, he was there. He was in my room in the basement, looking through my things."

"What did you do?" I asked.

"I told him to get out. We had ... we argued," he said.

"Did it get physical?"

"He didn't ... he didn't hit me. But I threw things at him. I wasn't going to let him touch me."

"What was his reaction?" I asked.

"He was livid. Like white-faced, bulging eyes."

"Cole," I said. "Did your father ever cause problems between you and the girls you dated?"

"Yes," he said. "He's the reason why I would always find excuses not to be there with any friends or girlfriends. I just never knew what kind of mood he'd be in. And he ... he liked to try to embarrass me in front of my girlfriends."

"How so?"

"He'd flex his muscles. Alpha male stuff. Parade around in his damn underwear and shirtless. The whole attitude was like ... he wanted them to see him and think he was bigger and better than I was. Like he was the *real* man of the house. He'd say that sometimes."

"Objection," Rafe said. "Hearsay."

"Mr. Mathison," the judge said. "Do you understand the objection? It's not proper for you to testify about what your father or any other witness might have said."

"I understand," he said, then mouthed 'sorry' to me.

"What else would your father do regarding your girlfriends?" I asked.

"He was ... you have to understand. One of the running themes of my parents' dysfunction was me. How they had to get married because my mom was pregnant with me. So he was always ... well, I got the impression he thought all girls were sluts. Anytime he caught me even kissing a girl he'd go ballistic. It was like he wanted them to think he was the big dog, but he also didn't want them coming near me."

"Okay, let's go back to the early morning of September 1st after you got home from the bonfire. What happened after you and your father argued?" I asked.

"I turned my back on him and walked inside. I went downstairs, and I went to sleep. When I woke up the next morning, my dad was gone. I had breakfast with my mom, then I went to work. Then ... everything just fell apart. I got the word that Lauren went missing."

"What did you think?" I asked.

"I couldn't believe it. I blamed myself for not driving her home that night. I knew something was wrong. I had a bad feeling. But I ignored it. I shouldn't have ignored it."

"Cole," I said. "When was the last time you saw Lauren?"

"At that bonfire sitting on Grant's lap. I didn't talk to her after that. I didn't see her on the side of the road. Kaylin's wrong. It wasn't me. I swear. It wasn't me. I didn't do this. I didn't kill Lauren. I wouldn't. I couldn't. We were friends. I still loved her a little in the way that you do with exes. I didn't want anything bad to happen to her. I swear."

He was sobbing by then. Great, ragged breaths escaped him.

I stepped behind the lectern and folded my hands. "Thank you," I finally said. "I have nothing further."

I left the lectern and slipped into my chair. Beside me, Tori had already written a note.

It read. "He's not objecting? Why isn't Johnson objecting more?"

I picked up the pen and scribbled my answer. "He thinks he's feeding Cole enough rope to hang himself. I would have done the same. Pray he doesn't succeed."

Chapter 29

"Mr. Mathison," Rafe started, putting heavy emphasis on the mister. "Isn't it true that in the afternoon of September 1st, you were questioned by the police?"

"Yes," he said. "I already said they came to ask me questions while I was at work."

"Do you remember what you said to them? Your exact words?"

"My exact words?" he said. "No. Not my exact words."

Rafe pulled the addendum from Detective Lewis's report. "Detective Lewis wrote that you reported seeing Lauren Rice at the party in the woods the evening before. Isn't that true?"

"It's true I told her I saw Lauren at the party," Cole said. "And it's true that I saw her."

"But when you first spoke to the police, you failed to mention your dating history with her. You failed to mention the fact you had an argument with her. Isn't that true?"

"She didn't ask me any of that," Cole said. "She only asked me if I saw her. I told her, to the best of my recollection, the timeframe."

"Two weeks later, you had occasion to speak with

Detective Lewis again. This time, you were brought down to the police station. And your lawyer, Ms. Leary, was present, wasn't she?"

"Ms. Leary was with me, yes," Cole said.

"In that interview, you said nothing about your communications with Lauren in the weeks leading up to the party, did you? You never mentioned the texts she sent you, did you?"

"I don't ... I don't think she asked me about those," Cole said.

"You want us to believe you had nothing to do with what happened to that girl. You wanted Detective Lewis to believe it. And yet, you withheld information about the nature of your relationship with the victim, didn't you?"

"I didn't withhold," he said. "She didn't ask me. I was trying ... that detective came and found me at Lauren's wake. In front of all of our friends. I was scared to death. I wanted to help but ..."

"You wanted to help?" Rafe shouted. "And yet you didn't cooperate. In fact, you withheld critical information about your communications with the victim."

"Objection," I said. "Defense counsel is no longer asking questions, he's giving speeches."

"Sustained, Mr. Johnson," the judge said. "Ask your questions."

"Detective Lewis asked you whether you and the victim were having a sexual relationship. Do you remember what you told her on September 15th?" Rafe asked.

"I believe I told her that no, we weren't sexually involved," Cole said.

"But that was a lie, wasn't it? You were having a sexual relationship with Lauren Rice as recently as January of last year."

"That's not what she asked me," Cole said. "Detective Lewis asked me if we were having sex. We weren't. Our relationship was over."

"Over?" Rafe said. He pulled up the transcripts from the text exchanges Cole had with Lauren. "That's also a lie. You and the victim were texting back and forth on topics of an intimate nature as late as four days before she disappeared, weren't you?"

"She was texting me," he said. "I wasn't texting back. I can't control what Lauren did."

"You never told your girlfriend Emma about these texts with Lauren, did you?" Rafe asked.

"No," Cole said. "I didn't."

"And you didn't tell her because you didn't want to get caught communicating with your old girlfriend, did you?" Rafe asked.

"That's not true," Cole said. "I hadn't done anything wrong. But I wasn't about to break Lauren's confidence either. I knew she was going through something. I was trying to still be her friend as much as I could."

"Be her friend," Rafe said. "And yet you never told the police about these texts, did you?"

Cole sighed. "They never asked me. I would have told them if they asked me."

"How convenient," Rafe said.

"Your Honor," I said. "This topic has been asked and answered. The transcripts from Mr. Mathison's interviews with the police have been entered into evidence. Once again, Mr. Johnson is speechifying, not cross-examining the witness."

"Sustained, Mr. Johnson," Judge Niedermayer said. "Let's move on."

I sat back down, but feared the damage on that score had

been done. But the facts were the facts. Cole's caginess with the cops was a self-inflicted wound. I could only hope his explanation made sense to the jury.

"Mr. Mathison, you were angry with Lauren Rice the night of the party, weren't you?" Rafe asked.

"Angry? I don't know if I was so much angry. I was worried about her. And I was frustrated," Cole asked.

"Frustrated ..." Rafe repeated. "Several witnesses reported seeing you arguing with the victim. You admitted you were arguing with her off to the side of the circle. You were pissed off, weren't you?"

"I was frustrated."

"This girl was trying to mess with your life, wasn't she?" Rafe asked.

"She was ... she was confused, I think," Cole answered.

"You thought she was trying to trap you, just like you say your dad trapped your mom, didn't you?"

"None of that had anything to do with me," Cole said.

"Which thing?" Rafe asked.

"All of it. I can't control how I was born. And if Lauren was claiming she was pregnant with my kid, it wasn't true. I knew it wasn't true. We hadn't been together in like eight months."

"She was lying," Rafe said, his voice coming out as a hiss. "You'd moved on to someone new. And Lauren was trying to get in the way of that, wasn't she?"

I understood Rafe's tactic. He was trying to get an anger reaction out of Cole. Make him lose his cool. Let the jury see it. Let them imagine the kind of rage it would take to kill someone and find it in Cole's eyes.

Stay cool, I thought. I said it over and over in my head, as if I could transmit it straight into Cole's brain.

"She was lying," Cole said, though his tone came out as a whine rather than rage.

"Lying," Rafe repeated. "She threatened to go to your new girlfriend, didn't she?"

"She said a lot of things," Cole said. "She's the one who was angry. She wasn't acting like herself that night. She was ... even all her friends were worried. She was throwing herself at every guy there."

"And you didn't like that, did you?" Rafe asked.

"No," Cole snapped. "I didn't like it. I told you. It wasn't like her. She'd been drinking. I was worried she was going to ..."

He stopped himself.

"Going to what?" Rafe asked, striding closer to the witness box. "She was going to what, Cole?"

"I was worried she was going to get herself in trouble. Going to get hurt! And it looks like that's exactly what happened!"

Rafe's lips curled into the beginnings of a smirk. He caught himself, straightened his suit, and stepped back behind the lectern.

"So you say Lauren Rice was a liar," Rafe said. "What about Kaylin Dwyer?"

"What about her?" Cole asked.

"She says she saw you talking to Lauren by the side of the road closer to one a.m. Is she lying too?"

"I don't know," Cole said. "I just know it wasn't me."

"Wasn't you," Rafe said. "You've known Kaylin since elementary school too, haven't you?"

"Yes," he said.

"And you saw Kaylin at the same party on August 31st, didn't you?"

241

"Honestly, I don't remember if I saw her. I didn't talk to her that night," he answered.

"But she has to be lying about you, right?" Rafe asked.

"I don't know if she's lying. I don't know what she saw. I only know it wasn't me," he said.

"And if Lauren Rice said she was pregnant by you, she was lying too?" he asked.

"Yes," Cole said.

"They're all liars, aren't they?" Rafe asked. "Even your mom? All these women around you lie, don't they?"

"Yes!" Cole snapped.

I rose to my feet.

Rafe straightened his back. "Let's talk about your parents. You claim they had to get married because your mother was pregnant with you, don't you?"

"That's what they told me, yes," Cole answered.

"And he got angry with her over it. Held it over her head for as long as you can remember, isn't that right?"

"Yes," Cole said.

"How many times did you hear that?" Rafe asked.

"What do you mean?"

"How many times, if you can guess, how many times did you hear your mother's unplanned pregnancy get thrown in your father's face over the years?"

Cole's face contorted. "I don't know. I didn't keep count."

"Too many, right?" Rafe asked.

"It was constant," Cole said.

"The theme of your life, right?" Rafe asked.

"Yes," Cole said, his voice barely above a whisper.

"He resented her for it, didn't he?" Rafe asked.

"Yes."

"Lashed out in anger. In violence, didn't he?"

"Yes. All the time."

Rafe walked a dangerous line. So did I. If I objected to relevance, I undercut my own alternate theory of the case. At the same time, Rafe's strategy was brilliant. Show the jury that Cole had been groomed to use violence against women.

"And maybe she lied," Rafe said. "He said that sometimes, didn't he?"

"Objection," I said. "Calls for hearsay."

"Your Honor," Rafe said. "My question elicits the defendant's state of mind, not the truth of the matter asserted."

"Mr. Johnson, if you're asking this witness about something his father said, I'm inclined to agree with Ms. Leary. Rephrase."

"You said if Lauren said she was pregnant with your baby, she'd be lying, right?" Rafe asked.

"Asked and answered," I said. "And it's been conclusively established as a scientific fact that the victim was not pregnant at the time of her death."

"It doesn't matter," Rafe said. "What matters is she led the defendant to believe she was."

"He's right on that," the judge said. "But Ms. Leary is right that this is ground you've already covered."

"But you were raised to believe your very existence had ruined your father's life, weren't you?" Rafe asked.

"Yes," Cole said.

"And if Lauren was pregnant with your child, that would have ruined your life, wouldn't it?"

"Except she wasn't!" Cole said. "She wasn't pregnant. And even if I didn't know that, I knew it wasn't mine."

"But she could have jammed you up, anyway? Your girlfriend would have found out. It's something you would have had to deal with one way or another."

"Yes!" Cole said.

"So you were angry with her?"

"I was frustrated," he said.

"And she wouldn't stop, would she?" Rafe asked.

"No."

"She kept coming at you. No matter what you said or what you did, Lauren just wouldn't take a hint, would she?"

"No!" Cole shrieked. "I tried to be nice. I tried. I swear I tried!"

Rafe took another step back. He was good. He stopped just before asking the follow-up question, the one he'd just cemented in the jury's mind. Cole tried to be nice, and it didn't work. So did he then resort to the only thing he'd seen play out over and over again within his own home?

"I've got nothing else," Rafe declared.

"Ms. Leary?"

I was still on my feet.

"Mr. Mathison," I said. "Did you strike Lauren Rice that night?"

"No."

"Did you kill her?"

Cole closed his eyes. A shudder went through him. Slowly, he opened his eyes and faced the jury.

"No," he said. "I didn't kill Lauren Rice."

A moment later, he stepped off the witness stand. The jury sat motionless, expressionless. And I had absolutely no clue what they were thinking.

Chapter 30

"It went well," Jeanie said. "I'm telling you it went well."

Nine o'clock at night after the first day of presenting my defense, I sat in the conference room wearing sweatpants, and a clean tee shirt. No point going home tonight, or likely any night this week.

"It's not enough," I said. "I'm telling you. It's not enough. Rafe gave that jury just as much reason to doubt Cole as I gave them to believe him. If I don't find and present a plausible answer to how that underwear got on that tree with Cole's DNA on it, none of this matters."

"You already have," Jeanie said. "It's Lewis. It had to be Lewis."

"I think I've proved she was sloppy," I said. "That's all. And it's not enough. Not by a long shot."

"She's green," Jeanie said. "She's the first woman detective Delphi P.D. has ever put in violent crimes. It's her first solo case. She's trying to prove herself. It all tracks, Cass."

We had the evidence photos and a copy of Lewis's case file spread out in front of us on the table. I'd sent Tori and Miranda home hours ago. I tried to send Jeanie home, but she wasn't having it. She also kept a change of clothes and a toothbrush in her office. At seventy-two, this stuff still jazzed her as much as it did me.

"What are you looking for?" Jeanie said, standing over my shoulder.

"Well, it would have been great if those underwear were just lying here on top of everything else," I said.

The crime scene unit had diligently photographed the contents of Lauren Rice's drawers, closet, and laundry hamper as they were found the morning after she disappeared. My job would have been easy, the case would have been closed had I found a shot of the underwear found later in the brush. But no such luck.

"This doesn't mean anything," Jeanie said. "Like you said. Lewis didn't catalog any of this. She just had these photos taken. You can see the stuff lying on top. You can't see the layers underneath. She didn't count how many pairs of socks or underwear or anything else. At best, this is neutral evidence. You just need reasonable doubt, Cass. I think you're almost there. Get the dad's cell phone data in. You can put him near the scene of where Lauren's body was found ... before it was found. That's the clincher. And Lewis never, ever followed up on that. That's a fact. It's not that hard of a stretch to go from shoddy work to downright evidence tampering."

Gritting my teeth, I had to nod. It just wasn't clean enough for my liking. But Jeanie was right. Sometimes it was all we could do.

"So," she said. "How's Eric handling all of this?"

"Eric? We ... uh ... we've kind of gone to our neutral corners until this trial is over. I can't say he's too thrilled with me for going after Megan."

"Come on." Jeanie waved a hand. "I know him. I think

behind the scenes he's just as pissed at Lewis as anyone. I think we both know damn well Detective Wray would never have signed off on this case as is."

"Maybe," I said. "But it doesn't make me feel any better. I don't relish ruining that woman's career."

"Sure," Jeanie said. "But Eric would have cataloged the damn underwear."

"Yeah," I sighed. "He would have."

I jumped as someone started pounding on the back door downstairs.

"The hell?" Jeanie said. She went to the window and looked down at the parking lot. When she turned, her smile melted into a frown.

"What now?" I said.

"I think it's Emma," Jeanie said. "Looks like she's alone."

"Terrific," I said. "So she's AWOL from Joe. I sent him to the house to pick up the dogs for me."

"We could pretend we're not here?" Jeanie wiggled a brow. "Hide under the table?"

"Nice try," I said. "What are you, fifteen?"

I moved past her and headed down the steps. Emma kept pounding so loud the walls shook. I unlocked the deadbolt and swung the door open.

"What are ..." I started.

She was red-faced, crying, her skin all blotchy from hives. This was full-on panic-attack mode.

"Emma," I said, opening my arms to her as well as my door. "Get in here. It's freezing out."

Her jacket was soaked with melting snow. I helped her peel it off and led her into Jeanie's office downstairs. I couldn't have her upstairs where we'd laid out all the evidence and case strategy notes.

I flicked the switch to start up Jeanie's gas fireplace and

took Emma to the closest couch. I grabbed a tissue from Jeanie's desk and held it over Emma's nose.

"Blow," I said. "That's an order."

She did. I wiped her nose and cheeks like I'd done when she was little. I threw the tissue away and sat down beside her. By then, Jeanie had also entered the room. She took the other side of the couch and wrapped her arms around my niece.

"Okay," I said. "So what's this all about? Did you get into a fight with your dad?"

Emma shook her head. "Not anything we haven't been having for months. Aunt Cass, I'm worried about Cole. You have to win this case. You just have to."

Jeanie and I looked at one another over Emma's head. I left her side and took the chair opposite her so I could really look in her eyes.

"Emma," I said. "Your dad told me you and Cole broke up."

"He broke up with me," she said. "It wasn't my choice. He thinks he's protecting me. Doing what's best for me. I am so sick of people making those kinds of decisions for me. He didn't even ask me what I wanted."

"Sure," I said. "Honey, I'm so sorry you're caught up in this."

Emma's eyes widened. "You have to put me on the witness stand, Aunt Cass. You just have to. I can tell them. Cole would never do anything to Lauren. I know him. I know him better than anyone. I can help. I know I can."

The next sound that came out of Emma tore straight through me. A shriek, not a sob. She pulled at the collar of her sweater as if the fabric itself was too much pain to bear.

"Emma," I said, going to her. I knelt in front of my niece and put my hand lightly on her knee. "Honey."

"Don't tell me I'm hysterical," she said over a hiccup.

"Don't tell me I'm not thinking straight. Aunt Cass, I know Cole. He's told me things. Confided in me. He didn't kill Lauren. He just didn't."

"Okay," I said. "And you know I believe you. I never would have let myself get involved in any of this if I didn't."

"It was his dad!" she yelled. "You have to make sure that jury understands what happened to him."

"I'm trying," I said.

"He's evil," she said. "Pure evil. And he's jealous of Cole. It's sick. I told you. Looking back, I really think Rudy Mathison could have hurt me too if he'd had the chance. You have to let me say that on the witness stand. Let me help him. He needs me. I'll do anything for him."

"Oh honey," Jeanie said. "That's the problem."

But Emma was beyond reason in that moment. We both gave her a minute to try to collect herself. Jeanie got a fresh bottled water out of the small cube fridge she kept in the corner of her office. Mercifully, Emma took it from her and drank. It helped.

"Emma," I said. "I know this is hard to understand, maybe. But you have to let me do my job and put on the best defense I can for Cole. That's what I'm doing."

"I know," she said. "I'm sorry. I'm not trying to accuse you of anything. It's just ... This is killing Cole. I see it. I know it. Every single day, little by little. If he loses ... if they try to put him in prison, he won't go."

"Let's just take this thing one step at a time," I said. "Are you still talking to Cole? Your dad said ..."

"No," she said. "Not since the trial started. Not really. He won't answer my calls. I've tried to go over to his house, but he won't come to the door. I told you, he thinks he's protecting me."

"Emma," I said. "Have you thought maybe that Cole is trying to protect himself?"

She got quiet for a second. "He's given up," she said softly. "Hasn't he?"

"I didn't say that," I said. "But his main focus has got to be on this trial. Then what comes next after that. I know you're hurting. This is a lot. It's too much, really. But I think Cole's right. I think you need to give him some space for a while."

"But it's a lie," she said. "You know that, right? That detective. I don't know. I just know that evidence was planted. I think I can prove it. So you have to put me on the stand."

I felt the blood rush from my head and go straight down to my shoes. I took a steadying breath, rose from my kneeling position and sat back in the chair across from her.

"What do you mean you can prove it?" I asked.

Emma's face contorted, as if the words she meant to speak caused her physical pain. She blushed. "Aunt Cass, this is hard. And embarrassing, but you have to know. I'm not afraid to get on that stand and say it if it'll help Cole. His life is worth it to me."

"Say what, Emma?" Jeanie said.

"Cole doesn't ... what I mean to say is ... when we ... look, there's another reason Cole knew Lauren was lying about the pregnancy. Or at least he knew for sure it wasn't his."

"Okay," I said slowly.

"He's careful. All the stuff he said about his dad is true. He grew up being blamed for existing. He learned that lesson well. Cole always wears a condom when we ... always."

"I see," I said.

"And I'll get up there and say that. And all the fears he had about his dad trying to hurt me. It's why we stopped hanging out at his house whenever his dad was home. He was creepy, Aunt Cass. Really creepy. It's like I told you. The way he'd look at me. I just thought he was doing it to get a rise out of Cole. He succeeded most of the time. It's just ... with the way he acted around me, I could see him doing the same to Lauren if he thought Cole was still into her. Or if he knew she was trying to say Cole got her pregnant. I can tell the jury all of that. You have to let me."

I wanted to be gentle with her.

"Have you said this stuff to your dad?" I asked. "I mean, about you and Cole being intimate."

Emma bit her lip. "I tried. I think he'd rather just think I was ten years old and only romantically interested in my Ken doll."

This got a smile out of me. "I know the feeling. Look. I'll take everything you said to heart."

"Cole won't even listen to me," she said. "Like he won't hear of it. He's so concerned with protecting me, it doesn't even occur to him that I might be able to help protect him. But this could help, right? If I said that to the jury. If I made them understand ... that would help Cole, wouldn't it?"

I folded my hands in my lap. "Emma, it's complicated. For one thing, anything you've heard Rudy Mathison say ... well, the judge would never let that in. It's hearsay. Your impressions of looks he might have given you, I doubt that could come in either."

"It wouldn't, honey," Jeanie said. "Like it or not, your story would be viewed as self-serving. You said it yourself. You're in love with Cole. You might want to help him, but there's an equal chance you might hurt his case without meaning to."

Slow tears fell down her cheeks.

"I'm sorry," I said. "Part of my job when deciding what witnesses to call is a risk benefit analysis. I'm afraid the risk of harm in calling you would likely outweigh any benefit. And you weren't there that night. You can't corroborate Cole's story."

There was more to it. Much more. Just a few short months ago, I'd heard my niece offer to lie to provide Cole with an alibi. Just a few seconds ago, she said she'd do anything to help him.

She wiped her tears. "I just wanted you to know," she said.

"I do," I said. "I really do. And I'm so sorry you're caught in the middle of this. It's not fair. And I know you feel hopeless and helpless."

"I trust you," she finally said. "I do. If you say you know what's best, I believe you."

She moved off the couch and into my arms. She was calmer now. Her cheeks started to dry.

"Just go home, Emma," I said. "Stay close to your dad. Let him be a dad. He's a good one. Even if he drives you nuts."

"I know," she sniffled.

She let me walk her to the back door. I watched from the window as she climbed into her car and drove away.

I went back into Jeanie's office. She'd poured herself a drink. A shot of vodka over ice and some Sprite. I waved her forward when she offered me one.

We clinked glasses and drank.

"Oh boy," she said. "You think she took that to heart?"

"I hope so," I said.

"You can't put her on the stand. You just can't."

"I know," I said.

"Rafe Johnson would rip her to shreds on cross. She wouldn't know what hit her. He'd twist her own words against her. That bit about doing anything at all to save him. Ooh boy. She'd probably give Rafe the rope he needs to hang Cole for good and not even realize it."

"I know that too," I said as I finished my drink. When Jeanie raised a brow, I gestured for her to pour me another one.

As I downed the second and my head began to swim, I couldn't help feeling the noose tightening around my own neck as well.

Chapter 31

I'D PASSED by this spot on Lumley Road probably a thousand times in my life. Farm country, mostly, Delphi natives knew you could get to U.S. 23 from it without having to go through town. I don't know what brought me out here that evening. I don't know that I believe in ghosts. Spirits, definitely. The ones that stay with you after your loved ones die.

Lauren Rice wasn't my loved one. I didn't even know her. But that evening, I prayed her spirit might find me.

Lauren's friends had set up a makeshift shrine to her. A chicken wire cross with ribbons and plastic flowers stuck through it. After the snow we'd had, it was bent nearly parallel to the ground. I leaned down and straightened it. The earth was wet, soaked from melting snow. It would freeze up again overnight making this stretch of road treacherous at best. Lauren's wasn't the first shrine to a dead teen ever to have been erected here. My senior year, Ellie Vaughn took a sharp corner too fast in the same kind of ice and flipped her Taurus. She too had a scholarship she never got to use.

"Talk to me, Lauren," I whispered into the night. "Who did this? Who came out here?"

Rising, I used my phone's flashlight to illuminate the nearby path into the woods. I was looking for something, anything.

It was just past dinner time. Joe said he'd be at my place with a pizza in about an hour. I made him promise not to bring up Emma or Cole's trial. We'd see if he could honor it over the pepperoni.

My boots sank into the soft earth as I found the trail. These woods stretched all the way to Shamrock Park on the eastern edge. Beyond that, you could get to the high school track. The cross-country team practiced out here and ran races in the fall. I'd tried that one year and hated it. After that, I swore I'd only run if someone was chasing me.

I stuffed my hands in my pockets and tried to figure out which bush had concealed Lauren Rice's underwear. There were so many, most weighed down under the heavy burden of melting snow.

I turned. You could see the road and the ditch from here. The scene was familiar. I'd viewed it a thousand times in crime scene photos.

"Where are you?" I whispered again. I didn't know what I expected to find.

Ahead of me on the trail, a dog barked. I stiffened as he came into view. A giant brown Great Dane with one ear cocked sideways, the other flat against his head.

"Malfoy!" his owner shouted.

I put my hands to my sides, hoping not to spook him into taking a chunk out of me. Though I'd never met a Dane who wasn't a lover.

"Sorry," his owner yelled as she ran down the trail toward me.

I knew her. Tracy Tenley. We went to high school

together. She was Tracy Muldoon now, if I remembered from her Facebook profile.

"Hey! Cass!" She smiled. She got a hold of Malfoy's collar. He slathered her free hand with kisses.

"Sorry about that," Tracy said. "Malfie's got his nose on a squirrel."

"No problem," I said. "We were just getting to know each other." I stuck my hand out, palm downward. Malfoy sniffed me and kissed me with as much gusto as he had Tracy.

"Surprised to see you out here," she said. "You looking for another clue?"

I smiled. "Something like that. So I guess you know how my life's been going."

"Uh, yeah," she said. "We're pulling for you. Awful stuff. I knew both those kids. Well, more their parents, anyway. Gil's a client of mine. I sold the house he used to live in with Julie. Found him the smaller one he lives in now. So sad. All the way around."

"It really is," I said.

"Well," Tracy said. "I just can't believe Cole Mathison could do something like that. I'm glad you're representing him. That tells me all I need to know."

"Thanks," I said. "And you know I can't really talk about the case."

She waved a hand. "Oh, I know. No worries."

I looked back up the trail. "Tracy," I said. "How often do you walk Malfoy this way?"

"Lots," she said. "About three times a week."

I debated what I could say to her. Most of what I wanted to know had been reported in the local news, anyway.

"Tracy," I said. "You know Lauren was found near here."

"Sure," she said. "I was part of the search party. My sisters too."

"And you know they found ... um ... evidence later. Right about where we're standing."

She cocked her head to the side.

"They did?" she asked. "I knew they found her underwear somewhere out here. But right here?"

"Tracy, three times a week," I said. "Down this trail. Every week? Since before Lauren's disappearance."

"Every week for about three years. Since Malfoy came into my life," she said.

"Did you see anything out of the ordinary? At any point from when Lauren went missing to, well, now?"

She clipped Malfoy's leash back on his collar. "No. Although I'm not sure what you're getting at."

"Has anyone ever talked to you about this?" I asked.

"You mean the police? No."

"Do you know anybody else who routinely walks along this trail?" I asked.

"Lots of people do," she said, her breath misting from the cold. "But you know that. The high school track team, for one."

"Right," I said. "So let me just cut to it. You never saw anything amiss out here. Nothing hanging off any of these branches?"

"What, like a noose?" she asked.

"No," I said. "Like clothing. Like ... that underwear."

Tracy looked up and down the trail. "No. There's litter like you wouldn't believe. Plastic bags. Cigarettes. Water bottles. But Cass, I didn't see anything out of the ordinary. If you know what I mean."

I did. And it was weak. I knew that. But it bothered me that Detective Lewis never questioned Tracy or the scores of other people who frequented this trail. It wasn't dispositive proof she'd planted the evidence. But at least it was another way to show she hadn't been diligent. It could backfire, though. The more people traipsed through here, it widened the pool of suspects who might have planted the evidence.

"Tracy," I said. "If I called you as a witness in this trial, do you think you could explain that?"

"What," she said. "That I didn't see anything? Sure. Though I don't see how that could help."

"It might not," I said. "But it might. You mind if I keep your number handy?"

Tracy shrugged. She reached into her fanny pack and pulled out a business card. Savvy. A real estate agent is always working.

"Thanks," I said. I scratched Malfoy behind the ears. He licked my arm, then started to bark as a squirrel darted down one of the trees.

"Here we go." Tracy laughed. Malfoy nearly pulled her arm out of its socket. I waved goodbye.

It was thin. So very thin. But it was something.

Chapter 32

Joe's wasn't the only car in my driveway as I pulled up. Eric's was there too. I could see a third set of tire tracks, so I knew the pizza guy had already come. Smiling, I wondered if those two knuckleheads would save some for me.

I pulled my Jeep into the pole barn. Joe was building a table for me in the garage. It had better light and heat this time of year. The wind picked up, and I pulled my coat around me as I headed up the walk.

I heard deep laughter coming from the kitchen as I went in through the mudroom. It warmed my heart. Not long ago, Eric and Joe didn't get along. They'd drawn old battle lines. Eric was a westsider. The Learys had always been pure eastside trash, though Eric had never once treated any of us that way, even as kids. He was also a cop. My father had bred mistrust of them into both my brothers. Now, though, they bonded over beers at my kitchen island. I was about to crash their party when my ears perked up.

"She tell you where her head's at with this judicial appointment?" Eric asked my brother.

I froze, holding my breath. It was sneaky of me to

eavesdrop. Probably. I flattened my back against the wall, hiding in the shadow of the doorway.

"Won't give me much of a straight answer," Joe answered.

"How do you feel about it?" Eric asked.

I saw my brother raise a brow. He went to my fridge and pulled another beer out. Gesturing to Eric, he got a second one for him.

"I think it'd probably be good for her on paper. But I don't know. I'm just not sure Cass is built for that kind of work. She likes her lost causes."

Eric laughed and twisted off his beer cap. "Yeah. She sure as hell does."

"Steady money though," Joe said. "Government benefits. The Learys have never, as a rule, sucked from the public teat. That's more your style."

Eric laughed at the dig. "It's a good teat. Most of the time."

"Yeah," Joe agreed. "So what's she said to you about it?"

Eric put his beer down. "She's been cagey. I don't know if she even knows what she wants."

I sensed a tinge of frustration in his tone and knew he was talking about more than just my career. I felt equal parts defensive ... and lousy.

"Oh man," Joe said, picking up on the same thing I did. "You're that far gone, huh?"

I started to sweat.

I watched Eric run a hard hand through his hair. At that moment, I wasn't sure what I wanted him to say. My heart fluttered as I waited.

"I'd say I'm not messing around," Eric said. "And I think the district court seat would solve a lot of things for her and make her life easier. I'm just getting sick of worrying about her all the time."

Joe clinked his beer bottle with Eric's in a toast. "Welcome to the club," he said. "But as a founding member, I can give you some advice."

I crossed my arms in front of me, feeling fire race up my spine.

"The minute my sister senses fear, she'll eat you alive. The more you try to get her to do something she doesn't want to do, the harder it is to deal with her. Trouble is, she's smarter than the rest of us."

Eric laughed. "Too smart for her own good most of the time."

"You're not wrong," Joe said. "You tell her how you feel yet?"

"I've tried," Eric said. "It's kind of complicated. There's the Wendy issue."

"I see that," Joe said. "You got plans on how to deal with that?"

Eric set his beer bottle down. "Are you asking me what my intentions are with your sister?"

Joe leaned forward, resting his arms on the counter. "Sure as hell am."

"You know her better than anyone," Eric said. "So you tell me, how far gone is she?"

Joe laughed him off. "No. I don't think so. I'm not walking into that fire pit. You ask her yourself."

"I've tried," Eric said. "And I've tried to tell her how good a judgeship would be for her."

My brother was still smiling. "Oh man. Did you actually try to tell my sister you know what's good for her? She eat your face off?"

"A little. Let's just say, your sister has a way of crawling inside your argument, busting it up, then using the jagged shards to stab you in the heart."

Joe laughed so hard he snorted beer out of his nose. "Yeah. I guess she does. She's been that way since we were little kids."

Marbury sat at my brother's feet. He picked that moment to come off his obsession with the potential for dropped pepperoni and realize I was standing nearby.

He howled with joy and scampered across the floor. I flung myself backward, then opened and shut the back door as if I'd just come through it.

"Hey, Marby!" I shouted. Madison was far more sedate as she waddled through the kitchen to greet me.

"Did you two save anything for me?" I asked. Joe slid an entire pizza box my way. "Got you your boring pepperoni."

"Great," I said. "I'll leave you two to your manly meat lovers then."

I leaned in and kissed Eric on the cheek, then slid on to the bar stool next to him. He and my brother exchanged a knowing glance. I played blissfully ignorant.

"Where've you been?" Joe asked. "Thought you'd be here like a half an hour ago."

"I needed to take a walk," I said. "Clear my head. Come up with a game plan for tomorrow in court."

Things grew silent then. I knew Joe was trying hard not to talk about the other elephant in the room. Emma. Megan Lewis. All of it. I saw Eric's wheels turn as he struggled to find a way to navigate to a safer topic as well.

As I bit into a slice of greasy pepperoni, I knew what he was thinking. Yes. Life might get far easier if I'd get out of the defense chair and onto the bench. No matter what happened with the Mathison trial, I had big decisions to make for all of us. Soon.

Chapter 33

TRACY TENLEY MULDOON made a decent witness. So did three other dog walkers who made a habit of taking the trail out by Lumley. Their testimony largely followed the script I laid out, using it as a drumbeat.

I pulled the map and crime scene photos detailing the area where Lauren was found in relation to the hiking trail.

"Ms. Muldoon," I asked. "How often do you walk this trail?"

"Three times a week, rain or shine," she said. The other witnesses were less definite. Once a week. Twice a week. But all testified to knowing the trail and using it as a habit.

"At any point during the period of Labor Day to December 5th of last year did you notice anything unusual on that trail?"

"No, ma'am," Tracy answered.

"Not that I recall," another witness, Bob Clemmons answered.

"Just the usual trash," junior high cross country coach Sean Gorman answered. "Once or twice a year, the junior high honor society kids go out there and clean it as part of an Adopt-a-Road service project."

Unfortunately, I couldn't establish that said service project took place within the timeframe I needed.

One by one, my witnesses confirmed that no, they never saw a pair of pink underwear hanging from a bush just off the trail.

And one by one, Rafe Johnson elicited the same information on cross.

"How closely do you look at the bushes on the side of the trail, Mr. Gorman?"

"Well," Gorman answered. "My main focus is on the trail ahead of me. Other runners. You gotta watch for dips in the ground after the rains. Loose branches."

"You're running, aren't you, Mr. Clemmons?" Rafe asked.

"Generally, yes," Bob answered. "That trail leads downhill. It's a little treacherous if you're going fast enough and not watching your footing."

"You say you always have your dog with you, isn't that right, Ms. Muldoon?"

"Yes," she answered.

"Malfoy never stopped to sniff anything hanging off branches, did he?"

"He stops and sniffs all the time," Tracy answered. "I don't recall him stopping at any bush in particular, no."

By the end of the day, I could only hope I'd given the jury something to hang their hats on if they so chose. In two and a half months, on a well-trafficked trail, nobody else had noticed anything hanging off that bush. What I hadn't conclusively proved was that it wasn't there at all.

Tuesday morning, January 16th, I called Roxanne Mathison to the stand. Like Cole, I think she'd lost at least twenty pounds since this whole ordeal started. She'd stopped dyeing her hair. She wore it in a bun, the front of it peppered with gray, the base of it jet black. She had on a navy-blue blazer and white linen pants. Her hand shook as she raised it to take her oath.

"Good morning, Mrs. Mathison," I said. "Will you tell the jury how you're related to Cole Mathison?"

"He's my son," she said, looking down at her shoes. "He's my only son."

"I know this has to be uncomfortable for you," I said. "If you could speak up and talk directly into the microphone."

"Sorry," she said. "Cole is my son."

"Does he live with you still?"

"He does," she said. "We live at 1421 McGrath. He was born in that house."

"Who else lives there with you?"

"My husband Rudy, it's still his legal address," she said.

"How long have you and Rudy been married?" I asked.

"Twenty-one years," she said.

"Mrs. Mathison, I know this is a personal question. But I have to ask. Were you pregnant with Cole when you married Rudy?"

She nodded. "I was. I was just over five months along."

"Thank you. Do you work outside the home?"

"I do now," she said. "I got a job at the Costco in Ann Arbor. I work in the deli department, since just before Christmas."

"But prior to that," I said. "Where did you work?"

"I didn't," she said. "I'd been ... Rudy always said he didn't want a wife of his working. He's old-fashioned that way."

"I see. So has he changed his mind that you're working at Costco now?"

She squirmed a bit. "No. Rudy ... he's not ... he's not providing for the family right now."

"Why is that?" I asked.

"He left his job at Comstock Trucking. He's out of work."

"Mrs. Mathison," I asked. "Are you still in contact with your husband?"

She looked at Cole. She looked at the jury. Blinking widely, she answered. "No. It's been a little while since I talked to Rudy."

"How long?"

"Um ... a while."

"Mrs. Mathison, do you recognize these documents?" I asked to approach the bench.

She leafed through a thirty-page stack of cell phone records registered to her number.

"They look like my cell phone bills," she answered.

I moved to have the documents formally admitted. They'd been self-authenticated by an affidavit from her phone company during pre-trial.

"Mrs. Mathison," I asked. "What is your husband's cell phone number?"

She rattled off the number.

"Do you remember the last time you actually spoke to your husband on the phone?" I asked.

"Not off the top of my head, no," she said. "It's been a while."

"Mrs. Mathison, would it help refresh your recollection if you looked at your cell phone records?"

Biting her lip, she looked down. "I could try," she said.

"Please do," I said.

She ran one finger down the columns, flipping back several pages. Finally, she looked back up.

"It says here I called him on August 30th," she said.

"August 30th of last year? How long was that outgoing call?"

268

She looked back down. "It says five minutes."

"Do you remember that conversation?" I asked.

"I don't ... not specifically. I probably would have called to ask him when he thought he'd be home from his latest route."

"Was your husband living in the home with you on August 30th of last year?" I asked.

"Off and on," she said. "He and Cole weren't getting along very well back then. It's like that with fathers and sons as they grow up."

"Are you aware of an argument your son had with your husband in July of that year?"

"They argued a lot," she answered. "Like I said, it's hard for fathers when sons start to become adults."

"How hard?" I asked.

She blinked.

"How hard, Mrs. Mathison?" I asked again. "Did you ever witness your husband physically abuse your son?"

She withdrew into herself. Part of me wanted to reach out and comfort her. She'd been through so much. I couldn't even begin to understand her pain right now.

"Mrs. Mathison," I said, speaking more softly. "Have you ever witnessed your husband physically abusing your son?"

"Yes," she said, shoulders drawn up.

"How many times?" I asked.

"I don't know."

"More than once?"

"Yes."

"More than ten times?"

"Yes." She nodded.

"More than a hundred times?" I asked, horrified by the words coming out of my own mouth.

"I don't ... I can't count." She was full-on crying now.

"Mrs. Mathison," I said. "What was the nature of that physical abuse?"

"His fists," she said. "His ... mostly his fists."

"Mostly?" I asked.

"I don't know!" she shrieked. "When he tried to ... I would try to stop him. I tried to stop him. I'd tell Cole to go run through the woods. Behind our house. Get out of sight. Go find a place to hide. If he'd just get out of Rudy's sight, for a little while."

"What happened when Cole got out of Rudy's sight?" I asked.

She leaned far to the right of her chair, as if she feared another blow might come at her. I took a step back.

"Mrs. Mathison," I said. "What happened when Cole would run out?"

She squeezed her eyes shut. I knew she could see the scene play out behind them. I hated this. Every second of it.

"It was okay if he would just come after me," she said. "Then I knew Cole was okay. He would hide. He'd be safe."

I took a breath. Going as slowly as I could to give her a moment, I walked back behind the lectern.

"Mrs. Mathison," I asked. "Did you witness the fight between your husband and your son in July of last year?"

She nodded. "Cole had had enough. When I told him to run out, he wouldn't. He stayed. He ... he made Rudy listen. Got him to pack his bags. Then Rudy left. I didn't hear from him for a few weeks or so after that."

"But you did hear from him again?" I asked.

"Yes," she said. "Maybe the middle of August. He was so sorry. He was getting help, I think. He was kind. Calm."

"Did you take him back?" I asked.

"Yes," she said. "But I made him promise not to be around when Cole was. It wasn't so hard. Rudy would be gone for days and weeks at a time on the road. He'd come home sometime when Cole was at work at the lumberyard. And Rudy would leave again before Cole came back. Also ... Cole was at his girlfriend's house a lot of the time. It was easy for them to avoid each other."

"Okay," I said. "Mrs. Mathison, I'd like you to tell me about the night of August 31st. Do you remember it?"

"Yes," she said. "Rudy came home. He was going to stay the night. Cole had to work the next day. And he was going to go to a party."

"He told you that?" I asked.

"He did." She sniffled. "I thought it was a good idea. Cole had been working so many hours. I thought it would be good for him to get away from that computer game and go see some of his friends. He was going to work by eight. I thought Rudy would be back and in bed before Cole ever saw him."

"I see," I said. "When did Cole leave?"

"I'm not sure," she said. "I went down to check on him before I went to bed. He said he was getting ready to go. He was putting a shirt on and I helped him find his shoes. He looked so handsome. I told him that. I told him to have a good time. Then I went to bed."

"Mrs. Mathison," I said. "When did your husband come home?"

She bunched her shoulders again as if she were waiting for yet another blow. "I don't know. I went to bed."

"Did you speak to Rudy after nine p.m. the night of August 31st?" I asked.

"I went to sleep," she said. "I just went to sleep. When I woke up, I think it was around seven thirty. Cole was home. He was getting ready for work."

"Where was Rudy?" I asked.

"I don't know," she answered.

"Rudy's truck was already in the garage that morning, wasn't it?" I asked.

She was lying. Why the hell was she lying?

"I don't ... I'm not sure."

"In fact," I said. "It's still parked there now, isn't it?"

"It's there, yes," she said.

"And where is your husband?" I asked.

"I don't know," she said.

"You're aware Comstock Trucking terminated his employment in mid-September, aren't you?"

"Yes," she said.

"Do you know why?"

"I don't ... that's Rudy's business."

"He stopped showing up for work, didn't he?"

"Objection!" Rafe called out. "Your Honor, counsel is leading the witness."

"May I?" I said, gesturing to the judge's bench.

"Let's have a sidebar," she said.

I strode up to the bench with Rafe at my heels.

"Your Honor, I'd like to treat this witness as hostile for the remainder of her direct exam," I said. "She's become evasive. By her own admission, she hasn't seen or spoken to her husband since the night Lauren Rice disappeared. She's covering for him and everyone here knows it."

"She's the defendant's mother," Rafe said. "That's her only son out there, and defense counsel has called her. I didn't."

"Be that as it may," Judge Niedermayer said. "I agree with Ms. Leary. The witness is evading questions where it concerns her husband. I'm going to grant her request. You may proceed."

My heart pounding, I marched back to the lectern.

"Mrs. Mathison," I said. "When was the last time you spoke to your husband?"

"I don't recall," she said.

"Isn't it true you haven't had any contact with him whatsoever since August 31st of last year?"

"I ... I ... he travels a lot for his job."

"But he lost his job," I said. I reached for another stack of records.

"Comstock Trucking reported his last check in to dispatch on August 30th," I said. "Were you aware of that?"

"If that's what they say," she said. "You can ask them."

"Are you concerned about your husband's whereabouts?" I asked.

"What? I don't. I don't know."

"Did you ever contact the police to report him missing?" I asked.

"No."

"Mrs. Mathison, do you and Mr. Mathison share a bank account?"

"Yes," she said.

"Checking or savings?"

"Both," she answered.

I grabbed my copy of her bank records and showed them to her.

"Can you tell me what those are, Mrs. Mathison?"

"It's ... these are from our savings account. We have one at Delphi Bank and Trust."

I moved for their admission. Rafe objected.

"Your Honor," he said. "For about the thousandth time, Rudy Mathison's whereabouts aren't at issue."

"They should be!" I shouted. "Your Honor, Detective Lewis testified that she did not pursue any other leads after arresting Cole Mathison. Her bias, the thoroughness of her detective work or lack thereof is very relevant."

"I'll allow it," the judge said.

"Mrs. Mathison," I said. "Can you read the entry dated September 2nd for that savings account?"

She cleared her throat. It didn't help. When she answered, her voice cracked. "There's a withdrawal."

"In what amount?"

"Eleven thousand dollars," she said.

"At what time?" I asked.

"9:13," she said.

"And what was the balance in that account after that withdrawal?" I asked.

"It says ... it's eight dollars and fifteen cents."

"Your husband made that withdrawal, didn't he?" I asked.

"He ... I guess so."

"Did you make it?" I asked.

"I don't ..." She looked helplessly at Cole. He couldn't meet her eyes.

"No," she said.

"Mrs. Mathison," I said. "You and your husband share the same cell phone plan, don't you?"

"Yes," she said. "We have two lines. Mine and his. Yes. Rudy set it up that way."

"So those records in front of you show the calls into Rudy's line too, don't they?"

"Yes," she said.

"Can you tell me the last outgoing call from Rudy Mathison's phone?"

She looked back at the records. "Um ... August 31st. There's an outgoing call at ten thirty."

"And who did he call?"

"He ... it's my number."

"It's a missed call?" I asked.

"I didn't answer," she said. "I was probably already asleep. Just like I told you."

"If your son came home by midnight, Rudy would have been there, wouldn't he?" I asked.

"Objection," Rafe said. "Calls for speculation. The witness just stated she was asleep."

"Sustained," the judge said.

"There was an argument that night, wasn't there?" I asked.

"I don't ... I didn't hear anything. I was asleep," she said.

"Was it your habit to sleep through arguments your son and husband had?" I asked.

"I didn't hear anything," she said. "I was asleep."

Her cadence was odd, like a mantra, like she was praying the Rosary. Every time she uttered the phrase, she didn't change tone.

"The argument your son and husband had in July was violent, wasn't it?" I asked.

"Yes," she answered.

"Your son ordered your husband out of the house, didn't he?" I asked.

"Yes," she said.

"And for the six weeks after that, you let him back in, didn't you?"

"He came back when Cole wasn't home," she said.

"That was by your design, wasn't it?" I asked. "Your way of trying to appease them both."

She didn't answer.

"Were you worried what would happen if Rudy and Cole were ever in the same room together again?" I asked.

"It's hard with fathers and sons," she cried.

"On the night of August 31st, you knew Rudy was coming home, didn't you?"

"Yes," she said.

"And you knew Cole was going out. You told Rudy the coast was clear, didn't you?" I asked.

No answer.

"You told Rudy it was a good time to come home because Cole would be gone, didn't you?"

"He was going to go to bed," she said.

"So you arranged it," I said. "You tried to make sure Rudy and Cole wouldn't run into each other. Cole was going to that party. You told Rudy to park his truck in the garage, didn't you?"

"I don't remember. I went to sleep."

There was her mantra again. I heard it. I knew it. The jury knew it. She'd been coached. God. She was protecting her husband to the detriment of her son.

"And you want us to believe that you weren't at all concerned about keeping Rudy and Cole from running into each other? That you went to sleep knowing that was a distinct possibility and what might happen?"

"I don't remember," she said. "I just went to sleep."

She shut down.

"I have no further questions," I said.

Rafe stepped up beside me. His ears were red.

"Mrs. Mathison," he said. "You never saw your husband that night, did you?"

"I went to sleep. I didn't wake up until after seven."

"So from roughly nine p.m. until seven a.m. the next morning, you have no idea who came and went, do you?"

"I went to sleep," she said again.

Tori leaned over with a note. "She's protecting him. Cass,

I think she knows Rudy's guilty. Why the hell is she protecting him?"

I didn't know. It seemed impossible. But then, as Rafe recommitted Roxanne Mathison to her story, it was as if a bell clanged and echoed through my head.

She's protecting Rudy. She knows he's guilty. She'll throw her own son to the wolves instead. I grabbed my trial notebook and quickly thumbed backward through my witness notes.

It felt like every organ in my body dropped straight down to the floor. How had I missed it for this long? All at once, I knew exactly what I had to do.

Chapter 34

I BARELY PAID attention to Rafe's cross-examination. He underscored almost everything I touched on in direct. Cole knew violence against women. Roxanne could not confirm her own son's alibi. He spent less than an hour doing it, and by the time he finished, I rocketed out of my chair and went back to the lectern.

What I was about to do was crazy. I knew it. I knew it flew in the face of every single thing I'd been taught about trial practice. Except, I knew I had the answer right in front of me, even if I could scarcely believe it.

"Mrs. Mathison," I said. "You've known the Rice family a very long time, haven't you?"

"Yes," she said, her face falling with relief. "Yes. Julie was a good friend of mine from way back. I feel so awful for him about all of this."

"Of course," I said. "You went to Lauren's funeral too, right?"

"Why, yes," she said. "Since Julie died, there's been a group of women from the church who have looked in on Gil from time to time. I'm afraid we kind of lost touch over the past few years. But I was so happy when Cole started dating Lauren. It was good to see she was doing so well."

"Yes," I said. "Mr. Rice testified about the kindnesses bestowed upon him from the church bereavement group. What sorts of things were you involved in?"

"Objection," Rafe said. "We've gone far afield of anything relevant to the issues in this case and counsel is reaching beyond the scope of cross at this point."

"Your Honor," I said. "This witness's familiarity with the events of August 31st and her relationships with the defendant and victim are both highly relevant and within the scope of cross. If you'll allow me a little leeway, I think you'll both see just how relevant."

"Get there quick, Ms. Leary," Judge Niedermayer said. "The witness and the jury need a break."

"Mrs. Mathison," I said. "I'll repeat. Exactly what kinds of things did the church bereavement group do for Mr. Rice after Lauren died?"

"What they always do," she said. "Cooked a lot of casseroles. Once a week, they'd send someone to look in on Gil. He stopped coming to church."

"And they'd bring the casseroles over to Gil's house, wouldn't they?"

"Once a week," she said. "There was a sign-up sheet."

"You were on that sign-up sheet, weren't you?" I asked. I picked up a piece of paper. It was nothing more than the back page of a subpoena I'd been using to scribble notes on. But no one else knew that.

"I was on the bereavement committee," she said.

"You cooked a casserole for Gil Rice, didn't you? What's your specialty?"

"Um ... I do a broccoli chicken bake."

"Sounds delicious," I said. I might as well have been on the edge of a high dive. One question. One chance. Roxanne's answer would represent my drop onto concrete or the water below.

"And you brought that broccoli chicken casserole to Gil Rice the week of December 5th last year, didn't you?"

"I don't ... I think ... I might have."

"But it was after your son had been arrested for killing his daughter, wasn't it?"

"Y-yes."

"You went to his house. He invited you in, didn't he? In spite of all of that?"

"Gil is ... he ... he's struggling. He doesn't ... we've known each other for a very long time."

"Your kids dated for over a year," I said. "Gil knew Rudy too, didn't he? In fact, he testified how much he worried about you and Cole. He said he kept his door open because he knew coming over to his house with Lauren offered Cole a respite from the chaos at home."

"If he said that," she said. "That sounds like Gil."

"So Gil never blamed you for what happened to Lauren. For what he thinks your son did to her. He let you into his home with your broccoli chicken casserole?"

She fidgeted. I expected her to start repeating that she was asleep again.

"I brought him the casserole," she said.

"You brought him the casserole," I repeated. "He let you into his home."

"Yes," she said.

"He let you into his home the week of December 5th. The church still has a record of the date you signed up for, don't they?" God, I hoped they did.

"I don't, maybe they do," she said.

ROBIN JAMES

"And your son," I said. "Cole's been living with you since he was arrested, hasn't he?"

"Yes," she said.

"And in that time, he's had visitors, hasn't he?"

"Yes."

"And in fact, one of those visitors was his girlfriend, Emma Leary, wasn't it?"

"Yes," she said. "Emma came over some. She doesn't anymore."

"But in that very first week of December of last year, they were still dating, weren't they?"

"Yes," she said. Her face had gone white.

"You were in Lauren Rice's home," I said. "The first week of December."

"Yes," she said.

"And your son had intimate relations with his girlfriend in your home in early December, didn't he?"

"I ... I don't ... I can't ..."

"Objection!" Rafe launched himself forward. He'd figured out where I was going with this.

"Mrs. Mathison," I shouted over his objection. "You took out your son's trash, didn't you?"

"Yes," she cried.

My God. My God. My God.

One member of the jury, a mother, covered her mouth in horror as she connected the dots.

"Your son learned the lessons of his parents well, didn't he?" I said, my voice dropping. Sweat poured down my brow.

"I don't ..."

"He used a condom. And you took out his trash, didn't you?"

Beside me, Cole let out a choked sound. A retch.

"Mama?" he cried, sounding like a little boy. "Oh God."

282

"You went into Lauren Rice's bedroom that day, didn't you?" I said. "You took something. What did you take, Roxanne?"

"No. No. No. No. No," Roxanne murmured. "I went to sleep. I didn't see anything. I tried to do the right thing."

"Your Honor!" Rafe shouted. But there was nothing he could do. There was nothing anyone could do.

Roxanne Mathison let out a shriek. "You don't know. You can't know. What he did. What he'd do. I had to. I had to! Cole. I'm sorry. I'm so sorry! I'm so sorry! It's okay. It'll all be okay."

Except it wouldn't. Not ever again.

Chapter 35

I COULD FEEL the heat coming off of Cole as his mother stepped down from the stand. She'd invoked her Fifth Amendment privilege on every question of Rafe's recross. Cole's eyes had gone blood red. His skin, purple. If he looked at her. If she tried to speak to him, I knew he would break.

I wanted to comfort him. I knew that pain. Betrayal. Abuse by the person who was supposed to protect you from the world. How many times had I intervened when my father hurt Matty or Joe? How many times had I comforted my little sister Vangie when she cried in the night for a mother who could never come to her again?

But there was no time for any of that. Not now. I had teed up the ball. I had to take the next swing.

"Your Honor," I said. "At this time, the defense would like to recall Gil Rice to the stand. I understand he's out in the hallway. Could we have the bailiff show him in?"

Judge Niedermayer gestured to her bailiff at the back of the courtroom. The commotion in the hallway bled into the room as Roxanne exited. I had to get Gil in here before news got to him about what had just happened. There were other ways to get in everything else I needed. And I would. But I had one chance to preserve Gil's testimony while he didn't know what I was after.

He looked bewildered as the bailiff pointed him back to the stand. He'd seen Roxanne leave, of course, but she'd passed him stone-faced. She'd gone back on autopilot.

"Mr. Rice," the judge said. "Let me remind you that you're still under oath from your previous testimony. Do you understand?"

"Yes," he said. He wasn't prepared to take the stand today. Last time, he'd come in a freshly pressed suit, his Sunday best. Today, he wore blue jeans. Two-day-old stubble framed his face.

"Mr. Rice," I said. "I just have a couple of follow-up questions for you. It shouldn't take long."

"Anything," he said.

"You're still a member of the First Presbyterian Church, isn't that right?"

He cocked his head to the side, puzzled. He gave Rafe Johnson a look for guidance. Rafe was still busy scrambling and writing notes to his paralegal.

"I suppose on paper," he said. "I don't go to church much. Lauren tried to get me to after her mom died."

"Isn't it true that members of the church bereavement group have come to your house in the weeks and months since Lauren passed?"

"Yes," he said. "They bring me food. Not so much lately. I asked them not to. I'm only one person. It's too much."

"Mr. Rice," I said. "Isn't it true that Roxanne Mathison came to your house on at least one occasion with the church group?"

"She did," he answered. "She came once."

"I'd like to ask you about that visit," I said. "Do you recall how long she stayed?"

Gil shrugged. "I don't remember specifically."

"But you invited her inside your home," I said.

"I did," he said.

"Did you sit down together?"

"I believe so. For a little while," he said.

"She came alone, didn't she?" I asked.

"Yeah," she did. "I knew she was having a hard time with everything. It was ... I gotta be honest. I was curious about what she'd have to say."

I knew both Rafe and Gil assumed I'd cross that hearsay line and ask what Roxanne said. Only I didn't care one bit.

"Mr. Rice," I said. "You haven't changed Lauren's room since she passed away, have you?"

He looked down at his hands. "No. Not yet."

"You haven't removed any of her clothes, have you?" I said.

"No," he said.

"Did Lauren keep a laundry hamper in her room?"

He looked up. "Why are you asking me this? What difference does that make?"

"Please answer the question, Mr. Rice," I said.

"Yes," he spat. "She had a laundry hamper in her room. And a waste basket. What in God's name is this about?"

"I just have a couple more questions," I said. "When Mrs. Mathison came to your house, were you with her the entire time?"

"What?"

"Did she use your restroom?" I asked.

"What the ... what are you talking about?"

"Did Roxanne Mathison use the restroom during her visit to your house?"

"I don't ... she might have. What kind of sick question is this?"

"She might have," I said. "So, is it fair then to say that you didn't have your eyes on Roxanne Mathison the entire time she was there?"

"What? Jesus Christ, lady. No. I didn't follow Roxanne to the bathroom. Are you going to let this go on?" He directed his last question to Rafe.

"Mr. Rice," I said. "Mrs. Mathison came to your house well after her son's arrest, didn't she?"

"Yes," he said. "She's ... I've known Roxanne forever. I didn't think I blamed her for what happened. I knew Rudy was no good to her."

"Thank you, Mr. Rice," I said. "I have nothing further."

"Mr. Johnson?"

Rafe sprang up. "Mr. Rice," he said. "Did you see Mrs. Mathison take anything from your home?"

"Take anything? No."

"Did you give her access to any other part of the house?" he asked.

Gil rubbed a hand over his jaw. "I said she might have used the bathroom. But no, I don't think she was in any other part of the house."

His voice broke at the end. Color rose in his cheeks. Gil's eyes narrowed with hatred as he looked straight at me. He'd put it together. He knew what I was trying to prove.

"I have nothing further," Rafe said.

"Ms. Leary?"

Taking a breath, I rose. "Mr. Rice," I said. "There's only one bathroom you would have allowed Roxanne or any guest to use in your home, right?"

I knew this. I'd seen the crime scene unit photos cataloging the contents of Lauren's room. Gil lived in a ranch house in the Dalton Woods subdivision. Until she'd moved to the retirement community, Jeanie had lived in the same neighborhood. Her house had the same floor plan. All the ranch houses there did.

"You gotta be kidding me," he said.

"Your guest bathroom," I said. "It's down the hall from your kitchen, correct?"

"Yeah," he said.

"And it's directly across from Lauren's bedroom, isn't it?"

"I'm not doing this," he said. "I'm done. I'm not answering any more questions. You make me sick."

"Mr. Rice," the judge said, her tone kind. "I know this is hard. But I'm going to need you to answer Ms. Leary's question."

"Yes, goddammit!" he shouted. "Yes. The guest bathroom is across from Lauren's bedroom!"

"Thank you," I said. "I have nothing further."

Gil stepped down. He charged out of the courtroom. As the judge caught my gaze, Rafe stood up and gave me a gift. He was the one that ended up asking for a recess.

I needed one thing. I needed to get a copy of the church bereavement committee sign-up sheets. I saw Tori had already made a note about it.

The judge ordered the jury out. Cole had become like a statue beside me. Rafe practically ran out of the room.

"I can't breathe," Cole finally said. "I can't ..."

"Not here," I said. "We need to get back to my office. Just hold it together that long. Tori ..."

"I'm on it," she said. "One of my best friend's mom is on that committee too. I'll get the list. I'll get her or somebody else in here to authenticate it."

I mouthed the words "bless you." Then, I grabbed Cole's arm and started pulling him out of his chair.

Miraculously, the hallway was clear by the time we made it out there. I didn't want to take any chances of running into Roxanne before we made it to my office.

"We'll take the stairs," I said. "We'll head out the side alley."

"She did it," he said. "Ms. Leary ... my own mother? She did it, didn't she?"

"I don't know," I said. "That's the God's honest truth. But ..."

"She got that underwear from Lauren's room?" he said, his face contorting. Only we both knew that was the least of it.

"And she got ..." He covered his mouth like he was going to vomit. It was hard to fathom, even harder to process.

"Yes," I said, putting a hand on his arm. We'd reached the stairwell. "I think it's possible ... no ... probable ... that your mother put your ... DNA on that clothing."

"She went through my trash?" he said. "After I ... with Emma?"

"I know," I said.

"For him?" he shrieked. "To protect him? My father?"

"Let's go," I said. People started coming down the hall. I didn't want anyone to hear Cole talking.

I opened the stairway door and found myself face to face with a keyed-up Gil Rice. He looked just as shocked to see us.

"Let's ... I'm sorry ..." I said. "We'll take the elevator."

"You ..." he hissed. "You think you can use me to get ... to help *him* ... you killed her!"

He launched himself at Cole, pushing me out of the way. He shoved Cole against the wall, driving an elbow under his chin.

"Gil!" I shouted. "Stop!"

Cole's face turned blue. I tried to pull at Gil's arm. He was going to choke him to death. Right in front of me.

"Stop!" I screamed.

The stairway door opened behind me.

"Good Christ!" Eric shouted. He pulled me away and got an arm around Gil.

"I'll kill him!" Gil hissed. "I'll kill you! You killed my baby! You should have killed me!"

"Gil, no!" Eric shouted. He got the leverage to pull Gil off Cole. Cole crumpled to the ground, gasping for air. I went to him, catching him in my lap.

Eric held Gil in a bear hug. Gil snorted. Tears rolled down his cheeks.

"Not like this," Eric said. "Not this way. Lauren wouldn't want this."

"You don't know," Gil said. "You have no idea!"

"I do," Eric said. "I know. But you can't help Lauren, you can't help anyone this way."

"I have nothing left," he sobbed. "Nothing. He has to pay. He has to pay. That bitch ... she's going to get him off. She was my *baby!*"

"Take him out of here," Eric said to me. Cole was just starting to get his legs back under him. I helped him rise.

"You need to die!" Gil said. "It doesn't matter what happens in that courtroom. You hear me? You need to pay."

"Shut up, man," Eric said. "I'm begging you."

Gil had a burst of strength and threw Eric off of him. Eric backed off, holding his hands out, protecting me from Gil if he decided to charge again.

"You don't know!" Gil shouted, pointing a finger at Eric's chest. Then he got quiet. He went still. He squared his shoulders.

"She was my daughter. I was supposed to protect her. Me! I'd do anything for her. Anything. You're not a father. You don't ... You'd do anything for your child. Anything."

He tore at his hair. His skin. With a final, guttural cry, Gil Rice whirled backward and launched himself down the stairs.

I had an arm around Cole. Eric turned to me. "You okay?" he said.

"We're fine," I said.

Eric nodded. "Just ... get him out of here. I'll make sure nobody else gets in your way."

Gil's anguished cries still echoed down the stairwell as I took Cole back out into the hall.

Chapter 36

"She did this to me," Cole said. He sat in a corner chair in my office holding an ice pack to his neck. Deep bruises were already starting to form where Gil Rice had nearly strangled him. He'd said the same five words over and over, unable to even process the fact that Gil had just tried to kill him. His mind stuck only with the simple, horrifying fact that his own mother had apparently tried to frame him for murder.

"You're okay now, kid," Jeanie said. She'd been the one to insist on the ice pack. "You're here. You're safe. You're with people who want what's best for you."

Her words seeped through me. I'd heard her utter almost the same ones to my little brother and sister twenty years ago.

"I knew she'd do anything for him," Cole said. Red-eyed, he looked up at Jeanie. "I just never thought ..."

"I don't think your mother's in her right mind," Jeanie said. "It's hard for you to see this right now. But I think she's a victim too. She's so afraid of what your dad will do ... what he *has* done ..."

"I'm her son," he said, finally letting his tears fall. "Lauren's dad is right. Not about me. But you're supposed to

293

do anything ... everything to protect your kid. Why couldn't she do that for me? She'll only do it for him."

It was going to take a long time for Cole to be able to truly handle all of this. If we got through this trial, I'd do my best to get him into intensive therapy. He may never be able to fully trust anyone again.

"Cole," I said. "It's possible your dad has been in contact with your mother during all of this. In fact, I'd bet on it."

"You think he's been threatening her still?" Cole asked.

"I do," I said. "At least I think it's highly likely."

"Yeah," Cole said, wiping his eyes. "Yeah. My mom ... she's passive. She doesn't stick up for herself. I tried so hard to stick up for her."

"I know," I said. "Believe me, I do."

"This had to have been his idea," he said. "That sick mother-fu... My mom wouldn't have come up with this on her own. She wouldn't have gone into my garbage and ... ugh ... taken that kind of trash from me. Cass, I'm sorry. I let this happen. God. Emma. It's going to come out that it was Emma I was with. You're right. We were still involved in early December. I should have broken up with her sooner. I got her mixed up in all of this. My mom got that ... um ... condom with ..."

"I'm not planning on putting Emma on the stand," I said. "There's no need. Your mother admitted to pretty much all of it. Gil's testimony also helped. Tomorrow morning, I'll be able to prove the exact date your mother went to Gil's house and lifted a pair of Lauren's underwear from the laundry hamper. Then ... this is all over but the closing arguments."

"Rafe should dismiss the charges," Jeanie snapped. I gave her a look. This wasn't a conversation I wanted to have yet in front of Cole. He was far too fragile. The problem was, I didn't quite know what to do with him. Going back home wasn't an option. In the morning, I'd call Dave Carver and see if Cole could stay there for a while.

"Cole," I said. "I think you're going to need to crash on the couch here tonight. I'll have my brother bring something over for you to sleep in and run out and get you a toothbrush."

"I can't go home," he said. "Not ever. I can't ever go back there."

"One step at a time," I said. "Tori's having takeout delivered. Let's just get you some dinner. Like Jeanie said, you're safe here. I've got a few other things I need to take care of. But I'll be back."

Cole nodded. I gestured to Jeanie. She followed me out of my office and downstairs to hers.

"You need to demand Rafe dismiss the charges," she said.

"I've already called him," I said. "He's not gonna budge. Roxanne stopped short of a full admission to planting that underwear with Cole's DNA on it. He's still planning on taking his chances. There's still the problem of Kaylin Dwyer's testimony and the cell phone data."

"He thinks that's enough?" Jeanie said, incredulous.

"Apparently so," I said.

"Christ," she said. "You know Jack LaForge would never ..."

I put a hand up. "I think it's time we fully embrace the fact that we're not dealing with Jack. I can't wallow in things I can't control. What I can control is prepping for my last witness, and closing arguments tomorrow."

Jeanie pressed her fingers to the bridge of her nose. "This is insanity. Pure, sick insanity."

"I know," I said. "But there's still an innocent dead girl at the heart of this. No matter what Roxanne did to Cole, what happened to Lauren was so much worse."

"What Rudy did to Lauren," she snapped. "Why the hell

can't Rafe and Megan Lewis get that through their thick skulls?"

"I know," I said. "But I have no solid proof of that. There are far too many open questions. And Jeanie ... thank you. Cole trusts you. That's going to matter a whole lot in the coming weeks in spite of everything else. Can I count on you to help him through this last bit? Just so I can get through the next twenty-four hours?"

She put her hand on my shoulder. "You don't even have to ask, honey."

The back door opened. Tori came in with fried chicken and two liters of pop. Jeanie sprang into action. She rounded up paper plates and napkins from the kitchen.

"Here," she said, plating two drumsticks and a wing for me. "Do my heart some good and eat at least this much. Then I'll deal with that poor kid up there for you."

"Thank you," I said, though I knew I wouldn't eat. I paused for a moment before asking Jeanie the next question that weighed on my mind.

"Jeanie?" I said. "You of all people know ... Do you think ... Is Cole going to be okay after all of this?"

She leaned against the doorjamb, her expression grave. "Honey, I don't know. I honestly don't know. But we'll do what we can for him. And we'll just have to hope it's enough."

We'll do what we can. Jeanie had done that for me and my brothers and sister our whole lives. It had been enough. I just prayed the same would hold true for Cole Mathison.

Chapter 37

THURSDAY MORNING, the ninth day of Cole Mathison's murder trial. I called one remaining witness, Michelle Proctor. First Presbyterian Church secretary and chairwoman of the Bereavement Committee, Michelle was quiet, thoughtful, and extremely well organized. Once I established for the jury who she was, I asked her one simple question that I hoped would put to rest any doubt about what happened with Roxanne Mathison.

"Mrs. Proctor," I said. "Can you tell me what day Roxanne Mathison volunteered to bring a meal to Gil Rice's home?"

"It was December 5th, a Tuesday," she said.

"Thank you," I said. "I have nothing further."

Rafe tried to unravel Michelle's testimony in the only way he could.

"Mrs. Proctor," he said. "Just because someone signed up to bring a casserole on a certain day, that doesn't mean they actually went out, does it? Isn't it true sometimes committee members drop food off at the church instead?"

"Yes," she said. "But I don't believe Roxanne did."

"Why is that?"

"Because there's a checkbox next to her name on the chart. I'm the one who checked that box. I do that when the volunteer calls to tell me she dropped off the meal for that day."

"But you don't have any idea whether Roxanne actually went inside Gil Rice's home, do you?" he asked.

"Well, no."

"All she was required to do was drop off a casserole," he said.

"Yes," she said. "When you volunteer, you volunteer to bring the meal."

"Thank you," he said. "I have nothing further."

The judge looked at me, anticipating my next words once Michelle Proctor left the stand.

"Your Honor," I said. "The defense rests."

By one o'clock that afternoon, Rafe Johnson stepped to the lectern to deliver his closing argument.

He was stoic. Brief. And effective.

"Ladies and gentlemen," he said. "The defense has been very good at one thing throughout this trial: misdirection. But you're smarter than that. I trust you won't be swayed by their outlandish theories about what might have gone on a full two months after Lauren Rice was brutally murdered. They want you to focus on unknowns. Theories. Fantasy. You don't have to. You need only look at the facts.

"Fact. Lauren Rice was an imperfect person. She was insecure. Jealous, perhaps. She was in love with a boy who cast her aside when he was done with her. She made bad choices. The worst one of all was trusting Cole Mathison.

"She was with him the night of August 31st. That is not in dispute. They argued. Fought. Probably said awful things to one another.

"Fact. Cole Mathison left the party at Shamrock Woods just after midnight. He followed Lauren out. Kaylin Dwyer told you what happened next, and it's undisputed. They argued by the side of the road. She was last seen in a heated exchange with Cole. She either got into his car or left with him. That's a fact. We know this because her car was found just a half mile down the road from where Kaylin saw her.

"Fact. Lauren Rice's phone was shut off, put in airplane mode at nearly the exact same moment Cole's was. Why? Because he was smart enough to know it would be a way to track both of their movements. And he didn't want to be found. That's premeditation, ladies and gentlemen. That is cold, calculated planning.

"Lauren Rice was a problem for Cole Mathison. She was getting in the way. In the way of his relationship with his new girlfriend. In the way of his future plans. He felt she wanted to drag him down so he took care of it.

"The defense wants you to feel sorry for Cole. I understand that. There's no dispute that Cole grew up under horrible circumstances. His father is a bad man. His mother is too, probably. After years of abuse, Cole learned how to deal with women who get in the way, didn't he? When he realized Lauren Rice wasn't going to stop ... he did what he was always destined to do. It's in his DNA. It's what he knew.

"He killed her. He lulled that girl into a false sense of security. Had sex with her. Think about that. In her last moments, Lauren might have even believed the boy she loved had taken her back.

"It was a lie. Cole Mathison's entire story has been a lie. He smothered her that night. Dumped her body in a ditch.

"Think about all the lies he's told. Would an innocent kid have glossed over his relationship with Lauren when the police first questioned him? By his own admission, he wants you to believe he was worried about her that night. Blamed himself for letting her leave alone. So why in God's name wouldn't he have told the police everything he knew? Well, I'll tell you. Because he was afraid he'd get caught. He knew he was the last person seen with her. He lied about it. He knew Lauren's state of mind. He lied about it.

"The defense wants you to believe that Cole's father is to blame. There's no evidence he was anywhere near Cole or Lauren that night. They have all these theories, but conveniently, they've failed to produce Rudy Mathison as a witness.

"Ask yourself why that is. Why that really is. How convenient is it that the one witness the defendant claims can prove his alibi hasn't come forward? Because it's yet another lie. Another misdirection. He wants it both ways. He wants you to believe his father was evil. Maybe he was. He wants you to believe he hated his own son. Maybe he did. But at the same time, he wants you to believe his father was so angry about what Lauren Rice was *doing* to his son that he went out and killed her? It doesn't track. You know it doesn't track.

"The defense has concocted an elaborate story, when the truth is really right there in front of you.

"Cole murdered Lauren Rice to keep her from ruining his life. He believed her when she said she was pregnant. He was scared of it because he knew he could have been the father. So he told you another lie. He'd been lying to his current girlfriend too.

"Now, it's up to you to hold Cole Mathison accountable for all of those lies. It's up to you to give Lauren justice and send her killer to prison for the rest of his life.

"The facts are in front of you. Cole Mathison is guilty. Lauren is counting on you to render the only just verdict in this case. Thank you."

Cole bristled beside me. I gathered my notes, but knew I wouldn't need them.

"Ladies and gentlemen," I started. "This case should have been dismissed against Cole. You know it. I know it. I'd wager even the prosecution knows it.

"Even if we take all the prosecution's facts at face value, what do we have? Cole got into an argument with his ex-girlfriend on the night of August 31st. It's not pretty to talk about it, but Lauren wasn't herself that night. There's no dispute about that. She was acting erratic. Drinking heavily, trying to make Cole jealous by throwing herself at other guys. Guys who were also drinking heavily that night.

"Cole was upset, we're not disputing that. But he went home, leaving Lauren Rice very much alive. What happened next? Cole told you the truth. He ran into his father. They had an argument. Cole told him about Lauren's accusations. Then what?

"Then Rudy Mathison disappeared. His cell phone data puts Rudy at the site where Lauren Rice's body was dumped, not Cole. The prosecution raises one excellent question. Where is Rudy Mathison now? Why would a father disappear the exact same night Lauren did? Why would he drain his life savings the second the bank opened the next day?

"Logic tells you, it's because he killed her. Was he doing it on some sick notion of being on Cole's behalf? We'll never know. It doesn't matter. We only know that Rudy Mathison has hung his son out to dry. He's gone because he knows we would put him on the stand and force him to testify about what happened that night.

"And we also know what happened after that. Days after Rudy Mathison's cell phone records get subpoenaed—the same records as Roxanne Mathison's ... she knows about it—

Roxanne Mathison goes to Gil Rice's house. That's not in
dispute. She disappears down the hall, out of Gil's sight.
That's not in dispute. She has access to Lauren Rice's laundry.
That's not in dispute. And she has access to a DNA sample
from a condom her son used. That's not in dispute.

"Roxanne Mathison planted evidence to incriminate her
own son. Why? The answer is simple. Horrifying. Tragic.
Because Rudy Mathison wanted her to. She is helping her
husband get away with murder, ladies and gentlemen.

"You have one job. You must decide whether the
prosecution has presented evidence that Cole committed this
crime beyond a reasonable doubt. He hasn't. Doubt abounds
in this case. Because of it, there is only one verdict you can
render. Not guilty. The prosecution wants you to think the
only way Lauren can have justice is by convicting Cole. No.
The only way she can have justice is if the prosecution and
the Delphi P.D. do their jobs and reopen this investigation.
Detective Lewis never thoroughly questioned any of the
hikers on the trail where Lauren's underwear was found. She
never questioned Gil Rice about who else might have had
access to Lauren's laundry. She never even took a detailed
inventory of the clothing still in Lauren's room after she
disappeared. She has never tried to find Rudy Mathison. She
knows his statement is critical to this case. She's ignored it.
Why? Because prosecuting Cole is what she thought was the
easiest path. A way to get a conviction her first time at bat as
lead detective in a homicide. But she got careless. She got
sloppy. Just like the detective who trained her.

"You can uphold justice by holding the prosecution and
the police accountable. There is a killer still out there. Cole
Mathison did not kill Lauren Rice. He too is a victim in this
case. Of shoddy police work. Of an overzealous prosecutor
biting off more than he can chew in his first murder case in

front of you. And of a sick, abusive relationship between the two people who are supposed to protect him above all others.

"When you look at the facts. When you do your job and hold these people accountable, I'm confident that the only just verdict is not guilty. Thank you. I do not envy your task, but I know you'll do it well."

I gathered my notes and slowly walked back to my table to sit beside Cole. He looked at me, but had no emotion in his eyes. He was broken. I just hoped it wasn't too late to bring him back.

Chapter 38

Peals of laughter woke me from a dead sleep. The clock read 9:17 and I couldn't tell whether that meant day or night. I fumbled for my phone.

Lord, a.m. I hadn't slept in that long in months. Years, maybe.

Madison's howl brought me the rest of the way out of my bed coma. Only one thing elicited that from her. Jessa was nearby, and my brother Matty likely threw her on his shoulder. I made my way to the window. Matty had made an ice rink with the snow blower last night. He skated circles around my niece, making her laugh. Marbury chased after my brother, playfully nipping at his heels.

"Coffee," I moaned. "Lots and lots of coffee."

Vangie waited for me downstairs. "Bless you," I said. She had a new pot brewing.

"The gang's all here," she said. "Hope you don't mind. Jessa had a snow day and didn't want to wait until this afternoon to come out. She's been so excited and driving me crazy. Matty took the day off just for her."

I rolled my eyes. As if my minding ever had anything to do

with it. But it was good to have my family around me. Good to remember that as crazy as things got with us, it was normal. We kept the evil at bay. The weight of Cole's trial settled back down over me, though, as I slid onto a counter stool and watched our family Ice Capades from the French doors.

"Where's Joe?" I asked, blowing steam across the top of my mug.

"He went to get donuts. We promised Jessa those and hot chocolate whenever those two decide to come in."

"Sounds good," I said.

"Jeanie called," she said.

I looked at my phone. "I didn't hear anything."

"She called your landline," Vangie explained. "I think she figured the rest of us would be here and she didn't want to wake you. She just wanted to let you know she got Cole settled out at Dave and Maxine's. Maxine is okay with him staying there until at least you get a verdict."

It had been three days since the jury had got the case. They decided to deliberate over the weekend. Now, Monday morning, I knew I could get a call at any moment.

"That's good," I said.

"Did she really do it?" Vangie said. "It was all over the internet. I don't know how much you can talk about. But his own mother? Planting evidence? It's so ... gross."

I sipped my coffee. "Yeah. I don't really like to think about the logistics of it."

"Joe's pretty freaked out," Vangie said. "He's furious with Emma."

"Emma is almost nineteen years old," I said. "I suppose nobody wants to really confront their kid's sex life."

"Ah, no," Vangie said. "I think I'll just encourage Jessa to enter the nunnery."

I laughed. "Good plan. Let me know how that works out."

"Joe can't be mad at you," she said. "Is he?"

I shrugged. "I don't know. I think Joe knows on paper he's got no cause. He's conflicted."

"He loves Cole," Vangie said. "Or he did. He still wants to. It's just so ..."

"Complicated." I finished her sentence with her.

"And he knows it all makes him a hypocrite," Vangie said. "Cole's twenty-one. Joe was already a father by that age. And well, gross as it is ... he's got proof that he and Emma have been using protection."

"Right," I said.

"But geez," Vangie said. "Do you think Cole will be okay after all of this?"

"I don't know," I said. It was an honest answer. "I really don't. I think we just need to get through this verdict. One thing at a time."

"They have to acquit," Vangie said. "They just have to."

I put a finger to my lips. "Don't say it. Bad juju."

Jessa let out a shriek. Matty skated by and scooped her up. Her laughter warmed my heart.

Yes. This. I needed my family around me today. I needed the sun on my face and the crisp snowy air in my lungs. I downed the last of my coffee and laced up my own skates.

Marbury yelped with enthusiasm as I came out to join the fun.

A half an hour later, Joe pulled up bearing two giant boxes of donuts. He'd gotten two dozen for five people. My mother used to call that Leary food math. She'd always chastise my grandparents for ordering roughly five times the amount of food we would ever eat.

Vangie had the hot chocolate ready by the time we all went back inside. Joe was quiet, but not frowning. If he was mad at me, he hid it. I'd take my concessions where I could and reached for a bear claw.

My phone stayed silent into the afternoon and evening. The jury finished a fourth day of deliberations with no verdict. The longer it took, the worse I felt about our chances.

The next morning, I went into the office and got some motions filed on a few other cases I had put on the back-burner during the trial. I told Tori and Miranda not to drive in. Jeanie wouldn't listen and came in anyway.

We worked in silence. Me upstairs, she down. Then, at 2:17 p.m. on the fifth day of deliberations, we got the call. The jury had reached a verdict. The judge was giving us one hour to assemble all the parties and come in to hear it.

Chapter 39

BY FOUR FIFTEEN, forty-five minutes after the judge called for, we had all assembled except for Cole. My calls to Maxine and Dave Carver went straight to voicemail.

"Should we be worried?" Tori whispered to me. We sat outside the courtroom. Rafe and his team had already gone inside.

"I trust Dave," I said. "He'll get Cole here." Still, I texted him again anyway. I got three blinking dots, then nothing.

Judge Niedermayer's bailiff poked his head out of her office door. "Anything?" he asked.

"I've never known Dave Carver not to respect a judge's request." I smiled. "They'll be here shortly."

"She's not happy," the bailiff said. "The jury needs to be done."

"I know," I said. "We all need to be done."

I looked back at my phone. Those three dots appeared again. A second later, Dave's text came through.

"Parking."

"Five minutes," I told the bailiff.

"Get inside the courtroom then," he said. "I'll meet your client at the door."

"Right," I said.

I went in with Tori. My throat felt dry. Rafe didn't look up as I walked in. He was furiously scribbling notes on a pad.

"It's going to be okay," Tori whispered. "Even if it's bad news. We'll appeal."

"One thing at a time," I said. A few minutes later, Cole came into the courtroom. Dave and Maxine had their arms looped through his, almost as if they were holding him up.

Dave brought him to my table, while Maxine quickly gestured me aside.

I gave Tori a look, then stepped three rows back and tilted my head so Maxine could whisper in my ear.

"He's in bad shape," she said. "We had to drag him out of bed. I'm worried. No matter what happens today, I think he needs to be seen by a doctor."

"Thanks for the heads-up," I said. "Let's just get through this."

"All rise!" the bailiff barked. Judge Niedermayer stormed out of her chambers. She saved a particularly hard glance for me. My client had kept her waiting almost an hour. Which meant we'd kept the jury waiting that long, too.

I put a hand on Maxine's arm, then rejoined Cole at the defense table. He was standing, but barely.

"Hold my hand," I said to him. I looped my fingers through Cole's. His skin was cold and clammy, his tone positively gray. I wanted to tell him everything would be all right, though I had no idea if it ever would.

"Will you send the jurors in," Judge Niedermayer said to her clerk.

They filed in one by one. Only one woman looked my

way. Contempt lined her face as if she'd swallowed something sour. I squeezed Cole's hand as he saw it too.

"Members of the jury," the judge said. "Have you reached your verdict?"

"Yes, Your Honor," the foreperson said. She was juror number two, a retired factory worker in her mid-seventies. She'd made a point of avoiding eye contact with either me or Rafe throughout the trial.

Judge Niedermayer's clerk took the verdict form and handed it to the judge. She read it. Her lips disappeared into a gray line. She handed the form back to the clerk and gave her a nod.

The clerk cleared her throat and leaned into the microphone. The court recorder's fingers hovered over her keyboard.

"We the jury, in the above-entitled action, People versus Cole Daniel Mathison, on count one of the complaint, being murder in the first degree find the defendant, not guilty."

Cole's hand tightened around mine.

"We the jury in the above-entitled action, on count two of the complaint, being murder in the second degree, find the defendant, Cole Mathison, not guilty."

His palms started to sweat.

"We the jury, in the above-entitled action, on count three of the complaint, being abuse of a corpse, find the defendant, Cole Mathison, not guilty. On count four of the complaint, obstruction of justice, find the defendant, Cole Mathison ... not guilty."

"I can't ... I can't ..."

I put my other hand over Cole's. I could feel his knees start to buckle. He doubled over. He was holding me so tight, I went down with him.

"Your Honor," I heard Rafe say. "We'd like to poll the individual jurors."

I could barely hear them. One by one, each spoke their vote aloud. All in the end, as required, voted not guilty. Later, I would learn there were four holdouts who wanted to find Cole guilty. It had taken nearly five days for the other eight to convince them to change their votes.

"Cole," I said. His eyes were open, but he didn't hear me. "Cole!" I shouted. His eyelids fluttered.

Maxine and Dave were at my side, along with two deputy sheriffs.

"I'm okay," he said, his voice breaking. "Did they ... is it ..."

"It's over." I smiled. "They found you not guilty. It's going to be okay. Cole ... you get to go home."

The words just came out of my mouth without thought. It was a thing I'd said to scores of clients in Cole's situation. *You get to go home.* Except in Cole's case, it was likely the second worst thing I could have said.

Cole got to his feet. The jury filed out. I looked for Rafe. He'd already stormed out of the courtroom. People swarmed everywhere.

As Cole sank into a chair at the table and sipped a bottle of water Maxine gave him, I reached over and loosened his tie.

From behind me, I heard my name. Eric had walked into the courtroom. His eyes searched for me. My pulse jumped. I wanted to go to him. I wanted to fling my arms around him and celebrate. But he had a grave expression on his face.

"We'll figure this out, Cole," I said. "Just hang in there. Maxine, can he stay with you guys tonight yet?"

"Of course," she said. She was already tending to Cole in the way that a mother should.

I gave Tori my bag and weaved my way through the

gallery until I got to Eric. He took my elbow and led me to a quiet corner in the hallway.

"What's going on?" I asked.

"I've issued a warrant for Rudy Mathison," he said. "I just wanted to make sure you were okay?"

"Okay? Why wouldn't I be okay?"

"Cass," he said. "I also want to find Roxanne Mathison. She had an appointment to show up for further questioning. She didn't show. I also issued an arrest warrant for Roxanne Mathison an hour ago. She's gone. She's not answering her phone. She didn't show up at work. We think she's skipped town."

"He's not safe, is he?" I said, looking back at Cole. "Rudy's out there. He's not safe."

"Maybe," he said. "Maybe not."

"He's going to stay with Maxine and Dave at least tonight."

"Good," he said. "I can send some extra crews out and keep a lookout. It wouldn't be a bad idea if you got him a personal protection order against Rudy, in case he shows up."

"I will," I said, then something dawned on me. "Wait a minute. Why are you the one questioning Roxanne Mathison and issuing arrest warrants?"

He pursed his lips. "Megan's off the case. Word came down last night. If your verdict went ... well ... how it did ..."

"They're firing her," I finished for him.

"We'll have to wait and see," he said. "Just ... for now ... watch your back. Hopefully Rudy's long gone. But if he's not ... you have a bad habit of attracting exactly that kind of trouble."

I wanted to argue with him, but knew he wasn't wrong. In my concern over Cole, it hadn't occurred to me my own safety might be an issue.

"Got it," I said. "And thanks for having my back."

Eric placed a hand on my lower back. He leaned in quick and quiet. His lips brushed my ear as he whispered. "Always."

Then he disappeared into the crowd as Dave and Maxine brought Cole my way. Dave's eyes held a question. He'd seen me talking to Eric.

"Come on," I said. "Let's all get out of here. I'll explain everything on the way."

Chapter 40

THE NEXT NIGHT, Maxine and Dave had me over for dinner. Cole was still staying with them and we opted for a subdued, quiet, celebratory dinner.

Cole was shell-shocked. Silent. I knew it would take him weeks, months, maybe years to recover from what had just happened.

He sat at Maxine's kitchen table, barely touching the pasta she'd made from scratch. Emma sat beside him, her arm around Cole's shoulders. He gave her a pleasant smile every once in a while, and I think he was glad she was here. It was hard to tell. Emma tried to draw him out, but he stayed withdrawn, quiet.

Maxine cleared the rest of the plates. I got up to help her. When we finished, she poured us two glasses of wine and I followed her out to their heated, covered porch. From there, the woods behind Dave's house seemed to go on for miles. He'd framed the house with pine. With the light dusting of snow on each branch, it looked like a Christmas wonderland, though the holiday was a month past now.

"He's in pretty rough shape," she said.

"I see that," I said. "And thanks so much for letting him stay here a little longer."

Maxine shrugged as she took the seat beside me. "I couldn't exactly turn him out. I'm just kicking myself for not having thought to keep him here after he was first let out on bail. It would have saved a whole mess of trouble."

Roxanne Mathison wouldn't have had access to Cole's DNA then. Maybe the case never would have proceeded to trial.

"Well," I said. "The bright side is now we know. Or Cole knows. He can never go back to that house. He can never really have a relationship with his mother at all."

"Any word on what happened to her?" Maxine asked. "We've heard nothing within the family."

"There's a warrant out for her arrest. They're going after her for obstruction. Rafe's going to bring up new murder charges on Rudy. Kaylin Dwyer is changing her story, apparently. Now she's saying it could have been Rudy she saw Lauren with that night."

"Great," Maxine said. "Rafe can't possibly think having her testify at a new trial ... if it ever gets to that ... will help him."

"I don't know what he thinks," I said. "I just know I won't be the one sitting at the defense table."

"Ever?" She smiled into her glass.

"Not you too," I laughed. "I've got my brothers, my sister, and Eric driving me crazy about this judicial appointment."

"Well, it couldn't happen to a nicer chick, if you ask me," she said.

"Thanks. And I've got a meeting with the governor's office again on Monday. They want an answer too."

"So you've got the weekend to figure out the rest of your life?" she said. "No pressure."

"None at all," I conceded.

We sat in silence for a moment. Dave was out in the pole barn, puttering with something. I could see his silhouette.

"So," I said. "What's the bounty on Rudy Mathison?"

Maxine set her jaw to the side.

"Oh, come on," I said. "Dave can't resist a good hunt. I know he's probably already talked to Eric about it."

Laughing, Maxine finished the rest of her wine and set her glass on the table between us.

"Well, if anyone can figure out where that bastard went, it'll be Dave." Maxine's tone changed. I sensed the fear in her voice.

"Seems like maybe I'm not the only one who should consider another line of work."

I saw the worry lines in Maxine's face.

"I'm sorry," I said. "I didn't mean to make light of anything. I know you're worried."

"It's just ... I've got a bad feeling about this one. To kill that girl the way he did ..."

"Dave's careful," I said. "He's not one to take unnecessary chances. Besides, if Rudy's smart, he'll stay far away from Delphi."

"I don't know," Maxine said. "Guys like him ... he gets off on controlling the people in his life. Roxanne. Cole. I just hope we got to him in time. He's going to need a lot of support. I'm not sure he's got it, Cass. You sure your niece knows what she's in for? Your brother's family? Those two are so young, and Cole has suffered from abuse you and I can't fathom. She might be better off just making a clean break."

I looked over my shoulder. Through the window, I saw Cole rest his forehead against Emma's. He kissed her. I saw the hint of a smile on his face. It was good to see. At the same time, I knew what Maxine meant.

ROBIN JAMES

"Well," I said. "They're taking him back at the lumberyard. He starts Monday. It's a great thing you did getting him into that apartment on the other side of town. I think once he settles into a normal routine, it'll do wonders for him."

"I think so too," she said. "I'm just ... I'm worried about Roxanne too. She was ... is ... still family. Not close, but this is what I do. I should have seen the pain she was in sooner. Maybe I could have done something. I feel like I failed her."

"You didn't," I said. "Don't think that."

I let the silence settle between us. I knew if there was a bounty on Rudy, there was also one on Roxanne. Dave would pursue that too, even if she were family.

"Do you think she went to him?" I asked. "Roxanne?"

"To Rudy?" Maxine looked out at the pine trees. "Yeah. I do. And I'm worried about what that means for her. He won't let her live, Cass. You know that."

A chill went through me. I'd thought of that a thousand times too.

"Roxanne Mathison wouldn't have planted that evidence against her son unless she felt the alternative was worse," I said.

"Exactly," Maxine said.

"Christ," I said. "It's all just so tragic. I can hardly think about it."

I rose from my seat. Behind me, the door opened. Emma and Cole walked out together arm in arm.

"We're going to take off," Emma said.

Maxine raised a brow.

"I'm gonna head over to Emma's place," Cole said. "I haven't seen her ... um ... your brother for a while. I want to thank him. I want to explain."

"I get it," I said. "And I think he'd like that. I'm not

318

comparing it to what you've been through, but Joe's been having a tough time with all of this too. I think it'll do him good to see you."

Cole came to me. He held out his arms. It took me off guard, but I hadn't realized how much I'd wanted to do this. To hug him. He had to have felt so alone all this time.

I squeezed him and tousled his hair, much like I did to my little brother's.

"Don't stay out too late," I teased. "And make sure you get my niece home safe."

I hugged Emma then. I felt her whole posture change as if a weight had been lifted. I kissed her cheek. Then Maxine and I watched as Emma and Cole left together in Emma's car.

Two normal kids doing normal things. Yes. That's exactly what Cole needed right now. I just worried it wasn't what Emma needed.

Chapter 41

I MADE it home just after midnight. Maxine invited me to
have more wine and spend the night, but the lake beckoned
me more. I drew solace from it. I walked down the porch to
the edge of the ice and inhaled its magic powers.

Pure white. A frozen paradise that would soon melt away
to a fresh start. I don't think I'd ever looked forward to the
coming spring more. I just didn't know where I'd be when it
got here.

I felt suspended between figurative scales of justice.
Where could I do the most good? On the bench or in front of
the jury?

As hard, as excruciating as the last few months had been, I
had to admit that I loved it. For all its messy uncertainty, even
when I lost, trying cases gave me juice I couldn't get anywhere
else.

But for how long?

I had no other life. I never went out with friends. Hell, I
really didn't have any friends outside of the office or my
family. It felt good to sit and talk with Maxine, but even she
was little more than a work friend.

Then there was Eric. I couldn't deny how much easier things might be if we weren't at professional odds all the time.

There was also money ... and government benefits. Little prestige, but everyone knew the district court was merely a stepping stone. I could go farther. Circuit Court for sure, but maybe something even greater beyond that.

If I wanted it.

My phone lit up with a new text. Smiling, I picked it up.

"You home yet?" Eric texted.

"Calling you now," I answered, then punched the phone symbol next to his name.

He picked up before the first ring.

"Hey." Eric's sleepy voice reached me from the other end of the phone, sending warmth flooding through me.

"Hey," I said. "You still at the office?"

"Just finished up," he said.

"Any new leads on Rudy or Roxanne?" I asked.

"Nothing I can share," he said. "And nothing earth-shattering in any event. It's landing hard on Megan. She's been demoted to the property room for the time being. There's something else though. Gil Rice. He ... Cass ... he tried to kill himself tonight."

My heart dropped. "God."

"Neighbor found him. Dumb luck. He was passed out in the garage with his car running. He left the light on and his next-door neighbor came over to check on it."

"Is he okay?" I asked.

"He will be," Eric answered. "I just ... I wanted you to hear it from me."

"No," I said. "Thanks for that. Eric, it's so awful. I just ... I can barely let myself think of it. Rudy ruined so many lives. This sounds horrific ... but sometimes I'm left wondering if maybe Lauren suffered the least of it. I'd like to think she's at peace now."

"I know what you mean. And ... Cass ... I know it's late. And I know everything's still in flux. I was just wondering if ..."

"Yes," I said, reading his mind. Or more, he was reading mine. "Yes. I'd like it if you came over."

It was past ten. An expectant pause settled between us. I knew what Eric was waiting to hear me say. I could barely breathe. I was exhausted. Mentally, physically, and emotionally spent. At the same time, there was something else I desperately needed.

"Eric," I said. "I'd like it if you stayed here tonight."

I swear I could almost hear him smile through the phone. That infuriating smirk he gave me. That seductive twinkle in his eyes.

"You sure?" he said.

"I'm sure," I said. "Only don't ask me too many questions or I might change my mind."

"I'll be there in twenty minutes," he said.

My heart was still racing when we clicked off. All of a sudden, I felt like a teenager. Should I change? Did I have time for a shower? Hell. Had I remembered to shave?

This was nutty. I was still on an adrenaline high from the trial. There was still the matter of Wendy. It was just ... I needed him. And there was no one else I wanted to be with at that moment in my life.

I ran upstairs, jumped in the shower and shaved. When I finished, I put on a black tank top and yoga pants, throwing a hoodie over it all. Certainly not the sexiest thing I owned, but it was comfortable. It was me.

I went to the window and looked out at the driveway. Eric hadn't arrived yet. I heard a thump coming from behind the barn. I jumped. The motion light went on. Fear prickled along my spine. I held my breath.

Marbury and Madison tore down the hallway, barking. They each crashed against the window, clamoring to get out. I kept a .38 locked in a closet. I started to go to it. Then, a screech filled the air as one of the feral cats who patrolled the woods came flying around the corner of the barn. Another, bigger cat had chased it away.

I let myself breathe again. I shook off my fears.

I had just enough time to run a brush through my hair and twist it into a topknot before the doorbell rang. It occurred to me, I might have to furnish Eric with a key.

I ran downstairs and swung open the stained glass storm door, breathlessly expecting to see Eric's shining eyes and that trademark smirk.

Instead, Roxanne Mathison stood in the open doorway, stringy, unwashed hair in her eyes.

I looked behind her up the drive. I didn't see a car. I didn't see anything or anyone else at all.

"You shouldn't be here," I said, wishing I'd gone for the .38. I felt a mix of fear, sympathy, and rage upon seeing her. I'd left my phone upstairs on the charger. Roxanne was empty-handed though; she hugged her arms around her.

"I know," she said. "I shouldn't have done a lot of things. But you shouldn't have either."

"Roxanne," I said. "It's not safe for you here. You know the police are looking for you. They have questions ..."

"I didn't know where else to go," she sobbed.

"Anywhere!" I shouted. "Anywhere but here."

"You need to know," she said. "I tried ... it was going to be okay. I thought it was going to be okay."

She seemed altered. She stared off at some unseen point. Unfocused. Unhinged.

The hairs stood up on the back of my neck once more. This felt like a trap. Was Rudy lurking in the shadows. Was that the play? Lure me out into the open and then ...

"The police are on their way, Roxanne," I lied. "I've got a silent alarm. You're on camera."

She blinked. "That's good," she said. "You should be careful. I should have been more careful."

"Roxanne," I said. "You know you need to turn yourself in."

"Not until you know," she said, crying now. "He's dangerous. You have no idea what he's capable of. He charms you. He lies. I tried to protect him. I swear, I did. I tried to love him. I do love him. Even now. I know what you all think of me. I know how horrible it all was."

"Roxanne," I said. "They can help you. You're better off in custody. They won't let anything happen to you. You'll be safe. There's a way out. There's help."

"You don't understand!" she shouted. "You think you did a good thing. You think this was justice?"

She slammed her palms against the glass door separating us. I thanked God for it.

"I did what I had to," she said. "I know what that makes you and everyone else think of me. But you can't understand what he's like. He's a monster. I'm sorry. I'm so, so sorry."

It took a moment for her words to register in my brain.

"Roxanne," I said. "What are you talking about?"

"He's a monster! He'll find me. He always finds me. I thought he was just like his father. But he's worse. Oh God, he's so much worse."

Just then, Roxanne's face became a ghoulish mask of terror as headlights rounded my drive and beamed right at her.

"He's worse!" she shrieked. "And he's out here right now because of you!"

Something moved in the shadows. I stepped back, tried to close the door. Then Eric stepped into view. His eyes narrowed as he saw who was at my front door.

Chapter 42

SHE WAS UNGLUED. Babbling. Barely coherent. She let me
put an arm around her and I led her to my dining room tab'
Eric took a seat at the opposite end of the table. He gestur€
to me, indicating the need for something to write with.

I pulled a pad of paper and pen out of a kitchen draw
and quietly handed it to him. "Mrs. Mathison," he said.
"You're safe here. I know you're scared. I think I can hel'
but I'm going to need to hear everything."

She sat with her hands clasped, resting between hei
knees. It made her shoulders bunch together as if she w
bracing for a blow.

"Am I under arrest?" she asked.

"Not at the moment," Eric said. "But you do knov
am." He pulled out a business card and slid it across t
Roxanne didn't even look at it.

"Of course I know who you are. I'm not an idiot,
crazy."

"Nobody said you were," he said. "But I need y
understand that right now, I'm a police detective. /

Rice's murder case is still unsolved. I believe you have material information pertaining to it."

"Am I under arrest?" she asked again.

"You are not," he said, reassuring her once more. "But we've been wanting to talk to you. The prosecutor wants to charge you with obstruction of justice. You understand that. You understood it at trial, that's why you pled the Fifth on the stand. You can ..."

"You don't know what he does. You don't know what it's been like. I don't have anywhere else to go. He always knows where to find me."

"Roxanne," I said. "Rudy's been in contact with you, hasn't he?"

Her eyes got wide. "Rudy ..."

"Roxanne, why'd you do it?" Eric said, his tone more gruff. "Why'd you plant evidence against your own son?"

"I thought I could save him," she said. "I tried. You have to believe me that I tried. I protected him. So many times, Rudy wanted to hurt him. I made him hurt me instead. But I couldn't be everywhere all the time. I took him with me. Every time I went shopping. I quit my job. I was a bank teller before. But I was afraid to leave. Afraid Rudy would hurt Cole when I wasn't there to see it."

"That had to have been so hard for you," Eric said.

"I wanted to leave. I swear I did. I tried. But Rudy would always find me. He broke ... he broke my arm. He would cut me. He would ..."

She pushed back the sleeve on her right arm, showing criss-crossing scars going all the way up to her elbow.

"I tried to kill him," she said, her eyes widening. "He had a gun. He kept it beside the bed. One night, he was passed out drunk after a Lions game. I went and got it. I could have done it. I swear. But then ... Cole got up. He was maybe ten years

328

old. He saw me. He asked me what I was doing. He knew ... but he said, if I did it. If I killed Rudy, then they'd take me away, and he'd have nobody left. How could I do that? How could I murder his father right in front of him?"

Pain made her voice thick. So much trauma. So much abuse.

"Roxanne ..." Eric started.

"I tried to get him help! I thought if I loved him enough, it would be okay. I could find the good parts of him. Love the bad parts away."

"Only that never works," Eric said.

Roxanne shook her head. "No. I could see it in his eyes. He was one thing to everyone else. Charming. Outgoing. So smart. But then ... to me ... it's my fault. I tried not to hate him. I tried not to see that look in his eyes. I tried to believe his soul was different. But it's not. He doesn't just look like Rudy."

My heart turned to stone. I knew what she meant to say. I wanted to think she was just confused. Or that I had misheard. Misunderstood. Anything.

"Roxanne," Eric said. "What about Cole?"

"Little things," she said. "We had a cat. A barn cat. It used to live under the porch. I never had a pet growing up. My mother was allergic. So I fed it tuna. I named her Athena. She was so pretty. Black and white spots. But then ... I couldn't find her. He ... he stood in the window laughing as I stood out there with a treat calling her name."

"What happened to the cat, Roxanne?" Eric asked. The air felt thick in my lungs.

"I found tufts of black and white fur sticking to the bushes on the trail out behind the house. He ... he strung her up. Skinned her."

"Who did that?" Eric asked.

"He was only sixteen," she said. "Sixteen!"

"Oh God," I whispered.

"Roxanne," Eric said. "Did Cole hurt you?"

Biting her bottom lip, she nodded as fresh tears fell. Under the table, I pulled out my phone.

"I never thought it would go beyond that," she said. "Rudy and Cole, it was me they wanted to hurt. But then ..."

"What happened that night?" Eric said. "What did you see the night Lauren Rice disappeared?"

"I was sleeping," she said.

"Enough!" The word ripped out of me. "No more, Roxanne. You're here. You want us to hear the truth. So tell it. I can't help you. We can't help you without the truth."

"I was sleeping!" she cried. "I was. But ... I heard him come home. I heard the truck door slam. I went to the window. Rudy was ... he'd been sleeping beside me. But he was gone when I woke up. I heard shouting. They were arguing."

"Who was arguing? Cole and Rudy?" Eric asked.

She nodded. "Yes. But then ... I only heard Cole. Rudy must have left. I thought he must have left. So I went out to talk to Cole. He ... he had a shovel in his hand. It was so late."

"What did Cole do with the shovel, Roxanne?" Eric said.

She let out a choked sound. "I tried to stop it. Not this way. I said not this way. But he didn't hear me. It was like he couldn't hear me. Maybe if I just hadn't said anything at all, Rudy wouldn't have turned. But he turned. He ..."

"What did Cole do?" I asked.

She buried her face in her hands. "He hit him. He swung the shovel, and he hit his father in the head with it. That sound. God. That sound. Rudy fell. And he ... he didn't get up again."

"What did you do, Roxanne?" Eric asked.

"He was so angry. I thought he was going to hit me too.

330

He swung at me. I ... I fell ... he made me pray. Made me beg. Then ... he ... he made me help him."

"What did you help Cole do?" Eric asked.

"Rudy keeps blue tarps in the garage. For painting. We rolled him up. Cole told me ... he took the truck. He took Rudy's truck. We put Rudy in the back. Then he left. Cole left. I thought maybe he'd never come back. But he came back."

"Roxanne," I whispered. "What happened to Lauren? Why ..."

"He ... he told me. I didn't want to believe it. At first, Cole told me it was all a lie. What they were saying. He said he didn't kill her. Then, he told me he did. If I said anything. If I did anything wrong, he was going to make sure I paid just like she did."

"What happened to Lauren?" Eric said.

"He said she wouldn't leave him alone. She kept hounding him. He told me he tried to get her to leave him alone. I wanted to believe what he said at first. That it was Rudy who killed that girl. Just like you said. He showed me the texts. Said she was trying to trap him just like I trapped Rudy. It made sense. I wanted it to make sense. Rudy *would* have been so angry about that. But she kept following him. Cole told me he and Lauren left that party together. They stopped on the side of the road. Cole said he wouldn't have done anything, but that she made him. Gave him no choice. So, he put her in his truck. I don't know where he took her. But he said she didn't suffer. He said he made her happy one last time."

My stomach churned. "He had sex with her," I said.

"He said he made her happy." Roxanne's words choked out of her. "Told her what she wanted to hear. That he loved her, and they could be together. Then ... then he made her go to sleep. He said she didn't suffer."

I put a hand over my mouth, afraid I'd throw up, scream, something.

"You shouldn't have taken this case. If it had been anyone but you. Cole told me they had nothing on him. And then you decided Rudy was the one who killed her. Just like Cole said you would. Just like he planned it. It was his idea to take that money out of the bank account. He drove me there the next morning. You never asked anybody at the bank if it was me or Rudy who came."

I gripped the sides of the chair, afraid the earth would open up and swallow me. Hoping it did.

"Cole said that's what everyone needed to believe," Roxanne continued. "It was my fault ... if I hadn't let Rudy do things to him. I tried. God. I tried so many times. So I had to do this for Cole now. I owed it to him. But Cole said everything would be okay. Rudy couldn't hurt me anymore. He said that was why he had to do what he did. So he could protect me. I wanted to believe him. But after he got arrested, he told me ... if I said what I saw ..."

"He threatened you," Eric said. "Is that it? Cole threatened to hurt you again if you said anything about what happened to Rudy or Lauren?"

She nodded. Tears rolled freely down her face. "I thought it would be okay. Cole was wrong. He got arrested. I thought maybe it was finally over. It was all going to be okay. But they let him out. He got so angry. He put his hands around my neck. He said if I did what he said, it would be okay. I should say I was asleep and didn't see anything that night. It would all be all right if I said I was asleep. Just stick to my story that I was asleep. But you ..."

She couldn't finish. The horror of her words sank in. "But

I figured it out," I said. "I figured out Rudy disappeared the night Lauren did. His cell phone records ... the bank records. Just like Cole planned."

Roxanne wiped her eyes with her sleeve. "Cole took Rudy's phone out of his jeans when we ... after we put him in the truck. I didn't know what he meant to do with it."

"He took it with him when he moved Lauren's body," Eric said. "My God. He took Rudy's phone so it would hit the cell phone towers where and when he needed it to. And he left his own phone here at the house so it would look like he never left after that."

"Just like he turned off his and Lauren's phones at the bonfire," I whispered. God. He hadn't killed her in some heat-of-the-moment fit of rage. He didn't just snap. He planned it out before they left that party together.

"And you knew that would be enough," I said to Roxanne. "My God. You knew that might be enough for reasonable doubt. You were afraid Cole would be acquitted."

She wiped her tears. "He would have killed me. He *will* kill me. Don't you see? I had to do it. He can get help maybe, if he's in jail."

"You planted that evidence," Eric said. "And you called Detective Lewis, didn't you? You were the anonymous informant. Because you knew without it, Cole would likely get away with killing Lauren."

"He said he would," she said. "He said if I just told them I was asleep it would all be okay for him and he wouldn't have to hurt me anymore."

"Why didn't you just come to us?" Eric said. "Roxanne, why didn't you just go to the police?"

"He would know!" she shrieked. "He'd know I didn't do what he said. He would have killed me. You say you can protect me, but you can't. You don't know what he's like. You don't know. He said he would find me, always catch up with me. Just like Rudy used to. My way was better. I tried to save her. I tried to make it so Cole would have to pay for what he did."

Eric wiped a hand across his face. Panic filled my heart.

"I have to go," I said. "I have to ..."

Eric gave me a warning look. It didn't matter. I pushed myself away from the table and ran into the other room. Grabbing my phone, I punched in Joe's number.

Sweat poured down the back of my neck. My fingers shook. Joe's phone went straight to voicemail. I called Emma's number next. Same thing. I called Katy. It rang three times, then she answered.

"Hey, Cass," she said, her voice sounding weary.

"Katy," I said. "Is Emma there? Did she make it back home?"

"What's the matter?" Katy asked.

"Is she home!" I shouted. "Katy, please. Is Emma home? Check. You have to check."

"Cass, I thought she was with you. Over at Maxine's."

"She left," I said. "She and Cole were headed over to your place. Are they still there?"

"Um, no," Katy said. "Cass, what's going on? Emma isn't here. I haven't heard from her since she left to go to Maxine's."

I covered my face with my hand. With my back against the hallway wall, I slowly sank to the ground.

Eric came to my side. "Cass," he said. "I've got a crew coming out. They're going to take Roxanne into protective custody."

"She's gone," I said. "Eric, Emma left with Cole. I don't know where they are."

"Cass?" Katy was still on the other end of the line.

"Get Joe," I said. "I need to talk to Joe."

"Hold on, Cass," Eric said. "Let me talk to him. If he thinks ..."

Joe came on the line. "What's up, sis?"

Eric held my eyes. I knew what he was worried about. Cole could be anywhere. He might do anything if he thought he was cornered.

"Hey, Joe," I said. In the background, I could hear Katy filling him in on what I'd asked.

"What's going on, Cass?" he asked, his tone going flat.

"We just ... Joe," I said. How could I explain it? How could I keep everyone I cared about safe?

"I just ... I need to get a hold of Emma," I said. "Has she checked in with you?"

"What the hell is going on?" he shouted. "Cass, you better tell me right now!"

I knew the look in Eric's eyes. He wanted me to be careful.

"Joe," I said. "I just need you to get a hold of Emma. Get her home. I'm on my way over. I'll explain everything when I get there."

Roxanne came into the hallway. Her face had gone white.

"Cass," Joe said. "Emma's not here. She's over at Cole's house. I've got a GPS app on her phone. Says she got there over an hour ago."

Eric grabbed the phone from me. He could hear everything, Joe was talking so loud.

"Joe," Eric said. "Just hang out there. Cass and I are on our way."

Joe swore. He wasn't buying it.

"Like hell," Joe said, then hung up the phone.

Chapter 43

Two minutes later, blue and red lights flooded the windows as the patrol crew Eric called in arrived. He wisely called female officers.

"Mrs. Mathison?" Eric said. "These women are going to take you down to the police station. They're going to see that you have everything that you need."

"You have to find him," she said. "He knows I'm not home. He told me to stay home. He's going to be very angry if he sees I'm not at home."

Very angry. My God. Emma was *with* him and my brother was likely on his way to both of them.

Eric nodded over her head as the officers stepped in to deal with Roxanne.

"Eric," I said, my voice breaking.

"Cass," he said.

"Don't," I snapped. "Don't you dare tell me to stay put. He's my brother. She's my niece. So unless you plan on handcuffing me to this porch post, I'm going after them."

He set his jaw. "Come on," he said. "Dammit. We'll take my car."

I ran down the steps. Eric was right on my heels as I got to his car door. He climbed behind the wheel just as one of the officers helped Roxanne Mathison into her car.

Fifteen minutes. It was just a fifteen-minute drive from my end of the lake to the other side of town where Roxanne lived. I kept trying to get Joe on the phone. It kept going to voicemail.

"She'll be all right," Eric assured me. I wasn't sure if he said it to convince me or himself.

"I didn't see it," I whispered. "My God. This whole time. I didn't see it."

"Don't," Eric said. "You can't blame yourself for this one. And you weren't the only one he fooled."

Eric's radio squawked. He barked orders into it.

When we finally pulled into Roxanne Mathison's driveway, I thought my heart might explode. Emma's Ford Ranger was parked in the street. For a moment, I thought we made it before Joe. Then I saw his truck. In the dead of night, its black paint concealed it, but there it was, parked parallel to Rudy Mathison's detached garage.

Eric cut the lights, then pulled into the driveway. I started to get out when I heard shouting. A scream.

"Stay here!" Eric barked. He drew his weapon as the front door flew open.

"No!" I shouted. Eric relaxed his stance as Emma ran out, her face contorted with fear. Her shirt was ripped open in the front, exposing her bra. There were scratches on her throat.

"Emma!" I shouted. I went to her. She nearly blew past me, wild-eyed. It took her a moment to recognize me in the dark. Then she threw herself into my arms, sobbing.

"I didn't ... he wasn't ... he was ..."

"Shh," I said, pulling her with me back down the walk.

"He got so ... so ... angry," she said. "I just wanted to talk. I didn't want to do anything. It's too soon. He forced me down."

"Emma," Eric said, his voice sharp, all business. "Emma, I need you to tell me who's in that house."

"My dad," she hiccupped. "Cass. My dad's in there. He's going to ... Cole was ... he said ... oh God. Is this what happened to Lauren?"

Emma was nearly hysterical and stopped making sense.

"Get her in the car," Eric snapped. "Stay there!"

Then I heard my brother's shout, a crashing sound, and a cry of pain.

"Daddy!" Emma cried.

I let her go. I ran with Eric, thinking only about Joe. Eric pushed me backward, forcing his way into the house. But I saw it all.

Cole backed up against the kitchen table. A picture frame lay face up at his feet, the glass within it shattered. The family photo. The one that hung on the wall just off the kitchen with Rudy Mathison looking so much like Cole.

"Nothing," Cole spat. "There's nothing you can do. I was acquitted."

"No," I said, surprised at how calm my voice came out. "They can't lock you up for killing Lauren anymore. But you took the stand, Cole. You told a jury under oath that you didn't kill her. So that was a lie."

"Perjury?" He laughed. "It's nothing. You're good at what you do, Cass. I knew you'd be the one."

"Perjury will be the least of your charges, Cole," I said. "We know about your father."

His eyes glinted pure evil. He was a changeling. All of the innocence and vulnerability I thought I'd seen in his eyes vanished. A mask. A chameleon. A monster.

"Joe?" Eric said. "I need you to step back. I need you to show me your hands."

Eric saw what I'd missed. My brother was holding a gun trained right at Cole Mathison's head. What had he seen? What had he walked in on?

"Joe?" I said.

"No," Joe whispered. "You killed that poor girl. You son of a bitch. You took her away from Gil. From everyone. And you were going to do it again. If I hadn't got here when I did ... Cass ... I found them in the bedroom. He had a pillow over Emma's head."

"It's over," I said. "Joe, Emma's safe now. She's right outside."

"Come on, Joe," Eric said. "Let me take care of this."

"Take care of it?" Joe asked. "None of you took care of this. You bungled this case from the very beginning!"

"Joe," I cried. I went to him. Over Eric's shouts, I put a hand on my brother's arm.

"Joe," I whispered. "Come on. It's time to go. Emma's right outside. She needs you. I need you."

Something got through to him. He turned to me. He relaxed his arm. I started to pull my brother away.

Eric moved to the side to let us pass. Shoulders sagging, Joe turned his back on Cole. I reached for him, taking my brother's hand in mine. I pulled him toward me. Turning, I started down the stairs pulling Joe along with me. Maybe if I hadn't turned ...

Cole's sick laughter filled the room. "I knew you couldn't do it. I would have. She's sweet, Joe. So sweet. Tastes just like honey. Same as Lauren. Little bitches get just what they deserve. If they would just leave me alone!"

I was halfway out the door, down the porch steps. Joe

stopped moving. His hand in mine went rigid. I heard him take a breath. Then, he slipped his hand out of mine.

It happened so fast. Before I could even turn around. Someone cried no. Someone screamed. Then the gunshot cracked through the stillness.

I moved in slow motion. Emma ran toward the sound. Instinct fueled me and I held her back. I couldn't let her see. I couldn't let her know.

I pressed my lips to her ear. "Get in the car. Get in the car. Stay there. Don't look back."

She listened. I turned and walked up the stairs. Eric wasn't where I left him. He was hunched over Cole Mathison's body. Cole had a single, red bullet hole straight through his forehead. His eyes were gone.

Joe stood in the foyer, gun still drawn.

No. No. No.

"He's dead," Eric said. As he rose, I thought he'd go for his cuffs. I saw a scene play out where he read my brother his Miranda rights.

No. No. No. Not like this.

Joe stood with his gun at his side. He met Eric's eyes, then dropped it to the ground. He turned, putting his hands behind his head.

"Eric," I said.

Eric's lips formed a bloodless line.

No. No!

He blinked. He looked back at Cole. Then at me. Joe dropped to his knees with his hands on his head, waiting for Eric to do what he knew he had to. Cole was unarmed. My brother had turned back. He deliberated. He made a decision. Judge. Jury. Executioner. First Degree.

"Eric," I cried.

Eric took me by the arm. He pulled me aside. His eyes burned through me. He'd gone still as stone. With short, clipped words, he said, "Do you need me to tell you what to do?"

Time froze. It was as if the ground split open. Then everything got clear.

"No," I told him. "I know what to do."

Eric's jaw hardened. A moment. Another choice. An unspoken pact between us. He let me go. He turned away from me and went out the door.

Right and wrong. Black and white. I lived in the gray. We all ... lived in the gray. I took a step toward my brother. Emma's cries reached me. Eric was putting her in the car, distracting her. Sixty seconds. That's all it would take. Change the course of my life. Joe's life.

I wasn't dying, but my life flashed before me, anyway. The easy path. The hard one. The only one. There was no going back. There was only ever one choice, no matter what it cost me. I took it.

I went to the kitchen. Covering my hands with my sleeves, I pulled a knife from the block.

"Joe, get up," I said. My brother was still on the ground with his hands behind his head. He kept his eyes squeezed shut, waiting for what he thought was inevitable.

I took the knife. I knelt down and put it in Cole Mathison's right hand, closing his fingers around it.

Then, I went to my brother. He'd finally gotten to his feet. His jaw twitched. His cold eyes held understanding as he looked at Cole and me.

It was over. All over. The spirit of Gil Rice's words pierced through my thoughts. A father will do anything to protect his daughter. Joe did just that. Cole Mathison would never hurt anyone else's daughter. Another father ... my brother ... made sure of it.

"Let's go," I said to Joe through tight lips. His face hardened. Unblinking, he gave me a slow, nearly imperceptible nod. Yes. A father will do anything to protect his little girl.

And this sister will do anything to protect her brother.

Chapter 44

A FEW DAYS LATER, they found Rudy Mathison's body buried in a shallow grave, deep in the woods behind his own house. Roxanne Mathison's words were what had given me the clue.

When things got bad, she'd told her son to run there. Escape. Find a place to hide. It gave me a hunch. Eric sent cadaver dogs out there and they hit.

Cole had built a treehouse back there. A sanctuary long ago, and then on a crisp night on Labor Day weekend, it turned into something else.

"Grisly," Jeanie said. We sat on the front porch. February 1st and crazy Michigan weather had rolled in. The snow melted, and it was sixty-two degrees out. We had winter storm warnings for the upcoming weekend, though.

The lake was still mostly frozen. A couple of fools were out ice fishing, anyway. Always.

"It's awful," I said. "I want to be mad at Roxanne Mathison. And I am. If she'd told the truth from the beginning, it would have saved us all a lot of grief."

"I know," Jeanie said. "That woman ... I just don't know if

she'll ever be okay again. She's too damaged. Any word on what Rafe Johnson's recommending where she's concerned?"

"I don't think she'll do hard time," I said. "I heard she's going to plead out to obstruction and accessory after the fact. She'll get a long probation, community service, and she'll serve whatever times she gets in a state hospital. Hopefully, she'll get some much-needed mental health help. But you're right. I don't know how easily it would be for anyone to come back from this."

Marbury and Madison chased each other on the lawn. Then, as always, Madison decided when it was over. She nipped Marby's tail and the two of them settled down to watch the lake.

"You ever going to tell me what happened with Joe?" she asked. Her question caught me off guard. Though the official report hadn't yet been issued, Rafe called me just this morning to tell me he wouldn't be pressing charges. The shooting of Cole Mathison had been ruled self-defense.

"And good riddance," Rafe had said. "I'm sorry for what that monster put your family through. I wish things had turned out differently the first time around."

"It is what it is," I'd told him. "You were right on Lauren Rice. You had the right monster."

"That's the other thing I wanted to tell you," he said. "The lab results came back on the physical evidence recovered from that tree house. They found Cole and Lauren's DNA all over it. Sweat. Hair samples. It looks like he put her in his truck and took her up to that treehouse. He had a sleeping bag and other bedding up there. There was a pillow we're pretty sure he used to smother her with. We found traces of Lauren's hair and clothing fibers in the wood floor. Not that anyone had any doubt, but I just thought you'd like to know."

"Thanks," I said. "Like I said, you were right, Rafe."

"Yeah, but you were better," Rafe said. There had been no bitterness or sarcasm in his tone. He meant it. I took it as the compliment it was, but wanted to get to the point I never had to think about Cole Mathison again.

"Joe's angry with me," I answered Jeanie. "But he's really angry with himself. We both misjudged Cole Mathison, and it almost cost us Emma."

In the moments after Cole was shot and before the ambulance and police crews arrived, my brother and I came to an understanding. From that day forward, we would never talk about what happened. One more bond we shared. This time, Eric shared it with us.

"He'll come around," Jeanie said. "He loves you and needs you way too much. We all do. Emma holding up okay?"

"Katy's getting her into counseling," I said. "I think she'll be okay. Thank God."

The wind picked up, whipping through my hair. We faced east, and the mid-afternoon sun pierced through the clouds. Jeanie repositioned her Detroit Lions baseball cap so the bill shielded her eyes.

"Well," Jeanie said. "Things are never boring when you're around, I'll say that."

I barked out a laugh. "Thanks. Glad to provide your entertainment."

Tires crunched on the driveway beside us. Eric pulled up. He promised to bring Jeanie and me dinner from our favorite Thai place in Ann Arbor. He was early. I was glad to see him. He rolled down his window and threw a smile my way. It lifted my heart.

Eric and I wouldn't talk about what happened in Cole Mathison's kitchen either. Ever. In the official report, Eric hadn't seen what transpired after he'd gotten Emma, the victim, safely deposited in his car.

He'd risked his career for me that day. For Joe. But I knew he'd done it for Lauren and Gil Rice as much as anyone else. Still, my brother might have faced first-degree murder charges of his own. It seemed as though my life would never be just black and white. I would forever operate within the gray lines. Accepting it settled another question for me that day. If anyone ever looked too hard, they might find the lines I'd crossed. They might use them to hurt the people I loved.

Just then, my phone rang on the table between us. Jeanie looked down and saw the caller ID at the same time I did.

The governor's office. I had an appointment with them tomorrow morning.

Jeanie gave me a knowing glance as Eric stepped out of his car bearing an armful of Styrofoam boxes. The aroma hit me and my stomach growled.

"I'll leave you to it," Jeanie said. She went to meet Eric as I picked up my phone.

"Hello," I said.

"Cass," a female voice said. I'd only met her in person once, but Governor Finch had a bright, commanding voice. I swallowed hard, knowing she wouldn't have called me herself if her aids hadn't told her what to expect.

"Governor," I said. "I'm glad you called."

"I won't be there tomorrow," she said. "I've got a meeting I can't reschedule. I just wanted to congratulate you in person. We're looking forward to the good work I know you'll do in the district court."

"Thank you," I said as I watched Eric and Jeanie head into the house. "And I wish I could talk to you about this in person too. But I'm afraid I'm going to have to decline your offer. I don't think I'm quite suited for the bench."

She paused. Governor Finch was no one's fool. She would think there was only one reason someone like me might turn down an opportunity like this. I didn't want anyone digging into my life.

"I'm sorry to hear that," she said.

"Turns out, I like what I'm doing," I said, and that was the God's honest truth. For all the mistakes I might make. The stress. The low pay. The long hours. It was who I was.

"Well," she said. "You're damn good at it. We all know that. I'm not done trying. If this isn't the right time for you, that's your choice. I'll keep your number."

I laughed. "Please do. Never say never. But can I ask you? Who was it that recommended me to you?"

She hesitated. Went silent. "I'm glad I got to meet you," she said, evading the question. It only sparked my curiosity more. She wished me luck, then ended the call.

Eric opened the screen door behind me. "You coming? The food's going to get cold."

Smiling, I rose and turned to face him. "I'm coming," I said. "There's no place I'd rather be."

He cocked his head to the side, curious, then gave me that lopsided grin of his as I came to join him and Jeanie. Marbury and Madison scrambled in behind me as the sun began to set over the lake in bursts of gold and red ... for the moment ... chasing away all the gray.

Up Next for Cass Leary...

Click for More Info

Cass's latest case finds her in the witness box instead of the defense table as someone she loves most of all faces trial for murder. Don't miss it! Click the book cover for more information or head to https://www.robinjamesbooks.com/book/mercy-kill/

Newsletter Sign Up

Sign up to get notified about Robin James's latest book releases, discounts, and author news. You'll also get *Crown of Thorne* an exclusive FREE bonus prologue to the Cass Leary Legal Thriller Series just for joining. Find out what really happened on Cass Leary's last day in Chicago.

Click to Sign Up

http://www.robinjamesbooks.com/newsletter/

About the Author

Robin James is an attorney and former law professor. She's worked on a wide range of civil, criminal and family law cases in her twenty-year legal career. She also spent over a decade as supervising attorney for a Michigan legal clinic assisting thousands of people who could not otherwise afford access to justice.

Robin now lives on a lake in southern Michigan with her husband, two children, and one lazy dog. Her favorite, pure Michigan writing spot is stretched out on the back of a pontoon watching the faster boats go by.

Sign up for Robin James's Legal Thriller Newsletter to get all the latest updates on her new releases and get a free bonus scene from Burden of Truth featuring Cass Leary's last day in Chicago. http://www.robinjamesbooks.com/newsletter/

Also by Robin James

Cass Leary Legal Thriller Series

Burden of Truth

Silent Witness

Devil's Bargain

Stolen Justice

Blood Evidence

Imminent Harm

First Degree

Mercy Kill

With more to come...

Mara Brent Legal Thriller Series

Time of Justice

Price of Justice

Hand of Justice

With more to come...

Made in the USA
Las Vegas, NV
22 February 2021

18311148R00215